La Paloma

A Novel Inspired by Real Life Events

Willard Thompson

Rincon Publishing
Santa Barbara, California

Other Novels by Willard Thompson
The Chronicles of California
Dream Helper
Delfina's Gold
Their Golden Dreams
Also
The Girl from the Lighthouse
La Paloma

La Paloma

A Novel Inspired by Real Life Events

Willard Thompson

ISBN 978-1-7340056-0-8

Cover and interior design: Gwen Gades
www.beapurplepenguin.com

Names: Thompson, Willard, 1940- author.

Title: La Paloma : a novel / Willard Thompson.

Description: Santa Barbara, California : Rincon Publishing, [2019]

Identifiers: ISBN: 978-1-7340056-0-8

Subjects: LCSH: Illegal alien children—California—Fiction. | Children of illegal aliens—California— Fiction. | Children of illegal aliens—Family relationships—California. | Mexican American families—California—Fiction. | Hispanic American women—California —Fiction. | Illegal aliens—Family relationships—California. | Immigration enforcement—United States— Fiction. | Deportees—Family relationships—Mexico—Fiction. | United States—Emigration and immigration—Social aspects—Fiction.

Classification: LCC: PS3620.H698 L36 2019 | DDC: 813.6—dc22

Dedicated to the memory of
Durand Roburds (Bud) Miller
A Marine World War II Hero

"To live is to be separated from what we were in order to approach what we are going to be in the mysterious future."

Octavio Paz

CHAPTER 1

FOR ME, STEPPING off the bus from Westwood in Monte Vista is like stepping into my alternate reality. Two white-haired Mexican men wearing droopy mustaches and ostrich boots are sitting together on the bus stop bench. They talk to each other in short, machine-gun-like, bursts of Spanish. As I start my walk toward home, one looks up.

"*Hola, Señorita*," he says, smiling so I can see his tobacco-stained teeth, "Often I see you at this time. From where you are coming?"

I have no idea who he is, but I return his smile. "From UCLA," I tell him.

He nods. "Ah, Trojans," and lapses back into silence.

"No. Bruins," I say, and keep going, smiling to myself. It must have been the tenth time the old man had asked me the same question, and he still doesn't understand.

The air is heavy with the aroma of simmering pork from a *taqueria* I walk past, but it blends into the smell of warm *Bolillos* at the *panadería* next door. Farther along, three middle-aged women in drab house dresses, stockings rolled to mid-calf, stand at a table of Norteño CDs. They're listening to Ramon Ayala's voice coming from inside the store as they chatter back and forth.

Hurrying home, I pass two big-bellied teenage girls pushing baby carriages. They comment at the marquee of our movie theater showing "Sicario: Day of the Soldado" and then admire the riot of red, white, and green *piñatas* hanging in the doorway of a shop next to the theater, spilling all sorts of imported merchandise onto the sidewalk.

When Connie, my little sister, was a toddler, she used to be dazzled by the sights and smells of the stores along Peck Road. Even now, a curious fourth grader, she loves to linger over the assortment of trinkets when our papa takes her window shopping.

I never liked these shops the way Connie does. For me, Monte Vista is my nightmare, haunting me with the memory of little Antonio. It isn't my world. The bus to Westwood each morning is my escape—three buses actually, and two hours each way.

"This is your culture, Paloma. Your people," my papa used to tell me, holding my hand, walking together up Peck Road to Mass on Sundays. "Embrace it," he would say. "Es lo que somos."

"I hate it, Papa," I told him. "I want to be an American girl."

Two gangbangers in baggy pants, with shaved heads, begin following me down the street, trash-talking to my back.

"Did ya see the nice tits on her?" one of them says loud enough for everyone on the sidewalk to hear. "I was peeking at them on the bus. How soft they would feel in my hand."

I cringe and quicken my pace. I want to turn around and yell at them to leave me alone, but I know to keep my mouth shut. There are enough people and traffic on the street that I feel safe.

"But her legs, man," the other one responds. "Think how those long legs would feel wrapped around your neck."

I do my best to shut out their words. I speed up, but they keep pace. Men and women on the sidewalk give them a wide birth.

At Garvey Avenue, they turn left after shouting obscene good-byes that describe what they would do to me if they ever got me alone. When they disappear down the street, I let out a breath and feel tension release from my shoulders.

Only neighborhood people are sitting about on their porches when I reach Magnolia, my quiet street of small, pinched, two-story stucco houses, with iron-barred windows and doors, secure behind chain-link fences. Our little house, two in from the corner, is my father's pride. Even though it's rented, he always has the best-looking lawn and garden on the block. At Christmas, our house is a riot of blinking colored lights, and loud holiday music competing with the neighbors' over-the-top decorations for the gaudiest display award.

A loud diesel delivery truck rolls past a boy in a navy watch cap straddling his bike on the corner, chatting up three girls. They are twelve- or thirteen-year-olds, heavy with makeup and budding breasts, vying with each other for the boy's attention.

Across the street, an older couple sits in folding chairs by their front door. Protected by their chain-link fence, they watch the teenagers while tending a small hibachi on their front stoop, listening to their radio tuned to a mariachi station.

"Hello, Mama," I call out in the direction of the kitchen, heading for the staircase. "You home? I smell dinner."

"Teresa Maria, come back here."

My mother hurries into the hall. Wiping her hands on her apron, she comes to the bottom of the stairs. "Your papa not home yet."

"Probably stopped to talk about last night's World Series game with the other men, Mama. I'm late for work."

"You eat with us when he gets home," she scolds.

"Mama, I want to talk with Papa about taking an apartment close to UCLA. The bus rides are killing me."

"Too much money," she calls after me.

I continue to the top of the stairs. "I have a test tomorrow, Mama. No time to eat anyway. Hey, you," I call out as I go past my brother's room where the radio is going full blast. I get a grunt in return. I stop and backtrack to his doorway.

"How was practice? Turn down the radio."

"I did good, Teri. Coach says some guys from the junior college will be lookin' at me during the season."

"You, the man," I say, then give him a more serious look. "How was the math test?"

"Not so hot."

"I can help."

"Yeah. Maybe." It's Rico's standard response.

Connie and I share a room. Busy with scissors and paste on a school project, she looks up and greets me with an ear-to-ear smile.

"How was school?"

"I'm making a hand puppet, Teresa," she squeals with glee, sweeping her dark bangs out of her eyes with the back of her hand. "We're having a puppet show in class tomorrow. Do you like my wolf?"

"Cool," I tell her. "He looks big and bad."

I change into my uniform, throwing my hair into a ponytail and fastening the red and gold baseball cap around it. Before leaving the room, I kneel by the side of the bed, facing the small ceramic statuette of the Virgin on my night table. Connie stays respectfully quiet when I whisper a prayer for Antonio. When I finish, I hurry back downstairs. Opening the front door, I call over my shoulder, "I'll eat at work, Mama. Tell papa hello."

"No good for you," I hear from the kitchen as I start back up the street.

* * * *

I get off work at eleven. Dreading two hours of cramming still ahead, wishing I lived near campus. I hurry home on the quiet streets, throwing quick looks over my shoulder, thinking about the gangbangers. Thinking it would be safer in Westwood. Turning the corner onto Magnolia, I'm startled to see my house ablaze with light. I stop for a moment and stare. The house should be dark, with everyone in bed. I speed up. The front door is open. Silhouetted just inside the living room, mama sits hunched over on the edge of the couch. Coming closer, I see she's crying.

"Mama..." I run the last few steps to embrace her. "What's the matter?"

"He don't come home, Teresa Maria." A sob escapes her throat.

A feeling of apprehension creeps over me. "Did you call around, mama? That's not like him."

"No one see him." She starts crying again. I put my arms around her, holding her until she stops. We talk about what to do.

"Don't call the police," she warns me. "Wait. I get off work at eleven."

But she agrees to let me call County Hospital. I ask the woman who answers if José Diaz has been admitted to the Emergency Room. The woman is impatient, telling me there are four Diazes in her computer just now, and it would take her several minutes to pull up each one to see if any are in Emergency.

"I'll wait," I tell her, adding a little attitude to my voice. "This is important."

Papa is not there.

When I tell mama, she starts sobbing again, moaning softly in Spanish.

"Stop it, mama," I can't help snapping at her. "Speak English."

It becomes a night without sleep for both of us. A night of holding each other and hugging and crying. In the morning we are spent. If the night had been full of questions, the morning holds no answers. It feels as if our small house is closing in around me.

Rico rides around the neighborhood before biking off to high school. No one has seen papa. Mama calls her job from the kitchen phone, hesitantly pleading that she needs a sick day. Her boss is unhappy. He says she can't take more time off without jeopardizing her job. Then she punches in the numbers for papa's employer. She asks whoever answers if he's there. I move close to her, trying to hear the reply. There's a long pause. When the voice comes back on, mama winces.

"When he left last night?" She asks.

"Who's calling, please?"

"Dolores Diaz, *son épouse*."

Mama thrusts the receiver at me. "Here, you talk."

I take it and wait.

"You'll have to talk to his supervisor," the voice says after a pause.

"Put him on, please," I tell the young-sounding voice.

"Sorry, he's out in the yard. We're having a problem. I can't reach him. Call back later."

The phone clicks off.

My worry grows. I feel it deep in my stomach. I look at my mother. She looks back. We stay silent for several moments.

"I'm going to the plant," I tell her, getting up and going toward the door. "I'll find him."

I take our old Nissan and drive slowly to Whittier, not wanting to risk getting pulled over. Papa's workplace is a big yard where old wooden pallets are broken into scrap or repaired with new hardwood. I've only been to the plant once before in the six months he's worked here. That was when he had accidentally driven a nail into his leg learning to use a pneumatic nail gun, and they called us to take him to County Hospital.

I park near the office shack. Only a few men are working with claw hammers and iron pry bars, taking broken pallets apart. The yard seems lifeless, no sounds of nail guns now and only a few men working. I walk up to one of them and ask for his supervisor. The prune-faced old guy, gray hair hanging below a beat-up straw hat, shrugs. He points toward the office without a word or a smile, keeping his eyes downcast on his work.

I start in that direction. A burly man with a silver belt buckle and leather boots comes out of the office. He strides toward me with a rolling gait, out of breath when he stops in front of me.

"My father is José Diaz. He didn't come home last night," I blurt out, wishing I'd been more restrained. "When did he leave yesterday? Do you know where he is?"

The supervisor hunches his shoulders. He puts his hand on my back, steering me away from the sounds of the workers toward a corner of the yard. His hand feels inappropriate. I walk quickly out from under it and turn to face him.

"I'm sorry to tell ya your father was picked up yesterday," the man says without any introduction or small talk, coming right to the point as if he were impatient to get back to something more important. "Yesterday mornin' a team from ICE, y'know, *La Migra*, rolled in here. Musta been fifteen, twenty of 'em. Rounded up all the workers in the yard while their buddies went through our office. Made a helluva mess, I can tell ya. Carted off all

7

the men we didn't have proper papers for. Your father, maybe twenty-five, thirty other men. Left us in a helluva mess, I can tell ya. We got only a couple of old men left to work."

Looking around the yard, I only see the old man and a couple of other old men, all with their heads down, sitting among the piles of rotting pallets sprouting wooden splinters and half-naked nails. In the back corner of the yard, I spot papa's beat-up Toyota pickup. I try to fathom what has happened to him? What is happening to my life? Then I look back at the supervisor. He fidgets, shifting from left foot to right, then back. He backs off a couple of steps. I can see he's in a hurry to get back to something.

"My father quit gardening to work here," I tell him. "He was proud of the job he did." As I said it, I feel a lump forming in my throat.

"He was a good worker. We'll miss him."

"Where did they take him?"

"He's probably across the border by now. I dunno."

"How can I find out?"

"Call ICE, I guess. Look, I gotta start finding new workers."

He walks off toward a company pickup. I watch him go.

Halfway, he stops and comes back to me. "Look, Miss, I'm sorry," he says. "Your father was a helluva good worker. He was a good man, always on time, smiling and helping the others. We'll miss him. He had friends here. But he knew the risks." He pauses and looks me over. "You'd better be careful yourself, Miss."

CHAPTER 2

MAMA DOESN'T CRY when I tell her about the ICE raid, but her fingers go straight to the rosary in her lap. "What we do without papa, Teresa Maria?" She says. "How we get along?"

I'm at a loss for what to do, sitting beside her on the couch, holding her tiny, wrinkled hand in mine, The morning light, filtering through the curtains mama had sewn with those wrinkled hands years ago, finds the dust motes drifting around the tiny living room. Getting to my Econ midterm in time is now out of the question. Staying in college might be out of the question, too.

The junior high guidance counselor opened a whole new world for me.

"Your test scores are outstanding, Teri," she said. "There's a program for undocumented students at the University—UCLA." At that, she had tilted her head to the side and looked hard at me with her unspoken question. "You might be accepted if you are willing to work."

I kept my gaze steady, not letting on anything, the way papa had taught me.

One afternoon, Veronica Estrada, a big, tough Latina, cornered me in the hallway. Everyone at Madrid Middle School said Veronica carried razor blades hidden in her frizzy hair. No one ever dared to ask.

She put a hand on my shoulder, smiling a kind of snickering smile. Then she slammed me hard against my wall locker. The combination lock jammed into my shoulder blade, making me wince.

"You ain't no fuckin' white bitch," she growled. "You try to act like one, but you're still a skinny, flat-chested chica. You're one of us. Watch out 'cause one day I'll get ya for tryin' to act better'n us."

Mama and I are silent on the couch. I try to find a way to reassure her, but nothing comes to me, so I let my gaze wander around the room. It's filled with made-in-Mexico things mama and papa have bought over the years. They're good enough, but nothing special. It all seems wrong to me, out of place, marking us as different. Veronica Estrada was right, I'm no fuckin' white bitch.

The next morning, mama fixes breakfast for Connie and Rico and sends them off to school; Rico on his bike, Connie on the bus she catches on the corner. Mama is dressed for work, but we continue sitting at the table drinking tea for a few minutes.

"We okay," she says to me.

"Where could papa be? Where could he go?"

"*Muy difícil*," she says.

"Please, Mama, speak English."

"Very hard to cross now. Fences. Walls. Soldiers. Easier for us."

"Where did you cross?"

Mama tilts her head and looks at me.

"Where did you come from?" I persist.

She gives me a disapproving look, which is easier for her than trying to criticize in English. "You don't listen, Teresa Maria. We tell you and Rico about coming to Monte Vista. You don't listen."

She's right. Rico and I hadn't paid any attention to the stories we heard around the supper table about mama and papa's struggle to get into California. We thought they were only meant to convince us how easy we had it in Monte Vista compared to them.

"What village did you come from?"

"Uruapan. Michoacán."

"Where's that?" I have no idea what she is saying. "Would papa go back there? How far?"

"Sí, very far. Days on the bus to get to border." Her face shows her exasperation. She gives me a dismissive shrug and gets up. "I go to work. Don't worry, Teresa Maria. Papa left some money. I get paid tomorrow."

"He left you money before he got picked up?"

"You father always take care of us."

* * * *

The smell of stale grease in the deep fryer greets me when I go through the door to the fast food place where I work. I nod to the assistant manager and shake a few raindrops off my hat. He is a strange, older guy who gives me the creeps the way his eyes always seem to be looking me over. I hurry to the tiny room off the kitchen to punch in. The odor of Clorox greets me, rising like a mist from the tile floor. Adjusting the headset, I go to the cash drive up window to take over from a teenage boy.

Early-season rain is slowing Thursday evening traffic, rising from the warm asphalt in puffs of steam, glistening in the headlights, and on the windshields of the cars waiting in line.

When I slide the window open to greet my first customer, I inhale a lungful of exhaust fumes that make me cough. Freeway traffic is a steady humming noise. As each car rolls up, I take the money and make change, paying no attention to the drivers, thinking about papa and the text messages I'd had with Ryan before leaving the house.

He'd texted to ask if I would join him the next night. "Want you with me. Be interesting. After at my place."

I texted back "Okay," and added a smiley face.

I don't think I'm in love with Ryan, but he's an okay, gentle guy. Handsome. Easy to be with. An economics major. He had been my introduction to college life. The constant hum of activity on-campus—concerts, plays, poetry readings, parties— enthralled me whenever I could get away from Monte Vista. I've met a lot of girls who have cute clothes that I like at UCLA, but I haven't made any close friends with those girls yet. I guess that will take more time.

No question guys like Ryan could offer me a different life, but I'd held back from him, and hoped he didn't notice. Of course, he did notice, but I want to make sure he's the right man, not just my ticket out of the barrio, before giving myself to him.

I hand the wrong change to a customer.

"Can't you count, *Señorita*?" The man snaps. His car lurches on to the pickup window. Traffic slows on the freeway as the rain picks up, cars begins honking horns and revving engines in the distance, but loud enough to be annoying.

"$6.79," I tell the next car. I take the ten and reach out to give the driver his change, making sure I've counted right. The face peering from the car's window startles me so much I pull back. Its owner grabs my wrist. I'm used to gangbangers pulling up at my window, but this one is different. He seems much older than the teenagers who hang around on street corners. His eyes bore into me. His shaved head, large and lopsided, with ridges and knobs, reflects the building lights, glistening in the drizzle, as he leans his head out the window. A tattooed snake crawls down his left arm from under his T-shirt. I jerk my hand back, but the knobheaded man doesn't let go.

"I know about your father," he snarls. "They carted him across the border with the other men—"

"Let go my hand, Creep."

"I could help you, *Chica,* if you let me."

"Forget it."

"Maybe find your father."

"How do you know about my father?" This time I jerk my hand away hard.

"I know about him. I hear things. I have friends."

I hold back, just looking at him, not sure what to say. The car behind Knobhead revs its engine. Farther down the line, another one honks.

"We should talk," he says. "When you're done—?"

"I don't think so."

"Suit yourself. You got a better way, take it. I don't give a fuck." He keeps staring at me. "You're one of us," he snarls.

I return his snarl, "Never!"

He grins, and I can see his teeth are horribly stained, a couple in front are chipped. "You think you're so fair-skinned you pass for a *gringa.* You don't pass with us, *Chica.* We know. You're very hot. Best for you to be my *mujer.* I take care of you."

He grins, and his car moves on. Another takes its place at the window. "You spend too much time talking to your boyfriend," the woman, whose kids in the backseat are jumping around out of control, almost spits at me. "We're hungry, and it's raining, you inconsiderate bitch."

CHAPTER 3

BY FRIDAY EVENING, the sky is as clear as an L.A. sky ever gets. I get off the bus a couple of blocks from where I'm supposed to meet Ryan in Westwood. It feels good to be back. The streets are crowded with evening buzz. Restaurants are full, and the good smells of pancetta and garlic spill onto the sidewalk. Only Knobhead haunts my thoughts. How does he know about papa? It doesn't make any sense. Could he really help, or is he just hitting on me?

I compare the address Ryan has texted me with the number on the building. I have the right place, but I'm surprised to see it's a storefront with voices coming from inside. I take a deep breath and pull the door open.

A couple dozen college kids, all clean-scrubbed and well dressed in ripped designer jeans and tank tops, are huddled up in small groups, sipping wine from plastic cups and making loud conversation.

"Hi. Welcome." An energetic blond comes from a group to greet me. "Are you a member? She asks."

"Member of what?"

"Sorry. Immigration Reform Students." The girl seems to swell up with pride. "This is our new headquarters, isn't it cool? We're the IRS," she giggles.

I don't see anything funny. I study the girl, who is not really very attractive but isn't unattractive either—mousey blond hair, face that needs makeup and a body that's a little top-heavy. She's typical of a lot of girls on campus, sort of wannabe hot girls who aren't.

"Not a member," I tell her.

"Oh, I'll bet you're with Ryan then," she gushes. "He said you were tall and very pretty. I'm Jen. Teri, right?" Jen gushes again as she looks me over. "You're Hispanic, aren't you? But Teri's not a Hispanic name."

"No," I tell her, "it's not."

I think about being angry or hurt by her lack of sensitivity, but let it go. What's the point? She seems clueless. It happens a lot on campus.

I spot Ryan against a far wall, talking to a few other presumably IRS members. I give Jen a weak smile, then walk away. Ryan's face brightens when he sees me approach. His eyes flash a private hello. I put on a better smile.

As I reach his side, he ends the point he is making to the others with "...it all started way back with NAFTA, you know?" Then he pulls me into the group. "Everybody," he announces. "I want you to meet Teri Diaz, my beautiful Latina friend."

I stand silent at his side for as long as I can stand it, sipping from my plastic cup of oaked chardonnay, fuming about his comment. I let my gaze wander around the room while he rambles on, answering questions from his attentive audience. It doesn't take long for me to decide I've had enough. I tug on his sleeve. "Can we get out of here, please?"

We go to his apartment, a small studio not far off campus on Hilgard Avenue, like the one I'd like to have. "What was that all about?" I ask as soon as we are facing each other in the living room, furnished straight out of an Ikea catalog.

"Not much. A new group we started to protest our unsafe borders. You know, Teri, we need better walls and more men down there."

"Not much? What do you mean? Did you see that place? The walls were plastered with posters of tired old Mexican men— *compesinos*, my father calls them. They are lined up waiting for money wired from the U.S. Another one showed immigrants being herded off by Border Patrol agents. You've got a big nerve taking me there. People kept talking about closing the border to keep illegals out as if Mexico was like the UCEN on a fraternity weekend."

Ryan steps close and tries to embrace me. This is always his response when we disagree. I push away from him. I can't even stand to look at him tonight, so I walk to the window and stare out over the darkened street.

"What is it, Ter—?"

"What is it?" I interrupt hotly. "What were you thinking? Asking me to an anti-immigration rally. How could you even think to do that? Who do you think I am? I'm Teresa Maria Diaz for God's sake."

"I know... I know who you are. We're not against Hispanics, you know. Only the ones sneaking in without documentation."

"So how do you know your 'Beautiful Latina' isn't illegal? Why did you call me that? You wouldn't call me your beautiful Americana would you?"

He goes silent. He stares at me with a look of incomprehension on his face. I let him look, feeling my anger rising inside of me. It must have shown in my eyes because he backs away. Then he sits heavily on the couch we usually make out on. "You're illegal?" He stammers.

I don't even have my coat off, so it only takes seconds before I am out the door, slamming it behind me.

CHAPTER 4

WE GET BY okay without papa for a couple of weeks, but then things start to change. Little things at first. Connie begins pouting about missing the treats papa used to bring home Friday nights for her. She's always been a happy child; now she spends much of her time whining.

As the days wear on, Rico complains at dinner more than usual. "Ma, why can't we have more meat?" becomes his evening mantra. "I've got to put on weight. Coach wants me to wrestle at 157 pounds next meet. I can't live on just rice and beans. I need meat—the coach says so. I had to stop for a burrito from the roach coach after practice with some other guys today."

"*Ai, pobrecito!*" Mama mocks him, reaching out to pinch his arm. "Soon, you'll be a *sombra*," she says. I can see the hurt in her eyes.

We can't afford for her to miss work, so I start missing more classes. I try to be around as much as possible in the afternoons when Connie and Rico get home. I still work in the evenings at the fast food place, and now bring my paycheck home to my mother instead of buying the kind of clothes like the other girls wear on campus.

One afternoon, about three weeks after papa has disappeared on the other side of the border, I answer the phone. The caller introduces herself as Mrs. Jamison from Connie's school.

My heart pumps. "Has something happened?"

"Is Connie's mother there?" Mrs. Jamison asks in a very controlled way.

"She's at work," I tell her. "Is something wrong?" I ask again.

"Connie's fine..." She waits a few seconds. "There is a problem. Could you come to the school to get her?"

Mrs. Jamison is a stout black woman with straightened hair. Her classroom has a familiar smell that brings back memories. Smells of paste and chalk dust and floor wax, and other tiny smells you take for granted as a fourth grader but seem stronger when you haven't been around them for a while. Mrs. Jamison has a familiar smell too, a sweet scent that comes from her hair, I think.

"Come in...Teresa," she says. "Did I get your name right?"

"Teri," I answer. "Where's my sister?"

"She's fine. Waiting for you in the office. I wanted to speak with you first."

Mrs. Jamison points me to a fourth grade desk where I sit with my knees jammed up almost to my chest.

The empty room has a hollow sound. An old sound. Mrs. Jamison looks down at me from her desk with a smile that's both warm and condescending at the same time. She has a very expressive mouth, full-lipped, and turned down corners in a constant frown.

"Is Connie having any trouble at home?"

It's a question I've half expected. My eyes search around the room, looking for the right answer. There are simple math problems on the chalkboard, short essays penciled on wide-lined paper tacked to the corkboards. Models of California missions lined up on the tables in the back of the room. But no answers. At least no answers that need to be shared with Mrs. Jamison.

"No. No problems," I say.

Slowly, and with high drama, Mrs. Jamison opens her desk drawer, as if she is about to show me secret documents. She makes a big deal of reaching into it and shuffling some papers around as if they are important ones she doesn't want me to see. Finally, she slowly removes it and places it flat on her desk so I can't see what it is.

"We had some free time today," she says, dragging out her words, "so I let the kids draw."

Very slowly, she lifts the paper, still not eager to share it until its full impact is visible.

What a drama queen.

"This is what your sister drew."

She hands it to me. A simple crayon drawing, carefully done in Connie's typically neat way. It's a picture of her family: mama, Rico, me, and Connie holding papa's hand. We're smiling. I look the picture over, then at Mrs. Jamison, keeping a neutral expression on my face.

"Do you see anything unusual?"

I look again, hoping what I'd seen the first time won't be there now. It still is. There are holes, small, irregular holes, poked through the paper with a pencil point. Holes poked through Rico and me. Through our faces and bodies. I look up at Mrs. Jamison from my fourth-grade desk, feeling like a naughty child.

"Connie started crying," Mrs. Jamison begins. "It took quite a while to calm her down."

21

Connie holds my hand as we walk home but doesn't say a word. We stop at a street vendor's cart, and I buy fruit ices for each of us. I see tears form in her eyes as she licks at her ice when we sit on a sidewalk bench. Waiting while she licks her way down to the wooden stick, I wish mama or papa were here instead of me, and I pray for guidance. Other kids joke and jostle, yelling at each other as they pass by on their way home from middle school. They give us quick looks but pay no real attention.

When she's done, Connie takes my hand. "I'm sorry, Teresa. I didn't really mean it. I love you and Rico."

"I know you do, Connie. You must have been very angry."

She doesn't answer for a while. She watches the cars and buses going by on the street, so she doesn't have to look at me, I guess. For a silent moment we listen to the traffic noise and inhale exhaust fumes. Finally, she does look at me. "I *was* angry," she says.

"How can I make it better?"

"You can't." A big sigh escapes her. Her face looks more troubled than any nine-year-old face ought to look. She brushes her bangs away from her face before going on. "You can't make it better. Papa's gone, and you can't bring him back."

"Is that why you stabbed us in the picture?"

"It's not fair. You had papa the longest. Then Rico had him. But I only had him a few years. It isn't fair that I didn't get as long a turn with papa as you and Rico did."

* * * *

On Sunday, I help Connie dress for church in a pinafore mama made. I pick out a bright yellow blouse for her to wear with it and brush her black hair to a lustrous sheen. Together, with mama and Rico, we walk up Peck Road and across Orchard Street to Our Lady of Guadalupe. It's a warm morning. The kind of early October morning when the breeze sweeps down from the mountains behind Monte Vista, brooming it clean of the smog and exhaust fumes, and fetid smells from the river and railroad yard. It tingles on our skin and ruffles our hair. Not Santa Ana winds yet but holding the threat they might be coming.

The church stands on a quiet cul-de-sac, its computer-operated electronic bells peeling a summons to Mass. I hold Connie's hand, and she grips mine tightly, just as I used to grip papa's hand tightly when I was her age.

"Give thanks for your blessings," he used to tell me as we crossed ourselves.

"I pray for a different life, Papa," I whispered to him.

"This is your life, Paloma. God gives you only one. Take hold of it, don't let it slip through your hands. God works in mysterious ways, but he has a plan for each of us."

"What is God's plan for me, Papa?"

"Quién sabe, Paloma."

"Why did you bring us to California?"

"I thought here would be better for us.

"Why did you leave Mexico, Papa?"

He always smiled a mysterious smile when I asked him that because the place he described sounded like a fairyland to me. He always made it sound like a land where little Antonio and I could have played together in safety, and no one would laugh at me for the way I talked.

As Connie and I kneel in the pew, I think I can feel papa's mustache brush against my cheek. It brings a lump to my throat. In my prayer, I tell the Virgin how much I miss my father and ask her to protect Antonio.

Activity picks up on the street after Mass as Connie and I start our walk home. Mama lingers in front of the church, chatting with several other ladies. Rico melts off with some boys, calling out to mama he'll be home for dinner. We take our time walking together, swinging our hands. The fascination of the shiny treasures she sees in the shop windows makes her often stop to look.

At the sight of a small gold cross in a *Joyeria*, Connie stops. Her breath fogs the window as she presses her face close against it.

"It's pretty." She purrs, her voice full of adoration. "I want it."

"We'd have to save up a long time for a cross like that," I tell her.

A pouty look knits her brow. Her face pinches down as if my words have touched her in some sensitive place.

"But I want it!"

She stamps her patent leather shoes on the sidewalk. "Papa would buy it for me. I know he would."

She's probably right. Papa often spent money to please us. That was his way. He could never say no. There was always money for the shops on Peck Road. Where it came from, I never understood, but it was there for the things he wanted to buy for us.

"I'll buy it for her."

I didn't connect with the voice at first, but when I look up, the face reflected in the storefront window startles me. Knobhead is standing behind us, grinning so that all his teeth show. The scarring around his mouth gives him a perpetual grin, verging on a sneer. He is probably in his thirties, a large, tree-shaped man, all thick trunk with no branches. He's wearing baggy, knee-length jeans and his Sunday best T-shirt, his sleeves rolled all the way to his shoulders, so the snake can slither down his arm.

I grab Connie closer to me. "Go away, Creep."

Connie looks up at him, frightened but hopeful too. I give him a decidedly unfriendly look. It feels like he has invaded our private moment, unwanted, like the snake, hissing at us, ruining our time together.

"Leave us alone, will you?" That's the best I can come up with. My anger fights a standoff with the fear this guy triggers in me. There is a question of how far to go, how far anyone could go before he strikes. I feel threatened. He seems venomous.

"It's okay," he says. "I have money. Let me buy it for the *niña*. No big fuckin' deal."

I have to get a hold of myself before going on. "No! It *is* a big deal. And watch your mouth. What kind of Neanderthal are you? Butt out."

He backs up a step and looks me over, his eyes stopping here and there so that I feel naked. "You're very pretty when you get angry," he says. His face reflects his amusement. I feel as if I will throw up if he doesn't stop. Grabbing Connie's hand, I start pulling her away.

"I heard from your father."

"You what?" I spin around to face him not sure I'd heard right. "What do you mean?"

"He got in touch through friends."

"How could you and my father have mutual friends? You're lying. Leave us alone."

Knobhead laughs at me. "You're making a mistake, Teresa. I know about your father. Your family needs help just now without a man. I can help you."

"Dream on, Creep, we have a man," I almost spit the words at him, then feel silly. "Rico is old enough to take care of us."

He laughs louder. "Really? You need me. You need someone who knows the streets and how to get along. We can help you find your father if you let us."

"Who is 'us'?"

"Me and my friends."

25

"I told you never." Still holding Connie's hand, I start to move away.

Knobhead stays in front of the jewelry store watching us go. "Be very careful for your little brother," he calls out. "He's over his head."

CHAPTER 5

HARD KNOCKING ON the door startles me. It isn't late, only about 9:00 pm. Mama is lost in a TV daze, watching one game show and sitcom after another. I'm trying to deal with the phone call we got at dinnertime. It had come from the wrestling coach at Arroyo High School. "Was Enrique sick today?" he asked. "He wasn't on the bus for our match with Pioneer."

It caught me off guard. I couldn't give him an answer. "He's not here," I told him. I looked at my mother, her face was blank.

The coach's tone changed. "I saw him in school this morning. I hope he's okay, but I want you to know if there isn't a good reason for this... Well, it's the school's policy to drop an athlete from a team if they fail to attend a match. The guys were really counting on him today."

The knocking doesn't stop. It doesn't get louder either. It is measured, persistent, demanding attention, cutting through canned TV laughter, intensifying the apprehension that has become a permanent resident in our home.

Mama gets slowly to her feet, giving me a worried look. The kind she's been wearing ever since papa got deported.

"*La Migra?*" She points toward the door.

I stand just behind her when she opens it. She keeps the steel-reinforced screen door closed, peering through it at the men standing on the doorstep.

"Good evening, Ma'am."

It's a professional voice, free of emotion, and free of any hint of what will come next. The voice belongs to a tall, solidly built young man. I bite my lip for noticing how good looking he is. His uniform has sharp creases pressed into it. The name above his breast pocket says Nuñez. A black officer stands a step behind him.

"Is this Enrique Diaz's home?"

Mama doesn't respond.

Not far off, the air horn of a Santa Fe freight sounds truculent as it starts moving a string of cars. For the moment, it drowns out the I-10 traffic noise. But you could hear a pin drop on our doorstep.

"*Sí,*" Mama finally answers, taking a deep breath.

"Is he here?" Nuñez let his eyes stray from mama to me. He takes me in with a practiced, appraising eye as if I were a piece of evidence. His gaze goes quickly back to mama.

She struggles for words. I put my hand on her shoulder, ready to jump in if she needs me. The events of the past weeks have weighed her down so that she looks old to me. I never thought of my mother being old before.

"We have a young man says he's Enrique Diaz out in the squad car," Officer Nuñez breaks the silence.

The other officer doesn't move, but he keeps his right hand poised just above his holster.

I edge in front of my mother and take charge. "Has he done something wrong?"

"No, Miss," Nuñez smiles warmly at me.

28

"Then what's the problem?"

The black cop's eyes come alive. "Gangs," he says a bit too aggressively. "We found him drinking behind Ralph's Market with some older boys—gangbangers. He's pretty well tanked. We could've taken him in, but we brought him home instead."

I let out my breath, relieved Rico is safe.

"You hafta watch out for these street gangs," Nunez says, tipping his hat and heading back to get Rico. "They'll ruin your kids."

✳ ✳ ✳ ✳

Without papa, our family is disintegrating. First, Connie, now Rico. Nothing really serious, yet. But step by step, one minor incident after another minor incident, we are falling down a hole.

I can feel mama abdicating her role as family head, more and more counting on me to hold us together. I stop going to Westwood and stay home so she can keep her job. She shows no emotion. She seems frozen. In denial about what papa's absence is doing to us.

"Why doesn't he come back and get his old job?" I ask.

"*No se*, Theresa Maria," she tells me. "Maybe he can't cross."

"Then why doesn't he call us?"

"*No se.*"

"A bill collector phoned today."

Mama just shrugs. "We pay."

My sadness grows day by day. At night it turns to sobbing I can't stop. In the morning, I supervise Connie and Rico, making sure Connie is dressed for school, and trying to coax Rico away from a mistake he'll regret. I collect the mail each afternoon and see the bills that keep coming. When the house is empty, I weep for what we have lost. For what I've lost. And then I weep for what I've never had but desperately wanted—a life away from Monte Vista.

Rico blames the coach for being cut from the wrestling team. He starts ditching school, hanging with street thugs. He withdraws. When he does speak, his words are mean. The allure of gang life is seducing him. The way he dresses shows his contempt for the pride his father tried to instill in him.

My shift at the fast food becomes my escape from the cancer eating at our family. I trade rancid cooking oil, and Clorox smells for the worries of Magnolia Street.

Knobhead invades my life. I can count on a visit from him almost every evening. Usually, it doesn't last long, and I'm protected by the glass barrier. Still, he is an ominous reminder that my life is sinking into a pit. Each time he drives up to the window, I flinch, feeling a spider crawling down my back.

"Your father might be in trouble," he says without preface when he pulls up to the window.

His words catch me off guard. "You don't know that," I tell him, but I'm not sure. "Why do you keep coming around to bug me? If you know something, just say it."

"Too many questions. No more. Just shut up and listen. I have friends. They keep an eye on things for me. They told me he called."

"What do you mean?"

"I told ya before. Look, if ya want my help, say so. I told ya once it's no sweat off my back if you don't."

"Then why do you keep coming around?"

"What time do you get off tonight?"

I hesitate. Thoughts of the risks race though my mind. Thoughts about my options. "Eleven," I finally say.

"I'll be in the parking lot. If you want my help come over to the SUV. If you don't, just keep on walkin'. But this is a one-time-only offer. Pass me by tonight, and there's no deal tomorrow."

At eleven, with the burger place going dark and locking up, I head into the parking lot with a load of garbage for the dumpster. There is a lone SUV parked in the far corner. I can see the streetlights reflecting off the roof and smoke coming from the exhaust. I haven't paid any attention to Knobhead's car before. It gleams in the lights. No rust, no dents, the paint on all the fenders matches. It's big and looks like an Expedition SUV.

I think about how silly I look in my red and gold uniform walking across the parking lot. I don't want him thinking I'm just another *chica* from the *barrio*, so I decide to dump the garbage and keep on walking. But I'm getting desperate, and the question nags at me—what if he *could* help? We need to find my father. After I put the trash in the dumpster, I approach his car.

The passenger-side door opens when I come near.

I look inside to make sure Knobhead is alone. "I only have a couple of minutes," I tell him. Sitting beside him gives me a chill. I kick myself for making the wrong decision.

"You don't hafta be afraid." He looks at me, not smiling. "I can help you."

"Say how. That's all I want to hear." Sitting so close to him, I wonder if he is a house painter because he has a faint smell of turpentine.

"Your father was released across the border with the other men. Some snuck right back that night. He stayed in Tijuana."

"How do you know? Who told you?"

"Don't ask questions."

The front seat is soft leather. I sink down into it and try to look unafraid but press closer to the door with my hand poised near the handle.

"Who are you?"

"I said no questions. My buddies call me *El Niño*."

"You're kidding, right? That's creepy." I can't help laughing, but the look on his face tells me it isn't a joke. "Like the weather or the Christ child?" I ask, pushing my luck too far.

He doesn't laugh. Maybe he doesn't get it.

"Get to the point. How can you help find my father?"

"We can drive to Tijuana. I know people there. Both sides of the border. They'll know where he is."

"Cross the border? With you? Not even in your dreams."

"Do you want your father back?"

"The border?"

"I can get you back and forth no sweat. You don't hafta worry 'bout the border. Just get me a photo."

I look out over the empty parking lot, watching the headlights cruising along Garvey Avenue, feeling desperate, unable to believe this hulking man. I don't even want to be sitting next to him. My mind races, processing possibilities. Then I'm startled alert when a motorcycle with loud pipes races down Garvey. "I don't know," I tell him. "You and me in Tijuana? I don't think so."

"I'm not such a bad dude. I'll behave."

"Like the other gangbangers?"

"I'm not one of them. Those other *chavos* are nothin'. *Cabrones.* Dogs. All they know is playin' the fool. Fuckin' around, pissin' everybody off. I'm not a fool, Teresa. Most of those dogs don't know what to do with a pretty *chica* like you."

That is not an encouraging thing for him to say.

"Besides, what other choice do you have? You want your father back, don't ya?"

I open the car door and start to get out. "I do," I tell him, "but not with you."

His hand grabs my wrist. "Don't leave."

Startled, I look into his face. His eyes are burning. I want to run from the SUV, get as far from Knobhead as fast as I can. I don't.

"I don't think ya get it," he starts again. "*Chicas* like you think the world is safe. It's not. You think nothin' bad will ever happen. Let me tell ya, you're wrong. Bad things happen. Your brother is headed down a bad one-way street. He gets dead or goes to jail, whichever comes first."

He pauses to take a breath, and his solvent smell wafts over me. "Look, your father don't mean nothin' to me. You don't either for that matter...yet. But I'm willing to help ya. What other choice to you have? You're a good-lookin' *chica*, but you won't get far without a man. If you wanna see your father again, you'd better listen up."

It sounds like a threat. I brood in silence for several minutes. My life is on overload. I feel as if all my problems are pressing me into the soft leather seat, making it impossible to leave when I know I should, making my decision impossible, but inevitable.

We agree to go on Saturday.

When Knobhead drops me off, I take a small photo of myself from my wallet and give it to him. When I open the car door, he looks from the picture to me. "You're hot," he says.

CHAPTER 6

THE RIDE PAST the mega-mansions on the highlands overlooking the ocean through Orange County is stop and go. As we get near the border, it is all stop. What was I thinking? Going across the U.S border into Mexico on a Saturday? Every college kid in Southern California must be in the cars around us, heading for fun and frolic in the bars and cantinas down to Ensenada.

What was I thinking, coming to Tijuana with Knobhead? I'm afraid of his control over me. Still, I haven't figured out any alternative. I have to find my father before my family falls completely apart, before I can get back to my own life.

Knobhead has driven in silence the whole way, glancing over at me once or twice, but generally just staring straight ahead. Once, his cellphone rings, and he talks for several minutes in Spanish, mostly a *Si o No* conversation on his end, so I pay no attention.

He finally breaks his stony silence. "You miss your father." It isn't a question.

"Of course, I do." The faint chemical odor I'd smelled before drifts over me as he talks.

"I got no father," he says after a pause. "No mother neither. When I went home one day they were gone. Our building collapsed. I was on the street, just a young kid."

"Earthquake?"

No response.

"I'm sorry."

"Yeah. Sorry. Everyone's sorry, but no one did anything. I slept in the rubble and begged for food. Some friends brought me to Tijuana when I was a teen."

He turns silent again for a few miles. "You're goin' to school."

"UCLA."

"College." He thinks about that for another mile or two. "Why ya wanna be like a gringa? ...Never happen." He goes back to his silent driving.

I'm scared how completely this strange man controls me. I have no idea where we're headed, only a vague concept I have of the border. I have two fifty-dollar bills tucked in my bra for safety that I borrowed from Ryan, but I guess if it came to that, he'd look there, too.

* * * *

The stench, as we wait our turn at the border crossing, is a mixture of exhaust fumes, industrial wastes and street vendor food. The noise accompanying the stench is a composite of diesel rumblings, car horns and human despair. The slight stirrings of air coming through the window, as we wait to cross, waft the odors and sounds into the SUV. I want Knobhead to turn on the AC, but I'm afraid to ask. He seems happy letting his snake, slither down his arm and dangle out the window.

When it's finally our turn, we cross the imaginary line into Mexico. I shudder involuntarily. Desperate times, I remind myself again. I've got to find my father.

"What now?" I ask Knobhead.

"I wanna get somethin' to eat." His words knock me back in my seat.

"What do you mean?" I starting to feel something isn't quite right. Like a gnat bite; it goes almost unnoticed but itches just a little. "What about ICE?"

Knobhead's face toughens on being challenged. His eyes narrow down to a squint, drawing his brows into one continuous dark storm cloud across his forehead. "Sure. As good a time as any, I guess. Don't think we'll get much from 'em. No big deal." His voice takes on a 'who cares' tone.

We park and walk back to the complex of buildings at the Port of Entry. Inside a concrete block office a handful of wrinkled Mexican faces, wearing ragged clothes, sit along a wall. Across the room, a U.S. Immigration officer sits on a high stool behind a counter. He's a middle-aged man with salt and pepper hair sticking out from his ICE hat, a large paunch and bad breath. I'm trembling, trying hard not to let it show as I approach him. He looks me over, tilting his head to one side. "Yes, Miss?" It's a polite but distant voice.

After typing my father's name in his computer, he looks back up at me. "We keep excellent records on the illegals we deport. We hafta, you know? That's how we get funding from D.C. The more we catch and send back, the more money we get next year. Catch and release. It's like fishing." He chuckles.

"Is he in your records?"

"A José Diaz was brought in here about four weeks ago. Is that the right one? We get so many with similar names."

"Where is he now?" I'm close to losing it with this guy's flip attitude.

"We let him go after a couple of hours in the holding tank. Our usual procedure. Usual, I say, unless the computer turns up any crimes or outstanding warrants. Can't be too careful letting criminals go, even to Mexico. Know what I mean? This José Diaz didn't have any outstanding warrants. That the right one, Miss? Lots of Mexicans named José Diaz, you know."

"Where did he go when he was released?"

"Not a clue. For all I know, he could be parking cars on La Cienega again. Once we let 'em go, these guys scatter, like mice in a room full of cats. 'Course, we'll catch 'em again and add 'em to our records. Catch and release." He gives me another big grin. "You're a U.S. citizen, aren't you, Miss?"

We leave the immigration office quickly. Dead end. My hopes dashed. Papa has been here, that's all I know for certain. Nothing I really hadn't known before.

Knobhead shrugs a what-did-you-expect shrug. Then his face brightens. "We knew ICE wouldn't be much help, but it was worth a try. Now we'll go see my people. They'll know what happened."

"What people? Who are your people?"

"You'll see. No more questions."

With that, he reaches out to grab hold of my hand and starts leading me back to the SUV. It sends another chill up my spine. I shake it off. It seems his hand is always grabbing me, so I give him my best don't-try-that-again-or-I'll-knee-you-in-the-crotch look and walk behind him to the Expedition. "Where are we going?" I shout over the noise of the diesel tractor-trailers and buses idling as they wait to cross into California. The acrid smoke coming in burps from their exhaust stacks erases a lot of the sky and tugs at my throat. The flags—ours and Mexico's, hanging limply side by side, are smudged and dirty.

"Las Playas. The beach. You'll like it."

I'm not here to like any of it. And so far, I don't. Traffic crawls going west across the fallen-down city from Otay Mesa, giving me time to blame myself for being stupid for coming here in the first place. Knobhead seems to be on a different agenda now, not as interested in helping me find my father as he'd been back in Monte Vista. Am I a prisoner in his SUV? It's a frightening thought. Scrunching down into the seat, I rub my sweaty hands on my jeans. I have to get it together, so I straighten up and brush my hair away from my face. "How long will this take? When can we go home?" I ask Knobhead.

He doesn't respond.

When we reach Playas de Tijuana, he drives down a street overlooking the beach, stopping in front of a large house, really a mansion, if mansions exist in Tijuana. It sits yards back from the road, close to the beach, protected from everything around it by a chain-link fence topped with razor wire. I can't take my eyes off the razor wire.

Our reception committee consists of three rottweilers. They charge the fence barking fiercely. Then they stand with their noses pressed through it, teeth bared, tongues hanging out as if they hadn't eaten a girl in a week. Getting out of the Expedition, walking toward the house, I recognize the sounds of "Para Siempre" a Vicente Fernandez song, the same music I hear on Peck Road every evening when I get off the bus. At least when I used to.

What I see as we get closer sickens me. I turn back to the SUV, but Knobhead grabs my wrist again to stop me. Wide-eyed, I stare.

"I'm not going in there," I say.

"It's just a beach party," he responds to the shocked expression on my face. "Some of my friends."

Friends? The young women, wearing skimpy bikinis—G-strings or thongs, and some topless—are lounging around on the deck and on the beach below it. Several heavily muscled men in Speedos, tattoos, and dark glasses, talk near the rail. One of them vapes, a couple dance to the music, one rolls a joint.

"I'm *not* going in there."

"Yes, you are," Knobhead answers, laughing. It is the first time I've heard him laugh. It isn't pleasant. Tightening his grip, he pulls me forward.

Panic sets in. I resist, pull my arm away, but his grip is unyielding. He propels me toward the gate. I feel as if I am heading into Hell.

A little elf of a man, as bald as Knobhead, comes out of the house and shoos the dogs away.

"*Que onda, mano?*" Knobhead greets him. "What's happenin'."

The little man shakes Knobhead's hand hard. Then he leads the way toward the house, with Knobhead still pulling me along behind. In the front hall, we stop. A large woman, wearing a bright pink caftan hanging shroud-like from her shoulders over a large belly, plods slowly toward us. Her flaming red-orange hair is tied up with a pink ribbon.

"So, you brought her," she greets Knobhead, limping slightly and rolling from side to side slightly as she comes eyeing me from head to foot. "She's as lovely as you said." The smooth, powdered flesh on her face wrinkles into deep clefts as she smiles at me.

My knees are actually shaking. I glance over my shoulder at the open front door we've just come through. I have to get away.

I have to find my father. Get back to my life, which seems very far away from this Mexican beach house.

"I knew you would like her, Mama Gorda," Knobhead says, curling his lips into a simple grin that shows his stained, chipped teeth.

Trembling progresses up my legs to my back. I begin to feel faint. My eyes lose their focus. The loud music grows dim in my ears.

I yank my hand away from Knobhead, push him out of the way, and run out the door toward the gate. The Rottweilers come alert. Growling at first, they rise, sniffing the air, watching. Then, barking and howling, they race toward me. At the gate, I wrestle with the handle. It won't open. Damn! It won't open. The dogs stop short, right at my feet. They form a semi-circle around me. Teeth bared they growl deep in their throats. One of them snaps at the air. I try one more time to get the gate open. Someone is rushing up behind me. The little elf man charges from the side of the house. I cry out. It's the last thing I remember.

CHAPTER 7

I COME TO on a strange bed, with the sounds of barking rottweilers ringing in my head. I check if I am still dressed. I am. Is the money still in my bra? It is. I put one leg on the floor then the other to get up, feeling wobbly but okay.

I have to get out of this house to regain my life. I creep to the window, afraid to look down at the deck. The ocean shimmers in the late afternoon sun. To the north, in the distance, I can see a steel fence that runs across the beach, disappearing into the ocean. California and Monte Vista are on the other side, I guess.

When I look down, It reminds me of orgy paintings I'd seen in art appreciation class. Bodies are sprawled everywhere as if an artist has placed them for maximum shock effect. Loud music, pot smoke, wine, beer, tequila, and about a dozen half-naked men and a cast of barely clothed women, presided over by the fat lady in a pink caftan. She swooshes around the deck, grinning lasciviously, talking to everyone, catering to their needs.

"What was that all about?" It's Knobhead's voice from the doorway. I spin around to face him, feeling as angry as I ever have.

43

"I was introducing you to Mama Gorda, you ran out. Then you fainted," he says.

"You creep! Take me home right now."

"Can't happen. We're here for a party. Make the best of it."

"No, damn it, I won't. I want to leave now."

"You look hot when you're angry." His look is bland, no smile, just a steady stare from his dead eyes. "You wanna know about your father, don't ya? Mama Gorda says—"

"Shut up! I want to leave. What kind of name is Mama Gorda?"

"She says there are comfortable clothes to put on so you can come down to the deck. I'll meet ya there. Gimme your phone—mine's in the car—and I'll make a call to find out about your father."

He goes to my shoulder bag on the chair near the door and starts rummaging through it, before I can grab it away.

"Give it back!" The frustration of my predicament makes me stamp my foot. I feel like a child. Like Connie.

Knobhead disappears out the door, racing down the stairs holding my shoulder bag, the phone still in it.

Helpless, I sit on the edge of the bed.

Soon, a young woman with an angelic face taps lightly on the open doorframe replacing Knobhead. She stays poised on the threshold—a voluptuous girl—probably in her late teens, her breasts spilling out from her bikini top and blonde hair falling softly around her shoulders reminding me of a Rubens painting.

She speaks Spanish in a low, purring voice. I stare at her, not responding. She stops talking and looks at me through large, almost black irises set in bright white eyes. "*No habla Español?*"

I shrug.

"I talk English some," she says, smiling, her eyes bright, but timid. "Don't be afraid. No one here hurt you."

"What kind of place is this?"

"Party house. We make videos."

"Videos?"

"*Si*, sex videos, *mucho* porno. Mama Gorda wants you to party with us."

"No!" I feel sick to my stomach.

"Oh?" The girl looks perplexed, then frowns. She bites her fingernail, looking me over. "I thought that why Hector bring you here. For porno. Beautiful girl like you could be a star."

"Is that his name—Hector?"

I'm trembling. What has happened to me? It's like I've been transported to some alternate world. If there's a Virgin Mary in this new world I'm trapped in, I implore her to rescue me.

"Are you crazy?" It's hard to keep from shouting. "I don't do porn!" Even saying the words sounds absurd.

"*Si*, Mama Gorda wants you to make a movie with us. Not so bad." She half smiles. "You get used to it."

What kind of girl makes porn videos? The thought is more disgusting than I can deal with. And what kind of name is Mama Gorda? Why do all these Mexicans have weird names?

Too many questions.

I can see the girl is nervous, so I reach out to calm her, touching her shoulder. Maybe to calm me, too. Feeling a sensation when my fingers touch her skin. "I don't make porno movies," I tell her again.

She looks perplexed. "Before we come to Mama Gorda's *Casa*, none of us did porno."

She tells me her name is Vivian. I motion her to sit beside me on the bed. Awkwardly silent for a few minutes, with neither one of us knowing what to say, she finally reaches out to take my hand in hers. Soft as her touch is, it sends another electric

45

charge up my arm that startles me. She asks where I have come from, showing no surprise when I tell her California. I ask where her home is. "I live here with Mama Gorda," she answers. As she does, her face brightened.

"Don't you have a family you can go to?"

"My family live in Sinaloa. They give me to Mama Gorda."

Vivian responds to the stunned expression on my face. "Life is different in Mexico," she starts. "It not that they do not love me. My mother and father cannot afford to feed all their children."

In a bittersweet voice, she explains her parents have made a good deal with Mama Gorda. Her brothers and older sisters are working or begging in the streets of Culiacán to help out the family. It was only natural, she says, that she should be the one to go. She adds it has been good for her, too. "Mama Gorda sends me to school," she says. Then she adds, "Time for you to come downstairs."

When I tell her again I'm not going to, Vivian becomes visibly upset. She gets up, tugs at her cotton shorts so they aren't invading her crotch, and adjusts her top, unconcerned that most of her rich latté-hued body is bare. She looks worried she isn't accomplishing the mission she's been sent on.

"Not so bad," she tries to assure me, once more. "Mama Gorda take good care of us. Give pills to relax you. Anyway, no videos today. Please come down with me now."

When I tell her no, Vivian becomes confused and hurries out of the room.

In a couple of minutes, I hear someone dragging a lot of weight up the stairs, one slow step at a time, groaning, mumbling, and huffing for breath. Mama Gorda blocks the doorway. Flecks of white foam glisten on her lips, painted pink to match the ribbon in her hair. She gasps for breath.

46

"Sweet child, why you make Mama Gorda climb all those steps?" Her hair is sweaty and slightly matted from her effort. It's the color of rust but streaked with coppery-red tints that give it a kind of metallic glow.

Smiling as politely as I can, I tell her, "There must be a mistake. That man, Hector, brought me here to learn about my father. I don't...party." That sounds weird, but I hope she gets the message.

"A lovely *chica* like you? With your pure white skin? So tall, so statuesque. You're our type. Look through the closet and pick out whatever you want to wear. I promise we'll be gentle with you. Just get to know the others on the deck, we're not shooting today."

She goes to the closet, opening it to show me a wardrobe that runs the gamut from the bizarre to the ridiculous, skimpy lingerie suspended from hangers in every conceivable color. Garter belts, bustiers, thongs, fishnet stockings—costumes for every fantasy from French maid to farm girl to nurse.

She reaches for a hanger. "This one good for a college girl. Put it on."

I can't help but giggle, even as I try to keep a severe scowl on my face, at what she brings out of the closet. It is a very low cut, very short UCLA cheerleader's dress, light blue sleeveless top with gold letters across the chest, and blue and gold V-trim at the waist. A short, flared skirt trimmed in the same colors and a dark blue thong to go with it.

I'm having a nightmare, I tell myself.

"I want Hector to take me home now," I tell Mama Gorda.

She looks at me with a sad face. "He's gone, *chica*. He left for L.A. fifteen minutes ago."

I jump off the bed and rush at her. "Gone? Without me? What's going on here? I need to leave right now."

"Okay, go ahead, you can leave if you want to."

I reach for my shoulder bag on the chair. A wave of panic come over me, it's gone. My wallet with the fake driver's license, along with my cellphone, both gone. I give Mama Gorda an accusing look, but I know it was Knobhead-Hector who took it.

"How am I going to get home without my license?"

"I don't know."

"I'm a prisoner here."

"I said you could leave anytime you want to. But think what might happen to a girl with your looks wandering around Tijuana. And the beach fence is a dangerous way to sneak across. It's watched constantly."

"I *am* your prisoner."

My sense of terror is physical. I strike out at her with both fists. But my attack is useless against her soft flesh. The blows she doesn't block sink harmlessly into the soft tissue of her arms and shoulders and breasts. I keep hitting until I can't hit her anymore. Out of breath, I collapse in tears on the bed.

I think I see a trace of pity on her face when I look up at her. "Hector, the dude who calls himself *El Niño*, is a fool," she says. The compassion fades, replaced by a stern, almost angry look. She turns and starts down the hall, then stops and turns back again. "But he did make the call for you. Our people know your father got into a pickup truck when he was released at Otay. He was headed to the mainland and was going south.

I looked at her in dismay. "Your people?"

CHAPTER 8

I SPEND A lot of time lying alone on the bed, thinking about papa, trying to understand the things he'd taught me.

"Don't hold back on living," he'd *cautioned whenever he saw me afraid. "You take the life you're given—some good, some not—make the most of it. It's our way."*

With his words echoing in my head, I search for some escape, but I'm trapped.

The first night passes with me left alone, curled in a defensive posture on the bed. What is this life I've been given I keep asking myself? Over and over in my head during my waking hours the thought keeps repeating. A month ago, my life was on course. Get my degree, get a good job, raise a family some day in a middle class California suburb. I thought that was the life God intended for me. Now, I'm a prisoner in a Tijuana porn house.

The rumbling in my stomach begins around midday Sunday, but by evening becomes a steady gnawing. As the hunger takes control of me, my ability to think clearly fades. No one comes near me, no one releases me from the prison of the room overlooking the Pacific. I'm as alone as I've ever been, only vague sounds of life drift up from below. Safe enough, maybe, but with no way out. And no food.

I make it through a second day, worrying that my mother hasn't heard from me, fighting the pains gripping my stomach. I try to sleep so they'll go away. It doesn't help.

Vivian comes to visit once. I ask her to sneak some food to me. The look on her face is sympathetic but tells me it isn't going to happen. She says Mama Gorda has forbidden it.

"What would she do if she caught you?"

"She say anyone who bring you food must leave the house and cannot come back."

I try to think about how bad a punishment that might be. "Does that scare you, Vivian?"

"It safe here," is her answer. "Outside, not safe. Not safe for girl like me. Girls get caught by gangs. Used by men. Please come down."

✳ ✳ ✳ ✳

On the third day, I spend time looking out my window. The crowd of tattooed men I'd seen the first day has thinned out. The Norteño music is gone. Young women come and go on the patio. I guess there are not more than a handful of them.

From the doorway, I can see up and down the hall. I tip-toe out to the staircase. No one is around. I go to the top of the stairs. Still, no one. Driven by my hunger, I start down, wondering if I can find the kitchen before being spotted.

The rest of the house I can see from the stairs startles me. The rooms—several living rooms and parlors, all off the main hall—each have a different décor. All are over the top with theatrical lighting. Silent, too. I stop to listen. Just faintly, when I stand still, I can hear pounding music that is more vibration than sound.

I go down a long hallway in what I hope is the right direction for the kitchen. Mama Gorda's voice breaks the silence.

"So, you decide to join us. I'm glad."

For a second, I think about racing back up the stairs to my room and getting back on the bed. That's not going to calm the feeling in my stomach, so I turn around to face her. "I have to eat," I tell her, almost shouting, feeling like a bad young child who's been caught stealing cookies from my mama's kitchen. "You can't do this. Please, I'm hungry."

"Of course, you are." She smiles unctuously. "And you will eat... just as soon as I introduce you to the others. They're taping a scene just now, but as soon as they're done, we'll go into the studio, and then I'll take you to the kitchen. But first, the introductions."

It is tough to meet strangers who have just finished doing what I can only imagine. I can't make eye contact with the young women. Vivian rises from a couch, where she's been sitting, and rushes toward me with her arms outstretched, prepared to embrace me. I back up in horror at the thought. My impulse is to find a sink and bathe myself.

Around the room, one or two women are toweling themselves dry, another works on reapplying makeup, another wiggles into a thong. The men simply stand by limply, deeply muscled, prominently veined, looking like sculptures except for the garish tattoos that give them a surreal look.

Vivian stops just short of the embrace, quivering and jiggling, not timid, bare to the towel wrapped around her hips, smiling her pleasure at seeing me. Standing still, her golden curls cover much of her bare breasts, she looks almost angelic. Her large dark eyes glisten with joy

"It's good, Teresa, you come here. All of us will be your new friends." She points to the other girls who nod or wave at me. The guys study me intently as if they are eyeing a slab of meat at the supermarket. Vivian grabs my hand, pulling me away from Mama Gorda. She introduces me to the others, one by one— Angelina, Lindsay, Brittany and Penelope—not their real names, I assume. When we're done, Mama Gorda tells Vivian to take me to the kitchen and give me whatever I want to eat.

"*Bueno*," Vivian gushes. "Now you be like us."

CHAPTER 9

I HAVEN'T EATEN in three days. I crave a hamburger, maybe because it represents a taste of reality in this ongoing nightmare, reminding me of Monte Vista. A prune-faced old Indian woman, who rivals Mama Gorda for size but has a darker complexion, grills it to perfection. She tops it with onions, tomatoes and lettuce and a couple of *Jalapeños*. The kitchen is the old Indian's domain, and she seems to thrive on caring for Mama Gorda's girls. She hustles between refrigerator, stove and me, making sure I'm satisfied with her efforts.

Vivian has donned a robe and pulled her blond hair into a long ponytail. She sits beside me as I eat. "She does all cooking here," she says, pointing to the woman. "What we want, she make. She buy only best at Costco in Imperial Beach each week and bring back to us."

I think it might be a good idea to make friends with the cook, but for now, I'm satisfied to focus on the French fries that come with the burger.

"No more videos today," Vivian says. "We can go on deck and catch rays—is that what California girls say?" She giggles. "We find you bikini. I introduce you to the guys."

"I don't think so," Mama Gorda says, coming into the kitchen behind us, overhearing the end of the conversation. "We don't want Teresa to be out in the sun. We want to keep her covered up and as fair as we can for tomorrow."

The rest of the day goes by too fast. My mind plays with all the disgusting possibilities Mama Gorda's words, "for tomorrow," bring to mind. At dinner, I'm served a sirloin steak, medium rare, the way I like it, with mushrooms and onions on top. A side order of zucchini comes with it, along with a very fresh green salad—maybe fresher than what my mother can buy at the Ralph's on Garvey Avenue. The rest of the girls eat *carne asada* with rice and beans. But no dessert. "My girls stay trim," Mama Gorda insists. "We eat well here, but no junk."

"See how she take care of us?" Vivian croons in my ear as we eat. "This is best place for me."

"But..." I look into her soft and trusting eyes and stay silent. Is she right?

Everyone retires to their rooms early. Some of the girls are studying for school. Those who aren't needed in the studio the next day will go to the convent school in Tijuana.

Soon after settling on the bed in my room—how has it become "my room" so soon?—Mama Gorda wheezes up the stairs and sticks her head in the door.

"We talk," she says, coming in without waiting. She lowers her bulk into an over-sized chair that sags under the load. She studies me without speaking for several minutes.

"Hector made a big mistake, no?" She says, looking at me with more compassion than I've seen in her before. "I see you are not made for this, but I cannot let you leave. The other girls would not understand. You are a beautiful young woman," she says, after pausing to study me again. "How I wish I had other girls as lovely as you are. I had your beauty when I was young."

I look at her, waiting. What's coming next?

"How old are you?"

"Twenty."

"A virgin?"

I looked down at the bed and nod.

"You're the kind of girl who ought to marry a good husband and raise a lot of children."

"Perhaps. But I want a career... not doing porn."

"We will do nothing tomorrow to violate you," she assures me, then goes right on, "but you will participate in our taping. I want to see how you do." She gets up to leave but stops in the doorway. "You are blessed, Teresa. You could make a lot of money in Mexico. But sleep tonight without worry. In the morning, the maid will put out the clothes I want you to wear. Sleep well and look your prettiest tomorrow."

I'm surprised at the plainness of the clothes laid out for me when I awake. A wool cardigan sweater in a lovely raspberry shade that sets off my dark brown hair when I look in the mirror, and a plaid woolen skirt, too short, but not obscene. Almost like an American college girl. I dress and go down to the kitchen. It's empty. Only the cook hustles about, and she is startled to see me.

"You no eat," she snaps. "Rules. No one eat until work is done." Then, as an afterthought, she points down the hall. "They wait for you in studio."

Walking down the hall on very shaky legs feels like doing a convict's last mile. Stopping just outside the studio, I'm more afraid than I think I've ever been, and I cannot stop my tears. How has this happened to me? I have no experience with men, yet in the next few minutes, my life will be ruined. Despite Mama

Gorda's reassuring words, I visualize some form of burning Hell on the other side of that door. It makes me sick to my stomach to think of the naked bodies carousing in all manner of lewd acts in that studio. Acts I have no knowledge of. Only ugly fantasies. I start to retch and run for a bathroom. That only prolongs my fate. I return to the studio, reach for the handle, afraid to touch it. I'm sure the doorknob will sear my hand. In my head, I cry out to the Virgin to protect me. The door opens. Mama Gorda stands in the doorway, smiling. "I thought I heard you," she says. "Come in, Teresa."

And there I am, standing in the doorway, looking at Vivian and two other naked and semi-naked girls, reclining on couches. I wince. Close my eyes. Almost retching again and turn away to stop myself. I turn back. The revulsion I feel is tempered by curiosity when I do. I've seen naked girls before, of course, in the middle school locker room.

The locker room was Veronica Estrada's hangout—the girl with the razor blades in her hair. She strutted around the Madrid Middle School locker room like she owned it.

"Look at you," she laughed at me. Ya got no pubes. No tits. You sure you're in the right locker room?"

She was right on all counts. Middle School was not a good time for my self-esteem. I was tall and scrawny. Flat as a board. "Bet you haven't had your period yet," she taunted. "You're not a woman, just a little girl. Never get a man to fuck you. You're so flat and ugly."

More often than not, she had me in tears before the bell rang.

Some of those same feelings come back now looking at the women draped over the furniture like X-rated slipcovers. I can't turn away. I keep staring. Comparing their bodies to mine. Looking for their imperfections, trembling slightly even though I try to hide it. Their bodies are beautiful, soft, plaint, voluptuous, beckoning. All my nerve endings are sensitized. Is there something wrong with me? The thought brings another shudder.

There are a couple of men moving floodlights and large reflectors around the room to create the lighting effects Mama Gorda wants. Two other men lounge behind their cameras, one rolls a joint, paying no attention to the rest of the activity until Mama Gorda snaps at him.

I am the only one focused on the girls. Why can't I turn my eyes away when these men are oblivious to the bare female flesh? I can't. It is as if Veronica Estrada is standing in the room, laughing at me. What would it feel like to have my clothes off? Would those men taunt me like she did? Or would they ignore me?

Mama Gorda puts her hand on my shoulder. "I promised we would not force you to do anything you're uncomfortable with. I want you to do just one thing in this scene today, and then it will be over."

She hands me several schoolbooks she picks up from a nearby table. "When the camera starts, and I tell you to, I want you to open the door and walk into the room."

She turns away from me. "Miguel, move that camera left," she shouts to one of the men. "Brittany, easy with the makeup. Not too pale."

Then she's back. "Stand in the doorway long enough for the camera to get a good shot of you," she instructs. "Look around the room. Smile as you look at your roommates, big smile at the camera. Set the schoolbooks down on the table and walk over to Vivian. Give her a big smile. A kiss. Then reach down and gently touch her breast. Let your hand slide over it and down her belly as far as you're comfortable. Then walk out of the camera to the other side of the room. That's all."

She reaches out to unbutton the top two buttons on my sweater then pushes me out the door before I can react.

So, there it is. There *I* am, standing in the hall, holding a stack of books with my bra and the curves of my breasts exposed, waiting for a signal. About to become a porn star. My legs continue to shake.

Through the door, I hear Mama Gorda's voice. "Roll the camera," she calls. After a few seconds that feel like an hour, I hear her say, "Come in Teresa."

Then it's a blur. I remember my hand reaching for the doorknob and reaching for Vivian's breast. Touching her nipple. I remember looking at the camera, almost dropping the books when I saw it point at me. One of the men was staring. I feel as if I linger over Vivian too long, touching her softness, seeing the reassuring look on her face, before rushing out of the scene.

"Okay," Mama Gorda sings out. "Not bad, Teresa. Let's try it once more, a little slower, a little more relaxed, and then I think we can take a break for lunch.

CHAPTER 10

THE NEXT TWO days continue my nightmare. I take off more clothing than I want to, but less than Mama Gorda urges. I touch other women, but don't allow anyone touching me. The other girls show me respect and patience. The men in the studio seem to stare at me until Mama Gorda scolds them.

"Is this so bad for you?" Vivian asks after the second day.

"Yes," I tell her, "it is. I feel dirty when we do those things."

"I like the way you touch me," she responds, giving me one of her soft and lovely smiles. "Different than the others. I feel safe with you in the studio."

She's right about that. With any of the other girls, I would have panicked, run out of the room. With Vivian, it was almost comfortable. Almost. She is sweet and beautiful and passive. I feel bonded with her whenever we touch. I'm beginning to think of her as a sister. "I'm glad my scenes are with you," I tell her. "I don't think I could do what we did with anyone else."

Vivian beams at that. She reaches out to take my hand and gives it a gentle squeeze.

* * *

"You don't belong here."

I'm dumbfounded at Mama Gorda's words. We are sitting together in her private office. She called me there after dinner, after my third day in the studio.

"Of course, I don't. I told you that." My anger makes my voice bristle. "I'm your prisoner."

"No, my guest... For now. But that's not what I mean. You're not like the other girls."

"I'm not a Mexican whore if that's what you mean? I'm an American."

"You're wrong on both counts, Teresa. These girls aren't whores, and you're not American. You try, but you are lost—not American, not Mexican."

Her words cut me. I let them go, but they rob me of my anger and sting more than I expect. I try to calm myself and struggle for some dignity.

"You keep them here like prisoners, having sex while you video them," I blurt out. "How can you sleep?"

"Don't be naïve, I sleep very well." Mama Gorda pulls her bulky body up in the chair. The fleshy skin around her eyes tightens as her face gains a toughness I haven't noticed before. "My girls aren't prisoners. In fact, they're free to leave whenever they want. You can too. Do you know why they stay?"

"Vivian says she feels safe."

"Vivian knows what it's like to be afraid. So do the others. You've never had that worry. You've never really been afraid. In Mexico, young girls aren't safe. They're kidnapped; they disappear off the streets, some on their way home from school. Gangs take them, they become sex slaves on both sides of the border, made to do whatever men tell them. That's right! Don't look so shocked. Sex trafficking is big in the U.S. If the girls refuse, they're beaten, sometimes killed. Bodies turn up all the time along the roadsides."

Her words make me uncomfortable. She watches me squirm, a kind of sardonic look comes over her face.

"It's true, I don't pay them, but I give them a safe home. I send them to school, so maybe they can find a job when they're too old for porn. I feed them and make sure they have medical care. Do you think the porn makers in Los Angeles do any of that? The girls in L.A. get diseased, and when they can't get work, they're tossed off. My way is better."

I have no challenge to what Mama Gorda is telling me, so I don't argue. I had no idea there even was a porn industry in L.A. Besides, she'd said words I needed to hear. "You said I could leave. When?"

"Tomorrow."

She gets up ponderously from her chair and goes across the room to a desk. She returns with an envelope she hands to me. I'm startled to see five one-hundred-dollar bills inside. I stare at her.

"I said you're different," she says. "You could be a great star in Mexico, Teresa. In telenovelas or movies. I've seen the tapes of the last two of days. You have a quality—shy and innocent—it speaks to the camera. You could make a lot of money." She pauses for a moment. "Hector went too far. Perhaps he never should have brought you here. He's a fool, but I'm glad he did so I could meet you. He brought you here to please me. I would say I'm sorry, but I'm not."

"He lied to me."

"He did. He thinks being called *El Niño* makes him sound tough, you know. Hector is not quite right in his head, but generally, he's harmless. We took him off the streets of Mexico

City. He was a *Tragafuego*, a fire-breather. Do you know what that means?"

I said I didn't. So, she tells me about young boys begging on the Reforma in Mexico City by igniting gasoline or other flammables they blow out of their mouths. I shudder at the thought. I have no idea about porn DVDs made in L.A. and shown on the Internet, or fire breathers in Mexico City. I guess I don't know much about a lot of things because papa never told me about them.

Mama Gorda chuckles, "In California, I think you would say Hector is one taco short of a combo plate. He works for us, and we take care of him, just like we take care of our girls. When he left, he took another envelope with money to give to your mother." Mama Gorda goes back to her desk and comes back holding my cellphone. "Hector left your phone. You should call your mother and tell her you're safe, Teresa. Tomorrow I've arranged a ride for you.

* * * *

The phone rings in Monte Vista, and Mama picks up
"Mama, it's me, Teresa..."
"I'm fine, mama..."
"I'm sorry you were frightened..."
"I lost my phone for a few days..."
"Have you heard from papa?"
"I need to find him..."
"I think he may have gone south..."
"Michoacán?"
"From papa? Who else could the money have come from?"
"In the mail?"
"Did you get other money?"

"Forget I asked..."

"How are the kids?"

"You've got to put your foot down, Mama..."

"Don't let him leave after dinner..."

"Make him show you his homework..."

"How is Connie doing?"

"Good..."

"Tomorrow or the next day, I think..."

"Whenever I can get across..."

"It's a long story..."

"I gotta go, Mama. My phone's dying..."

"I'll be home as soon as I can..."

"Love you."

＊ ＊ ＊ ＊

I do a final scene with Vivian, not much different than my other scenes. When it's over, I feel a huge relief. I've survived. Maybe more. Maybe I've learned a lot about myself. I know I'm changed in some way. I've grown up.

I don't rush out of the studio when the camera stops. Without thinking, I go to Vivian. She is coming across the room to me. We meet in the middle and embrace. Just the embrace of two friends, nothing more.

Later that morning, Mama Gorda calls me into her office and introduces me to Javier Ugalde. Tall, solidly built, but lean-looking because of his height, Javier has close-cut black hair and a prominent straight nose. There is no question he's handsome, perhaps in his late 20s or early 30s. I study his face as we're introduced to see if there are any signs of judgment about what I've been doing here.

He turns south off Benito Juarez, just before it merges into Paseo de Los Heroes, the road that crosses the border, onto Boulevard Sanchez Taboada. A few blocks south, he turns into a stone-paved driveway and stops. Removing his helmet, he motions me to do the same.

"Why are we stopping?" Handsome or not, I don't know who Javier Ugalde is, don't have any reason to trust him—actually more reasons to distrust him—and no intention of blindly being led by him.

He looks at me for several moments before breaking out in a laugh. "No need to be frightened, Teresa," he says when he stops laughing. "With me, you are as safe as you can be in Tijuana. This is a restaurant. I brought you here for lunch."

"You said you were taking me across the border—"

"And I will. I thought we might spend an hour or so dining and getting to know each other first. I think you'll enjoy this restaurant. Then we'll talk about crossing."

✳ ✳ ✳ ✳

We are hardly in the door of the large restaurant when a man rushes over to greet Javier. "*Señor* Ugalde, such a special pleasure to see you again," the man gushes. "Your usual table? This way, *por favor*."

The room is trying to look like an outdoor patio. A stone fountain in the center splashes water, creating the fantasy of coolness. Around the walls, stone colonnades support a false wooden roof. Brightly-hued birds fly free about the room, tiny spots of living color—red, blue, green and gold—barely catching the corner of my eye as they flit from perch to perch.

The waiter hovers over Javier as we sit side by side in a booth on the wall facing the fountain. Javier doesn't ask, he simply orders two margaritas.

"So," he starts when the man rushes off to get our drinks, "what is a pretty American girl doing at Mama Gorda's?"

I feel flush and a little faint. It's one thing—on the verge of starving—to do what had to be done to survive. Quite another to have this good-looking man question me about it. I can't quite bring myself to look at him. "It was a mistake," I tell him, looking down. "A long story. I wasn't supposed to be there."

"I see." He grins.

He might have winked, I'm not sure. My eyes search around the room, looking for the birds, or something else, rather than looking directly at him. I see that most of the restaurant's customers are watching us.

"What you do is really none of my business." He smiles as the margaritas arrive, and changes the subject. "If you'll let me, I'll order lunch for you. They have some wonderful food here, not what you get in L.A. They specialize in authentic food going all the way back to the Mexica —The Spaniards called them Aztecs."

I sip the drink, feeling the tequila slide down my throat, a little hot and scratchy, but comforting, nevertheless, feeling like I'm in some kind of romantic fantasy. I steal a couple of quick glances at Javier as he looks at a menu. His clothes are casual and immaculate. His hands holding the menu are manicured. When he looked back at me, there is softness in his dark eyes.

"How does squash blossom soup and squid in three chili sauce sound to you?"

"Squid?" I tried to be casual, but the idea of eating squid catches me off guard. I've never eaten squid.

Squid was the bait papa used when he took me fishing in Long Beach on Sunday afternoons.

"Sometimes we get food for free," he would tell me whenever he managed to hook a rock cod or some other edible fish. I never ate papa's fish. Whenever I tried, I pictured the dirty waters he fished in, and the image made me gag. He'd shrug and turn to mama at the dinner table. "What kind of niños do we raise?"

"Trust me. It's wonderful." Javier reaches over to pat my hand for the second time in an hour, as if to reassure me. "A little garlic and onion, some olive oil, cooked with *ancho*, *mulato* and *guajillo* chilis."

It's then that I realize how out of place I am. The restaurant is charming if a bit *faux*. The food apparently goes well beyond Olive Garden fare. That was the way papa and mama usually treated their children. I look down at my jeans, grimy from almost six days' wearing. I feel cheap, no longer the bright college girl I'd been a month before, and I can't help wondering if that part of my life is gone forever. Memories of the past few days choke in my throat. I would have gotten up and run, if I had known where to run.

CHAPTER 11

THE SQUID IS a delicate blending of tastes, with the chilies adding just a hint of warmth. Still, thinking of papa and the Long Beach harbor, it's hard to swallow. Our conversation is friendly, a little strained as you'd expect between two strangers. Javier is polite and a little bit formal.

We are interrupted several times when the owner comes over to ask if everything is all right. Even as the restaurant fills with noontime customers, I'm aware he is giving Javier his special attention. Occasionally, people at other tables sneak quick looks at us.

I really want Javier to know I'm not one of Mama Gorda's girls, but I don't think I should come right out and say it. He seems like a nice guy. It's important to me to convince him I'm bright, articulate, and definitely not a porn princess. But I don't know what to say or how to say it. So, I let him lead the conversation, and I respond with one-word answers, feeling like a retard.

"Let's talk about crossing," he says as we are finishing. "I understand you don't have any U.S. or Mexican ID. Not even a driver's license."

The impact of his words hits me hard. "You're right. Is that a problem?"

"Not really. But we can't just drive through the Port of Entry, can we?" He gives me a bright smile that morphs into a chuckle, coaxing me to lighten up. "There are some places where I can drive the Kawasaki across. Out in the desert. Is that okay with you?"

I take a sip of the espresso Javier has ordered for us, thinking about sneaking across the border, not wanting to say a word. It burns my lips and all the way down my throat. I wince and hope he hasn't noticed. I keep quiet.

"What will you do after you cross?" He asks.

"Take a bus home, I guess. In the morning."

"Carmen—Mama Gorda—told me Hector brought you to Tijuana to look for your father," Javier says when the waiter leaves us. "She said he was deported."

Briefly, I tell him the story.

"Any idea where he might be?"

"Maybe Michoacán, wherever that is." I kick myself for sounding stupid.

"Have you given up looking for him?"

"I don't know what to do." I give Javier a weak smile along with a shrug. It is the kind of smile I hate to see on girls' faces when they try to act helpless to get something out of a professor. "I need to find him, but I don't know how to do it."

"I could help. I know my way around the country pretty well. I know people. I'm at your service if you'll let me—"

"I couldn't ask that."

"You can if you want. In fact, I'm going to Michoacán in the next day or two. To *Morelia*. I'd be happy to take you there, and we could make some inquiries."

In his dark eyes, almost as dark as the espresso, I can see he is serious. Who is he? And when did he get to be a superhero? I can see he isn't a gangbanger like Knobhead. He doesn't dress or talk like one. But what would I be getting myself in for traveling deep into Mexico with him?

Even with all the negatives my mind throws up at me, it's a tempting offer. A handsome man, eager to help. I consider it. What are you thinking? I ask myself. Can I trust this man?

Javier holds my gaze, returning it with a sincere look. I need to say something to break the silence. I need to say no. "On your motorcycle?"

He bursts out laughing. "My God, no. We would fly there. My plane's available, and it would be my pleasure to escort you."

"Your plane?" Who is this guy?

"My family's plane actually, but I'm a licensed pilot. What do you say? We could go to Patzcuaro for *Dia de los Muertos*."

This is definitely getting out of control, but I don't know how to act. How to stop it. "Where is Patzcuaro?"

He grimaces. "In Michoacán."

"Is *Dia de los Muertos* special there?"

"One of the best fiestas on the Mexican calendar. Like your Halloween. You'd have fun. And I'd want to show you the butterflies."

"Butterflies?"

"Yes. Each winter, millions of Monarch butterflies, maybe billions, winter in the Oyamel trees of Michoacán. It's an incredibly beautiful sight to see. Come spring, after they mate, they fly back north to drop their eggs and die. How they find their way to their overwintering site in Michoacán remains a mystery. Many of us believe the butterflies are the spirits of our departed loved ones. We can look for your father and celebrate our new friendship at the same time. You can stay at my family's house in Tijuana tonight, and we can leave in the morning."

Warning bells are going off all over in my head. This is going way too fast. Is Javier the key to finding papa? How can I know? I'm on overload. Yet I'm ready to say yes if I can find my father and stop our family from disintegrating without him. That's all I want.

Then I have another thought. "Sorry I can't go. The clothes I'm wearing are all I have. I've worn them for a week now."

"You can buy new clothes this afternoon if that's the only thing stopping you."

"I can't. I don't have a lot of money with me." It's a lie to get me out of this trap I've created for myself.

"Consider it taken care of. We'll get you a few essentials here, and tomorrow I'll introduce you to some shops in Morelia."

"I don't know," I stammer. My head is spinning, I'm feeling trapped. "It's too much to ask. Maybe you better just take me across the border—no big deal, right?"

Javier reached for my hand, holding it in his, giving it a little squeeze—again. "I'd be honored to help you find your father. Please let me. I promise to be a gentleman. So, it's settled," he says when I don't respond quickly. "We'll go shopping," he, signals for a check. "It will please me to help dress you."

I think I'm going to faint.

* * * *

The Sea of Cortez sparkles like a blue-green gem from 18,000 feet in the air, but I think I'm going to be sick to my stomach any second looking down at it. The steady drone of Javier's King Air 350's engines is a persistent warning I'm about to die even though the air is clear and calm. The sound of the propellers is a voice in my head saying over and over it will be my punishment for the things I've done at Mama Gorda's; for traveling in Mexico with this handsome man. I whisper a prayer to the Virgin, confessing my sins. The plane drones on.

Javier looks over at me from the pilot's seat. He must have noticed my clenched fists, or my white face, or the way I'm slumped down in the seat. "First flight in a small plane?" He asks.

"First flight, period."

He laughs. "An American girl like you has never flown?"

I think I hear a hint of sarcasm in his voice when he says, "American girl."

I am an American girl, but not a privileged one. Mama wasn't anxious to go any place that might require IDs. There was no extra money for vacations to places that required a plane ticket. At first, our family spent all our holidays with Rogelio and Lupe, but after Antonio died, mama and Lupe drifted apart.

"There's only one place I'd want to go," papa always answered when the question of travel came up, "back to Michoacán where your mama and I grew up. I'd like to show you the beautiful land we came from." At that, he always paused, getting a kind of sad-eyed look. "But we can't go there, my little dove. So, we'll go to Disneyland or Magic Mountain instead."

To Javier, I'm an American girl. To Ryan, I'm a *Latina*. Mama Gorda says I'm neither. She says I'm lost. Who's right? Who am I? I feel so out of place in this airplane. I sit up straighter in the cushy leather seat next to Javier, but I'm scared.

"I *am* American," I tell him. "I guess I'm a pretty naïve one though, jumping into a small plane with a man I barely know. You think I'm a fool, don't you? Or something worse."

"Not a fool, Teresa—please let me call you Teresa—but perhaps too trusting. That could get you in trouble in Mexico. Here it is better to trust no one."

"Not even you?" I tease.

"Not even me. Often in Mexico things are not always what they seem."

I hadn't expected that. "Tell me why?"

"Please call me Javier." His smile is warm and genuine, but he keeps his eyes straight ahead and his hands on the controls.

I wait for more.

Reluctantly, in little bits and pieces, as the plane flies south, he tells me about himself. He says his family is in the export and distribution business. They've done well, and he is benefiting from it. He says he hasn't done much to contribute to the family business since graduating from Stanford.

"So why were you at Mama Gorda's?" The question has bothered me from the start.

His eyes scan the horizon. It's several seconds before he answers. "Better to call her Carmen. Mama Gorda is only what they call her in Tijuana. We each have our embarrassments," he says. "Sometimes it's good not to ask too many questions. I won't ask you about what you were doing at Carmen's house, and I hope you'll do the same for me. Suffice it to say my family's company does some distribution work for her. Most of her business is over the Internet, of course, but we deliver some DVDs to L.A."

"Smuggling, you mean?"

"As I said, some questions should not be asked or answered."

We fly on in silence and land in Culiacán to refuel. Javier leads me into the tiny airport restaurant where we eat a quick lunch in silence. Questions ricochet in my head like the bullets that killed Antonio. Am I in danger with Javier? What kind of danger? Ever since I agreed to cross the border with Knobhead, it feels as if I've made one bad decision after another. My life is out of control.

Sitting at a table in the small airport lounge, Javier breaks the silence as I sip an iced tea. "Look, I'm sorry if I shocked you. I thought it was better to be honest with you from the start. You don't understand life in Mexico so let me try to explain—"

"Explain? What's to explain? You all but said you are a smuggler, Javier. What more is there to explain?"

"I'll try if you let me."

I nod half-heartedly. What choice do I have?

"Teresa, Mexico is like a tiny mouse living next door to a hawk. The mouse is very weak compared to the hawk. He can't even do what most mice do because if the hawk sees him, he'll gobble him up. So, the little mouse has to sneak around the hawk to find enough food to survive. Sometimes he even finds food in the hawk's nest when the hawk is away hunting other mice."

"That's great. I get it, you're a smuggler." His hurt expression shows me he understood my sarcasm. "You don't act like a mouse to me. And how does that help me find my father?"

"You're wrong about me being a smuggler," he says. "I was born into a family in the export and distribution business. You can't blame me for the family I was born into, can you? Any more than you blame yourself for your family."

He's right. I am embarrassed by my family. I love my father, mama and my brother and sister, too, but they embarrass me. I'm not proud of them or proud of the way we live.

"In my country, there aren't enough jobs for everybody," he goes on. "Mexicans have too many children, the government is inept and corrupt, it doesn't create enough jobs. Large American corporations have taken work in farming away from our farmers. Many of them now go to work in low paying jobs at factories near the border. Mexicans have to scratch for ways to make a meager living. Some sneak across the border to work in the United States. Carmen makes porn videos and my family helps her distribute them. We do what we must."

"It looks like you're doing more than just surviving," I tell him.

He laughs heartily. "We are. But you wouldn't punish us for that, would you? My role is to learn the financial end of the family business. I went to Stanford to study business and finance so I could contribute. But I don't go sneaking across the border if that's what you were thinking. All of us in Tijuana know how to cross the border without being stopped. So, I guess you could say I was going to smuggle you across when we first met."

Javier makes it sound respectable. No different than Ryan studying economics and polysci at UCLA so he could go on to law school and join his father's firm. Family business is family business, right? Still, it doesn't feel right. It feels wrong.

"We've got another five hours to Morelia," Javier says. "We'd better get going. Unless you want to turn back. In that case, I can get you a flight back to Tijuana and arrange to get you across the border. You decide."

I tell myself the only reason for continuing is to find papa. But I'm not sure I'm being honest. The fact is, Javier intrigues me. I've never known anyone like him. I know I'm taking a huge risk, but I feel so over my head already, it hardly seems to matter. We reboard the plane and I put my headset on and buckle up for the ride.

CHAPTER 12

THE REST OF the flight passes in silence. We fly over land that changes from dry brown to vibrant green. Mountains rise up to meet us, creating updrafts that bounce the King Air around, creating unpleasant feelings in my stomach.

Javier radios ahead for a car and driver. A balding middle-age man with a bushy white mustache picks us up at the airport. I pay little attention as he drives us into Morelia passing an assortment of houses randomly planted along the roadside, while I try to sort out the events of the most bizarre week of my life. I feel like Alice falling down the rabbit hole.

Javier checks us in to a small inn at the top of a rounded hill, overlooking the city. It's more like my fantasy of a private villa than a hotel. Entering the magnificent lobby, my breath catches in my throat. Dominated by a marble fireplace, with a wood beam ceiling arching high over our heads, the walls of the room are crowded with large oil paintings of Spanish cavaliers. White slipcovered couches and chairs, a rough-hewn oak coffee table and matching end tables form a conversation area on the tiled floor in the middle of the room. Two multi-colored ceramic urns guard the fireplace, and a finely made wrought iron chandelier with *faux* candles hangs over the sitting area. The simple elegance of the spacious lobby overwhelms me. I've never been in this kind of hotel before.

Holding the single plastic bag from Tijuana containing all my worldly possessions—a change of underwear, blouse and jeans—standing beside Javier at the registration desk, I feel out of place, wondering what the clerk must think of me. He greets Javier with a smile and respectful reserve. "Have a pleasant stay, Señor Ugalde," he says. Smiling professionally, he hands Javier two keys he takes from the wall rack behind him. He pays no attention to me, as if I'm part of the luggage.

Our driver comes from the side to grab Javier's suitcase. I feel humiliated when he takes my plastic sack. We arm wrestle just briefly before I let it go. "This way, please, *Señorita*." He grins at me as he says it. "I show you to your room."

Javier has reserved two adjoining rooms with a locking door between them. I throw the plastic sack on the large bed, maybe the largest bed I'd ever seen, as soon as I closed the door. Then I go to the adjoining door to make sure it's locked and collapse back on the bed, needing a few minutes alone.

After a few minutes, my solitude is interrupted by a knock on the adjoining door.

"Are you hungry, Teresa? We could go down to the dining room when you're ready." When I open the door, he's there, looking fresh after his long day of flying, not a strand of his dark hair out of place. I stare at him feeling miserable. I am bedraggled, wiped out. "I can't go looking like this," I tell him. "I'll just stay in my room."

"Then I'll call room service. We can eat on my balcony. Tomorrow we'll find you some more clothes to wear."

I shut the door and drop down on the edge of the bed again to gather my thoughts. Who is this very thoughtful man, I keep asking myself? So handsome. Seeming such a perfect gentleman. I hardly know him, yet he treats me like a princess. Ryan has never been so considerate. What's wrong with this picture?

"One of our most beautiful cities," Javier says.

The twin spires of the Morelia cathedral, illuminated by hundreds of small lights, dominates the skyline as we sit on the balcony outside his room.

"Wait till you see Morelia in daylight," he adds. He fixes his eyes on me and they don't waver. They are almost black in the flickering light from the candles on the table, flecked with golden specks. His lashes make me jealous. He seems unashamed to be staring at me, but it makes me self-conscious, so I let my gaze wander out over the city below us.

"Whenever I come here, I'm deeply moved by the history. The buildings and parks were all here when the Spanish ruled us." Javier pauses to sip from his tulip-shaped wineglass. Relaxed, glancing around the panorama of the semi-dark city before us, he sets the glass back on the table and gives me a smile that could melt concrete. "You look tired tonight," he says, resuming his inspection. "You need a good sleep."

Releasing me from his stare and setting his wineglass down, he asks, "Do you know much about our history?"

"Some," I tell him. Then, I stop myself. "No, not really, to be honest. My father always told me about the beauty of Mexico but not much about its history."

"Michoacán is truly one of our most beautiful states. You'll see that over the next few days as we look for your father. But for me, it's about all the history that has gone on here before us."

He reaches across the table to put his hand on mine. I feel a slight tingle at the back of my neck but leave my hand in place.

"Think about it, Teresa. We are sitting here looking out over that magnificent cathedral and other old buildings that were here more than five hundred years ago. And yet *our* history—yours and mine—is only days old, hours old really. It makes you think how transcendent our lives are, how important it is to capture all of life that we can."

I can't help laughing. "You sound like my father. He would have said *Carpe Diem* except he wouldn't have known the words, so he always told me I should take advantage of every opportunity that comes along."

"Life's an adventure, Paloma," papa would say to me when I was a schoolgirl. "Not always good adventures, but always challenges to be lived. You need to find a balance, M'hija. Be responsible for your actions but let the river of life flow around you, lift you up and take you wherever it leads. Find your balance. If you don't, you'll miss the wonder."

So far, I've tried to be responsible for my life, but it has been short on wonder. In Monte Vista, I tried to escape the barrio life around me. Living in Monte Vista meant a life of mediocrity or worse, of being less than I dreamed of being. For Antonio, it meant dying. The real Mexico is so different, it gives me chills. And I am beginning to admit to myself I'm attracted to Javier. Oh, papa, what would you think of me now?

"Your father sounds like a smart man. I hope you take his advice." Javier gives my hand a gentle squeeze.

I open it so his fingers are nested in my palm. I look out over the lights of Morelia but keep my romantic thoughts to myself.

Over a light supper, Javier tells me Morelia's history. The Indians here never succumbed to the Aztecs, he says. "They were light-skinned, called *Purepecha*. I can see their blood in you. They were proud people, tall and handsome. You have their strong features mixed with the fair complexions of the Spanish Conquistadores who intermarried with them. You are a real daughter of Mexico, Teresa."

I return his smile and reach quickly for my wine glass, uncertain how to respond. My heart is pounding.

"The *Purepechas* fought the Aztecs to a standstill but eagerly joined Cortez's men in overthrowing them," he pauses, "but perhaps I talk too much about history."

"My father was very proud of being from Michoacán."

"About your father... I made some calls from my room."

I let go of Javier's hand and sit straighter. "You found him?"

His face grows serious. "I'm not sure. Possibly. Let me ask you, was he an avocado farmer?"

The question catches me by surprise. I rush to say no, but then stop to think about what I remember growing up.

"When my father first came to California, he found work in some of the avocado orchards around Whittier," I tell him. "He didn't own them, but I guess you could call him a farmer. He said it was in Michoacán where he learned to care for the avocado trees. After a few years, when he got established, he started a gardening business. He had a truck and tools, he worked with my uncle."

"So, he had his own business?"

"He did very well. He said most of the gardeners working in the Pasadena and Sierra Madre areas were just mow, blow and go men who didn't love the gardens they tended the way he did. He and my uncle Rogelio concentrated on full gardening services, tree care, hedging, planting, those kinds of services. They could charge more—"

"You told Carmen your father was picked up in a pallet yard with the others—"

"He sold the gardening business to Uncle Rogelio six months ago and took a job in the pallet yard."

"I see."

"He said he was tired of working so hard."

"I think we've found your father," Javier says.

CHAPTER 13

THE NEXT MORNING golden light floods through the closed drapes, giving the room a buttery yellow hue. Reluctant to leave the best bed I've ever slept in. I consider how wonderful it would be to spend the rest of my life in the luxury of the past twenty-four hours. Then I hear a knock on the connecting door. Grudgingly, I get to my feet and feel my toes sink into the deep pile of the carpet as I walk across the room.

An envelope peeks out partway under the door. Picking it up, I flop into a chair by the window, amused that Javier is sending me notes, the way we did in junior high. But when I open it, I'm startled to see ten crisp one-hundred American dollar bills inside. Definitely not junior high. Javier's note says he has business to attend to for most of the morning, but he'll see me for the afternoon drive to Patzcuaro. He suggests I order breakfast in the room and then go to the address he gives me of a dress shop to buy whatever clothes I might need for another week or so. A week or so? This is not a vacation! I'm here to find my father and take him home. Javier even goes so far as suggesting a formal cocktail dress could be useful. I pause, thinking about the incongruity of attending a cocktail party with Javier, wondering what he has in mind and not feeling comfortable with the answers I come up with. For yet another time, I'm beset by the question of who he really is. And why I'm beginning to feel attracted to him? And how has he found my father so quickly?

I stare at the money several minutes. Am I being bought? It's an uncomfortable thought. But what other explanation is there? I set the bills and note aside on the table and dismiss the unpleasant images racing through my mind, resolving to return the money. When I open the drapes, the golden light explodes into the room. The cathedral and the surrounding ancient stone buildings seem close enough to touch. The view leaves me breathless. Opening the French doors to my private balcony, letting the softly floral-scented morning air embrace me, I let go of all nagging questions. Life feels too comfortable to worry. I pick up the house phone and order breakfast sent up.

At the round leather-topped table, warmed by the sun, sipping coffee, I sort through the contents of my shoulder bag, counting the remaining money I have, which includes what I'd gotten from Mama Gorda. I refuse to think of it as payment for porn. It doesn't include Javier's ten crisp hundred-dollar bills still lying on the table inside the room.

I can't escape the uncomfortable feeling two men have given me money. For what? Down payments for sex? I'm thankful Javier didn't come on to me last night. I've always assumed Ryan would be my first lover, but I'm in no rush. We have come close on several occasions, and it bothers him a lot that I wouldn't go all the way. He pleaded, almost begged, and pouted when I refused. But he keeps trying. He lent me the hundred dollars anyway.

It wasn't as if I was trying to use Ryan or mislead him. One part of me wants to be committed to him, but another part fights against it, always holding back. Any number of girls on the UCLA campus would trade places with me, stripping naked for him in a heartbeat. He has everything a girl could want, handsome, a great body, a wealthy family and a promising future. But I don't want to be "his beautiful Latina".

Sorting through my purse, my cellphone falls out on the table. I look at it, not sure if it has any battery life left. I dial home anyway.

"Hey, Rico, it's Teri..." I'm surprised when he answers. "I'm near where papa grew up, Rico. I think he's here. I'm going to find him if he is..."

"What do you mean, why bother? Don't be disrespectful..."

"Bring him home if I do, I guess. I've met some people who can get us across the border..."

"Don't rub it in. If mama hadn't been bounced around so much on the bus, I would have been born in the U.S. too. Is she there? Is everything okay?"

"At work?"

"What time is it there?"

"Oh, sorry. It's mid-morning here..." I stop for a moment to think. "Why aren't you in school, Rico?..."

A long pause.

"Don't give me that. You're ditching. Mama thinks you're in school, doesn't she?"

"Do you expect me to believe that? What about wrestling, Rico? The junior college...? You're throwing your life away..."

"Don't be a butthead like the guys you're hanging out with. You are better than they are. Mama and Connie need you to be there for them..."

"Listen to me. Don't blow me off. You're making bad choices. When I bring papa back, things will be good again..."

The phone goes dead. I don't know if my cell dropped the call or Rico hung up.

I have to find papa. Soon. I dress quickly and pray Javier will take me to him.

It's an easy walk down the hill to the *plaza*, but my thoughts are about Rico back in Monte Vista, so, I pay little attention to the people around me as I walk. The late October day is pleasant. A breeze fills the air with floral perfume. I hardly notice the older people sitting on benches around the park, reading papers or talking in low voices. I find the dress shop Javier recommended. Looking at clothes is hard because my mind keeps going over the conversation with Rico. The salesgirls chatter in Spanish and hover around me as I try on a few dresses and dress pants and tops. They bring clothes that aren't right for me and keep asking what it is that I want. I don't know what I want. I don't want a cocktail dress.

The younger of the two, with intensely black hair and eyes that shine against the whiteness of her teeth, the prettiest of the pair, finally gives me a questioning look. "*Es la señorita* Javier said was coming, no?" When I nod, she winks at the other girl. Together, they rush into the back room, returning with arms full of clothes, exquisite cotton dresses, tops, linen pants all in tropical shades, shoes and boots, a jacket and several silk cocktail dresses in black, red and a deep blue color, all nicer than anything I've ever owned. "These for you," the older girl says in her best English. "Javier say make sure they fit."

"How do you know Javier?"

Both girls reply with giggles and bashful grins.

Most of the clothes fit perfectly. When I start to pick and choose among them, the older girl shakes her head. "No, no," she insists. "All for you. All paid for."

I gasp.

They salesgirls make it clear they have orders I'm to take all the clothes that fit. I have no choice but to pick up the bundles. "No, no," the girl says again. We send to your hotel."

Dazed from the dress shop experience, farther along the street, I buy a cheap woolen *rebozo* and pay with my own money. Despite the warmth of the day, I throw it around my shoulders. It's comforting.

The sidewalks and outdoor cafes around the plaza are filling up along with the sounds of people coming and going on the street. I can't help watching as two well dressed young women approach me, chatting back and forth, shop clerks or office girls, probably. One wears a well-tailored, deeply V-necked dress in blood red soft cotton, gathered tightly and belted at the waist. Her friend wears a similar dress, looser fitting, in black. They remind me of young women on the streets of Westwood, definitely not the Veronica Estrada type. Their clothes set off their finely cut, shoulder-length hair, and their fair complexions. I admire them as they approach, and stand still while they pass, looking after them as they go on down the street. I follow a little way until I lose sight of them. What did they think about me, I wonder? What do all the other people on the street think? American or Mexican?

When the women disappear, I'm standing in front of the cathedral. The bells in the twin towers are peeling a call to worship so, without any thought, I follow other worshipers inside the iron gates and up the steps, through the imposing wooden doors into the nave. The long central aisle stretches ahead through a series of vaulted arches toward a distant altar, resplendent with gold. I walk about halfway, then kneel, cross myself and duck into an empty pew.

Diffused light fills the church, coming from windows set high above in the walls. The church air feels stale, as if dust motes that flutter in the light have lingered too long and can't find their way out. Pews are sparsely filled. When I turn to look behind me, I see a face that seems familiar seated a couple of rows back. The man turns his head away when he sees me looking at him, but I recognize the mustache. It's the driver who had helped us check in yesterday evening.

Ignoring him and giving myself up to prayer, I beg the Virgin to keep my family together; to pull Rico back from the dark pit into which he's falling. I pray for Connie, precious little Connie, too young to understand what's happened to her family. And for Antonio, who had been too young to understand when the gunshots rang out. I beg the Virgin's help in finding my father.

"Give me a sign he's safe," I whisper.

I lapse into a kind of reverie, kneeling on the stone floor of the old cathedral, built so long ago by Indian laborers who were my ancestors. Mexican history has never been important to me before, I'm an American. Today it seems real. And I do care.

A hand gently touches my shoulder. Turning, I see Javier kneeling down beside me, his dark eyes smiling. I move a little closer to him, so I can lean against his shoulder and let my tears flow.

It is as if he already knows my pain. He stays silent while I cry. He doesn't move, leaving me alone with my sorrow. After a few minutes, he hands me a linen handkerchief. Then he helps me to my feet. I dab at my eyes as he leads me from the cathedral, with his arm firmly around my shoulder. As we leave, I see the driver has already gone.

"Any news?" I ask as we walk back into the intense early afternoon light. The mustache man is now standing across the street, lighting a cigarette. He turns his back on us as we walk by.

"Yes," Javier says. "I think we've located him in Uruapan. We'll go there when *Dia de los Muertos* is over. Patzcuaro is on the way."

CHAPTER 14

THE TWO-LANE ROAD to Patzcuaro winds among wooded hills and down into deep green valleys. Javier drives the car the same way he flies a plane, eyes straight ahead, both hands on the wheel, turning only occasionally for a quick look at me.

"How did you find him?" It's the question I've put off since the start of our drive from Morelia.

His response is a kind of verbal shrug. "My family has some connections, so I asked our people to find him. He's in Uruapan, it's only a short drive from Patzcuaro."

"Just like that? Your people make some quick calls, and there he is? I'm grateful..." I stop without finishing the sentence, looking at him, wondering if I should ask the next question. I do. "I think you haven't told me all there is to tell about your family."

"Perhaps not." He keeps his eyes straight ahead.

"Are you going to?"

"There's no point." He gives me one of his quick glances. I see he's drawn a veil over his face. There is nothing there to read.

I've come into the heart of Mexico with this man I know so little about. And yet he's found my father in a day or two. A needle in a Mexican haystack. It seems like all in a day's work, not even work really. What is he not saying about his family? How important are they in Mexico? Questions nag at me as we descend from the mountains. It's time to get some answers.

I make a show of stiffening a bit and scrunch toward the door. "I *am* grateful, Javier, but I'm uncomfortable with you. You're too mysterious. Maybe this isn't such a good idea, us coming here together."

He checks the rearview and renews his gaze straight ahead without any response. We drive on in silence.

"Things are different in Mexico," he starts after a few minutes. He lapses into silence again before giving it another try. "In Mexico, many lines are blurred. Right and wrong are not always easy to know in our struggle to survive. Things are often not what they seem." He looks at me, studying the expression on my face, maybe planning his response. My expression is unyielding. "My father is a powerful man, and he has many connections," he says. "People throughout the country work for him. I could wish that he was in a different business, but my wishing won't change anything. We are what we are."

"Criminals?"

Another five-mile pause.

"I'll understand if you want nothing more to do with me, but I won't lie. After we find your father, you can be on your way home, and I'll understand. But I want you to know we do what we have to do. And I would miss you."

"Maybe I should go home. If we find my father, there's nothing to keep me here." I blurt it too quickly before thinking about what I'm saying. In the back of my head, I can hear papa saying some of the same kind of words Javier is saying. "You speak as if you have no choice," I continue, "as if you are the victim of some catastrophe that's out of your control."

"Let's drop it. I can't explain."

I need a graceful retreat from the path I'm heading down. As much as I want to know, I don't want to know. Relaxing some, letting my body shift toward Javier as we round a curve in the road, I can feel the tension. I try to relieve it.

"So, doing what you have to do has put your family in this powerful position?"

"It has."

"Planes, new motorcycles, the best restaurants, hotels."

"Are those things important to you?"

"Important enough, I guess. Every girl dreams of fine clothes, like the ones you bought for me in Morelia. They're beautiful, better than anything I've ever had. But they're a little over the top, don't you think? And the money in the envelope? I'm going to give it back. For me, respect is more important than fine clothes."

I have never felt comfortable around men. I never know what to say to them, don't really know what to think about them or how to judge them as boyfriends. Is Javier a good man for me? I like being with him. Even the question seems weird, but it rattles around in my head. It's the same question I've asked myself about Ryan. Probably Ryan and Javier ask themselves the same questions about me.

✳ ✳ ✳ ✳

A middle school dance in Monte Vista was the first time I became aware of my awkwardness. We were all awkward and gawky then. Boys on one side of the gym, girls on the other. No man's land in between. Only the very aggressive girls coupled up. I wasn't a couple. In fact, I didn't want to be there at all, but papa had insisted I go when he heard there was a school dance.

"Go, Paloma, find out what it's like to dance with a boy. Remember, he'll be as scared as you are."

No one could have been as scared as I was standing in that knot of girls when a boy started to cross no man's land toward us. I knew—I don't know how I knew, but it is a feeling girls have—he was heading for me. His name was Sergio Sanchez, the only boy in our class as tall as I was. A popular kid, too. I heard other girls talking about him in the girls' bathroom, dreaming about being his "chica."

On he came, straight at me. The other girls sensed it and backed off, leaving me alone, like Sandy, waiting for Danny Zuko in "Grease." I felt naked and frightened as he approached.

I wanted to be like Sandy—pretty, blond, popular, All-American. I wanted Sergio Sanchez to be those things, too. But I wasn't, and he wasn't. I trembled as he approached, unsure how to respond. I panicked. Just before he got to me, I turned my back on him. Then I ran clattering across the gym floor in my first pair of high heels and disappeared into the girls' locker room.

"You are one dumb bitch." It was the broken glass voice of Veronica Estrada standing in the doorway, hands on hips. "How could you embarrass Sergio in front of everyone in the school like that, you bitch. The other boys laughed at him. We get ya for this."

With no further words, she walked over and punched me in the stomach, then turned and left the girls' locker room.

* * * *

As we round the curve, *Lago de Patzcuaro* opens up before us, freeing me from the memory of Sergio Sanchez and Veronica Estrada. The lake lies in front of us, a study in blue. Depthless waters, a sky without edges, cotton clouds, perfect mountains surround and protect it. Islands bob about in the water, perfect dabs of brown and green from Claude Monet's pallet. It's as if I'm entering a new world of make-believe where princesses and princes rule with magical powers to banish bad thoughts, and everyone is like Sandy and Danny.

Then I hear the squeal of tires. A car races up alongside ours. Javier's head jerks around to see the other vehicle where two men are staring across at us. I see him tense. He comes back to his straight-ahead focus, both hands on the wheel. The other car moves slowly ahead until its rear fender is even with our front bumper. Then it starts crowding into our lane. Bit by bit, it forces Javier to steer toward the edge of the road overlooking the placid lake.

All of a sudden, Javier slams on the brakes and steers back toward the center of the road. I'm thrust forward, restrained from hitting the windshield only by my seatbelt. The other car keeps going, flying off the edge of the road. Javier stops the car.

"Are you hurt?" He looks over at me. I can see he's breathing hard.

"What just happened?" I gasp, too shaken up to speak, I put my hands over my face.

"I don't know." His face is pale, but I can see he's trying to act calm. Maybe for me. "All of a sudden, that car just swerved in front of me."

"You did a good job staying out of the way."

"Sure you're not hurt, Teresa? I didn't know what else to do."

"I'll be fine. You did the right thing."

Javier restarts the car and begins to put it in gear.

"Shouldn't we see if the other car is okay?"

He pauses and looks over at me. "Nothing I can do now. It's over the side."

"Should you call the police? They could be hurt."

I'll let the police know when we get to Patzcuaro," he says, pulling back onto the highway.

I stay quiet as we drive the rest of the way down the hill, too upset to say anything more. I look at him, see the set of his face, almost a mask, his eyes focused straight ahead, and wonder if he can explain what's just happened? Does it bother him? He doesn't say another word. After a mile, he seems to have forgotten it, relaxing just a little. I give his hand a squeeze but shudder to myself, still seeing the other car forcing us off the road in my mind's eye.

Nothing has prepared me for what has just happened. It only took a matter of seconds from start to finish, but the scene replays over and over in my head. I watch Javier, trying to read his thoughts.

Reacting to my silence and my stunned expression, he takes one hand off the wheel and reaches over to touch mine. "Each time I come here, it's the same for me. Always the same feeling of insignificance when I see the lake. It leaves me without words to describe God's handiwork. Did you know *Patzcuaro* means Door to Heaven?" he says.

Is that it, I think? God's handiwork?

✴ ✴ ✴ ✴

We park in front of another villa he has selected for us near the central square. He gets out and comes around to my side, extending his hand to help me out. I take it but lead him away from the inn's entrance. "Show me the plaza before it gets dark," I say to him, taking a deep breath, feeling my racing heart start to slow, trying to regain my composure.

The Plaza Grande is surrounded by ancient whitewashed stone buildings. Covered colonnaded arches along the street form a promenade, with restaurants tucked underneath and spilling out to the street. Each offering its own distinct aroma of spicy sauces, roasted meats and pungent sweets. The sounds of street vendors, hawking their wares in loud, sing-song voices, catches my ear. Without thinking, forcing the experience of the past hour to be still for a while, I lead him to a stall containing brightly painted ceramic skulls and skeletons in an array of poses and styles, each with his or her own mocking facial expression. Female skeletons wearing full-length Victorian ball gowns of yellows, blues and pinks, with matching wide-brimmed, flower-trimmed hats, stand alongside sombrero-wearing gentleman in full *vaquero* finery. Empty eye-socket skulls mock us with their grins.

"How weird. They're laughing at us."

The young woman tending the booth holds one out to me. I resist and cling to Javier's hand

He laughs. "We take death seriously, and they mock us for it," he tells me, pleased by my shock. "Especially on *Dia de los Muertos*."

Another stall catches my eye, farther down the promenade. I drop Javier's hand and run to it like a schoolgirl. The stall is filled with displays of candy in the shape of skulls, some pink, some white, some decorated in gaudy colors.

The old woman behind the counter gives me a deep bullfrog croak and hands me a sample. As I reach out to take it, she grabs my wrist. The heavily plowed cheeks of her sunken face crack into a smile, showing broken and missing teeth, mimicking the skulls on her table.

"It's a special time for romance, *Señorita*. You have a handsome *caballero* at your side. Love him tonight but honor the dead tomorrow. Pay them their due, the ones who went ahead of us, *La Malinche*, the *Mujer* who showed us the way."

She leans so close I can smell her garlic breath. Then, lowering her voice to a rasping whisper, say says, "Be very careful, *Señorita*. Very careful, indeed. I see danger all around you. My bones ache for the pain you will feel."

For a shriveled old crone, she has a powerful hold on my wrist. I wince, staring at the pencil points of blackness in her eyes. She stares back, sending silent messages through them.

"*¡Bastante!*" I scold her, pulling away and stepping back from the booth. She looks at me another instant then turns to a customer coming down the promenade.

"Pay no attention to the *bruja*," Javier says, coming up behind me. "These old witches love to scare young women."

I drop the candy and turn my back on the stall. I want to get away from her and her prophecy as fast as I can.

We continue walking around the Plaza, where flower stalls are filled with bundles of fresh chrysanthemums and marigolds in yellows, oranges and deep red tones.

"*Dia de los Muertos* colors," Javier says. "Tomorrow night you'll see how the graves are decorated with flowers. Always the same colors."

"Graves?" My look tells Javier the thought frightens me.

"Tomorrow night, we'll go to the graveyard."

I shiver at the thought. And about the old witch's words.

CHAPTER 15

"YOU'RE FULL OF surprises," Javier says.

We're seated at a table on the other side of the plaza where he's taken me for a drink. I suspect he has something else on his mind, too, that puts me on edge.

"How so?"

"Tu hablas Español. Carmen said you didn't."

"She was right. I didn't speak it in her house. I never speak Spanish at home."

"But you did to the shopkeepers in Morelia and the hotel doorman and just now to the *bruja*."

"Did I?" The realization makes me laugh. "How could I grow up in a Spanish-speaking house and not know the language, Javier? I didn't speak it at home because I didn't want to, and I didn't want my family speaking it. I wanted us to talk like other American families. Here? Well, here it's the right language, isn't it?"

He smiles and slides his chair a little closer, so he can put his arm around my shoulder again. "You're full of surprises, Teresa. The more I think I know you, the more I realize I don't. You enchant me."

I stay quiet, but the expression on my face gives me away. It's my turn to reach across the table to take his hand. A very tentative move.

"Am I misjudging the situation?" He says.

"Who was the woman the old crone was talking about?" I change the subject.

"She was paying you a tremendous compliment, comparing you to *La Malinche.*"

"Who is she?"

Javier smiles.

"Her real name was Doña Marina. She is the mother figure of all Mexicans. An Indian girl, *La Malinche*, was sold into slavery by her father. Her owner gave her to Hernan Cortez as a gift, and she became his mistress and interpreter—"

"Sold into slavery by her own father?"

"Yes. I'm afraid young women were not well respected back then."

"And now?"

Javier gives me an exasperated look, the kind my father often gave me when I interrupted him. "Let me continue, Teresa," he says. "*La Malinche* taught Cortez about the *Mexica*, and she had his baby boy—Don Martín. He was the first Mexican born after the conquest, the first *mestizo* of us all."

"A traitor to her people?"

"Some say so. But others believe her influence on Cortez saved many hundreds of Indian lives in the long run. To this day, *La Malinche* is a woman of controversy in Mexico. Like I said, the old woman paid you a big compliment."

"But she was wrong, wasn't she? I'm an American student, not a Mexicana."

Javier's expression sours.

"Why do you fight against that so much?" He says. "Many young Mexican women are going to college in the U.S. You're not unique. And it doesn't make you American. Your *Purepecha* blood is as Mexican as mine, Spanish and Indian mingled together. That was *La Malinche's* gift. Your beauty comes from a blending of old and new world blood. You should embrace your heritage."

We sit looking at each other across the table, holding hands without speaking, learning each other's faces and moods. I hear what Javier has said. I've always resisted papa telling me so proudly about being Mexican. Looking around Monte Vista, I never found anything to be proud of.

"I want to be an American girl," I'd expressed my frustration at papa one day on Peck Road. Tonight, as the twilight fades in Patzcuaro and stars appear over the lake, I can think about being Mexican. Javier is Mexican, deeply Mexican, I guess, and proud of it. I don't need a mirror to remind me of my bloodline—Veronica Estrada and Knobhead taunted me about it enough.

With the reflected torchlight off the old stone buildings around the plaza setting a romantic mood, we eat a quiet dinner, not in silence, but just making small talk, skirting around the more important feelings that divide us. Javier orders coconut shrimp curry for me that tastes as good as it smells, and a sizzling Argentine steak for himself. After we eat, I take the envelope, still containing the hundred-dollar bills, from my purse and hand it across the table. "I can't accept your money," I tell him. Then I thank him for the clothes he paid for in Morelia, squeezing his hand, "I don't know how I'll be able to repay you, but I will."

Taking the envelope, he laughs. He says seeing me in the pants and blouse I'd chosen to wear for the drive to Patzcuaro is repayment enough. "I have never been with such an attractive young woman," he tells me.

I blush.

"I've dated many women, but never anyone like you, Teresa." Then he takes half the bills from the envelope and returns it to me. "Keep this, just as a loan in case you need it later. Pay me back when you can if that's what you want to do."

Our fingers are interlaced. Javier sits close as we watch the street life slow with the coming darkness. The candle on the table cast a shadow on his face. I'm content to bask in the warmth of his words and let the languid evening air embrace us. It could be easy for me to forget the real reason I'm here. I haven't come for romance, but it has found me. I hadn't expected it, didn't really want it. I only want my papa back home in Monte Vista so my life could proceed again in the direction I'd planned. But the stars and moon shimmering off the lake make it easy to fantasize about a different world. They offer me a different direction.

"I've grown very fond of you, Teresa." Javier's words break my spell. "Is there reason to hope you might have feelings for me, too?"

A sigh catches deep in my throat at his words. For a moment, I can't speak. Looking at him, I'm helpless to find words to explain my feelings. I'm not really sure what my feelings are. I gulp for a breath and continue looking into his face. It seems as if minutes pass. Or maybe time is just standing still for me as feelings chase around in my body. Or maybe it's the thought we almost died a few hours ago.

Finally, I'm able to smile at him. "These past days, my feelings for you have grown and deepened, Javier. They scare the wits out of me, but, yes, I have them. I can't hide them. I'm sure you can see I'm fond of you."

"I must tell you," he says, gripping my hand firmly, "I only reserved one room for us here tonight. If that makes you uncomfortable tell me."

For only an instant it does. I'm beset by doubt. Only an instant. Then I move closer so I can whisper. "You are moving very fast for me. Please be patient. We'll see."

It's awkward for a few minutes, but Javier is a gentleman. He says he understands. We can have separate sleeping arrangements. When we get up from the table, I step close to him. We kiss.

Arm in arm, we walk through the darkened streets. The vendor stalls are boarded up for the night. The *bruja* is gone. A few young men and women stroll in the plaza. They speak softly to each other, under the watchful eyes of older chaperones, sitting on benches, jabbering with other chaperones, but always keeping an eye on their daughters and granddaughters. I take Javier's hand and lead him to our room.

CHAPTER 16

JAVIER AND I spend the daylight hours leading up to the eve of *Dia de los Muertos* exploring the treasures in the craft shops. A whole new world has opened to me. Am I really in love with this man? Or is it just the romance of Patzcuaro? Or the fear of death? Was last night real? It wasn't the trip to the moon I had fantasized about, but it was a start.

The town is alive with preparations for the coming night. Flowers in the stalls around the plaza are all but gone. Skeletons, skulls and death head candies are being gobbled up by tourists. The town is subdued, but an undercurrent of excitement is almost physical at the same time. Women carrying brightly colored mesh supermarket bags, imprinted with pictures of Frieda Kahlo, scurry about the streets on their daily shopping rounds.

We lunch at a sidewalk cafe overlooking the lake, holding hands, staring into each other's face with looks that reflect the passion of last evening. A mariachi trumpet at the far end of the plaza calls out for our attention. Drums and guitars follow. We crane our necks to see the musicians, but the crowds in the street block our view. Then, as the music grows louder, a procession comes in sight.

At first, I think a mariachi band of crippled old men, bent over and stooping low in pain, is approaching. It's a macabre sight, and I don't know how to react. How cruel to let these deformed ancients parade through the streets. But looking closer, I see something is amiss. I flinch at the sight but then begin to laugh. The dancing old men are wrapped in brightly colored serapes from head to foot. Each one shares the same grinning facial expression as his companions as they bob and whirl and hop their twisted bodies from foot to foot down the street.

"Wait a minute."

Javier turns to me, already laughing. "*Son Niños*, he says. "Children in masks dressed like old men." He has tears of laughter streaming down his cheeks. "It's Mexico, Teresa. Things are often not what they seem, I warned you. It's the dance of the *Viejitos*—the little old men."

The procession hobbles and limps its way past our table, continuing down the street toward the lake. The sight has everyone smiling and laughing, but it has a sad undertone for me. Some children never live to be old men. Antonio never did.

* * * *

As the afternoon merges into early evening, we start down the hill toward the lake with others in a kind of procession. A picnic basket and blankets have magically appeared on Javier's arm as we leave the villa holding each other's hands.

"Let's walk to the lake," I urge him. "It's all too beautiful to miss." I take his arm, laughing at all the sensual pleasures I feel.

Fishing boats glide from the middle of the lake toward shore over still water. Butterfly-shaped nets balanced across their bows, glow like fireflies in the setting sun. Javier leads me to a dock where we join a line to board a small ferry boat. Women hold children with one hand, and baskets and bags of food, or bunches of bright orange and yellow flowers, in the other.

On the short trip to the island of Janitzio, as the sun drops into the lake, Patzcuaro seems like a miniature village. The mountainsides surrounding it are bathed in soft shadows in endless shades of blue and purple. They deepen as the ferry takes us further out in the lake. It's a fairytale land where I feel like a princess with my prince.

On the island, we follow the crowd in a slow climb up a narrow, rock-strewn path to the cemetery on the hilltop. Tombstones there have sprouted bright flowers and religious icons arranged on makeshift altars of baskets and boxes. Silver and wooden crosses, ivory votive candles and images of the Virgin of Guadalupe are everywhere. These altars seem to hold endless arrays of objects. Some contain food, others are loaded with family pictures, favorite books, children's dresses, shawls, baseball gloves, and soccer balls. There is an abundance of Mexican beer and tequila bottles, mostly opened, some half empty.

Finding a small patch of grass in front of an untended grave, we spread out our blankets. People nearby pay us no attention, rushing to get their own preparations ready before dark.

"This is the strangest thing I've ever seen," I whisper to Javier, taking his hand. "It's bizarre."

He gives me a stern look. "In North America, you fear death, here we embrace it." He starts to unpack the picnic basket but stops and says, "Death is a part of life. Or perhaps a passage to a new life. It's important to our departed relatives. On this special night, we believe their souls return to be with us."

That gives me a shiver.

When he has emptied the basket, Javier turns it over and covers it with a cloth. I add the votive candle I bought in the plaza to light for Antonio. Javier takes a small, golden cross from his pocket and places it next to the candle. From other pockets, he takes brightly colored ribbons, several miniature picture books, and finally a gold-framed photograph of a little girl.

The photo stabs my heart. The laughing child in it is no more than four or five; a round-faced cherub, on the chubby side, with hair that looks as if it had been dunked in a bottle of ink Staring at it, I can see a resemblance to Javier. Is it his daughter? I think back on the questions I've failed to ask him over the past few days. My heart takes a swift elevator descent to the pit of my stomach.

He sees me staring. "My sister," he says. "Her name was Sophie. She died shortly after this photo was taken. Died of a fever we couldn't control. The doctors didn't know what it was or what to do about it. She'd be a teenager now, almost as old as you are, Teresa."

My heart rises, then falls again. I reach out and take his arm. "I'm sorry."

* * * *

Javier's altar and the photo of his dead sister cast a subdued mood over our picnic. We eat cold turkey with chocolate mole sauce in silence. The guacamole that accompanies it is the best I've ever tasted. Still, it sits heavy on my stomach as I think about the dead girl. And then, about Antonio. We wash the meal down with bottles of *Modelo Especial*. The beer tastes flat and bitter to me.

Breaking the silence when we've finished eating, I tell Javier, "I wish I had a photo of Antonio to put on the altar beside Sophie."

"A family member?"

"A cousin. We played together all the time."

Javier moves closer, puts his arm around me, and looks into my face with sad eyes reflecting the candlelight. He waits for me to go on. When I don't, he asks, "How did he die?"

I don't want to tell him. I have tried, without success, to forget. I keep silent, but the pictures play in the back of my mind. I can hear the sounds—gunshots, shouting, police sirens, wailing ambulances—etched there forever.

Tears roll down my cheeks. "Shot," I mumble. "Murdered. He was only five."

Javier continues to hold me, his face changes from sadness to disbelief.

✳ ✳ ✳ ✳

We were playing in a sandbox in a park near the apartment in Monte Vista where Lupe and Rogelio lived. Our mothers were nearby, talking, keeping their eyes on us to be sure we were safe. Teenagers and older men were playing basketball on an asphalt court next to us. Nobody paid any attention when a car came around the corner, slowing down as it passed. Someone stuck a gun out the window and fired several shots at the basketball players. Then the car sped away. One bullet hit a steel light pole on the edge of the court, ricocheting in our direction. Antonio and I were sitting together. The bullet hit him. Cops came. An ambulance took Antonio to the hospital. I never saw him again. No one ever caught the killers.

✳ ✳ ✳ ✳

We lapse into silence again. Javier sees my sadness. He cradles me in his arms. I cry on his shoulder. He kisses away my tears while he holds me.

After a few minutes, he stands reluctantly. "I need a couple of minutes alone," he says, "Just let me clear my head and I'll be back."

109

He moves off, moving quickly, but carefully stepping around the people with altars and blankets on the ground. How could they believe they can entice the souls of their loved ones back to the living? I can't bring Antonio back. What faith grips these people? Is Antonio's soul hovering nearby, searching for some sign? I reach in my pocket and take out a piece of skull candy I'd bought during the afternoon and place it on the altar just in case. But I don't have the faith of the others.

Women nearby glance over at me, making small signs of condolence—a smile, a raised hand, a sad eye—telling me they understand. Silently they create a sisterhood of sorrow.

Sitting on the blanket, in darkness, I watch a shooting star burst across the sky and die. Had I really seen it? Staring into the night, I say my prayer for Antonio. As I do, anger constricts my chest, forcing out an audible moan. My childish mind told me long ago Antonio's death was a punishment for being Mexican in Monte Vista. As foolish as that thought might have been, it stayed with a four-year-old girl, festering, making her afraid.

How can I reconcile that image of my childhood playmate bleeding to death in the sandbox with this land of my parents, of Javier, of all these prayerful women longing to hear from their departed loved ones? It was all a jumble.

It seems as if Javier has been gone for a long time. I guess he's walking in the darkness, thinking about Sophie. Taking a final sip of my warm beer, I try to wait patiently. As much as I try to stay with the somber thoughts the evening is about, my mind keeps bouncing back to him. I could accept Javier as a short-term fling in this romantic setting. Is there more? After all, I'm not looking for a serious relationship, but I keep reliving last evening together. Fantasizing into the future. The questions about his family still trouble me. I try to shake them away. Am I over my head? No doubt.

Time passes. Where is he? Should I get up and look for him? Or should I leave him alone to his solitude? Is this another aspect of him I need to accept?

At least an hour passes, and still he doesn't return. I start to worry. Romantic images fade, replaced by more fearful ones. What about the car that almost forced us off the road? When another hour goes by, I grow desperate. I get up from the blanket and walk around the cemetery. I search every corner and up and down the uneven rows of headstones. Stillness has settled on the graveyard as if a black drape has been spread over it. Most of the women are dozing or deep into their prayers. A couple of times I call out for him, and a woman on the ground nearby gives me an understanding look. Perhaps she thinks I'm calling for a departed loved one.

I retrace my steps, going back to our blanket and the makeshift altar. Then I search the cemetery again, with tears blurring my vision. I have no clue. No idea where to look. Javier's gone. The feeling of aloneness overwhelms me. Finally, I go back to the blanket and lie down, silently calling out to the Virgin to deliver Javier back to me. Tears flow a little longer. Then they dry up. My prayers dry up, too. He's gone. What has happened to him? Only fear possess me now, lying on the blanket. As the night air grows cold, I pull my knees up to my chest, pull the blanket tightly around me, and lie there shaking.

CHAPTER 17

DAYLIGHT REVEALS NO trace of Javier. He has vanished in the night. I force myself to leave the cemetery with the other women, but I have no idea what to do. I can't remember if he has his cell phone with him or not. The altar-draped picnic basket and Sophie's photograph seem to say he had expected to come back. I gather them up along with my candle for Antonio.

Has he abandoned me? It doesn't seem likely. Why would he? Nothing is making sense.

Walking back into the little village of Janitzio, I convince myself Javier has had an accident, perhaps a fall, so I search for a police station to report him missing. All I can find is one lone policeman standing at the ferry landing, watching people crowd around the gate to board the boat back to Patzcuaro.

"Get on the boat," the pot-bellied man says when I explain my concern. "Tell Polizia in Patzcuaro, *Señorita*, not me." He turns to bully the crowd of women waiting to board to stay in line. I can't help wondering if his words are intended to rid himself of me and my problem more than they are to be helpful.

When the ferry docks in Patzcuaro, I recognize a familiar face standing off to the side, intently watching people disembark. After a minute or two, it comes to me he's the driver from Morelia again. The man in the cathedral. He is wearing a straw sombrero now that covers his balding pate, but I know it's him by the droopy white mustache.

So that's it, he's come to Patzcuaro and gone to Janitzio to give Javier a message or summon him back to Morelia. And now he's waiting for me. I gulp a deep breath of relief, letting it out slowly to relax my anxiety, hoping things will be all right.

I push through the crowd of old crones rocking unsteadily down the slanting gangplank. The man looks in my direction then turns and quickly starts walking off. I hurry after him. "Javier," I call out a little too loudly. "Where is he?"

His blank expression freezes me where I stand, triggering new fears. He gives me a vacant stare.

"*Lo siento, Señorita.*"

Turning the palms of his hands up in a gesture of helplessness, he moves quickly away from me.

I'm desperate. I hurry toward our room at the villa to see if Javier is there. Or if he has left a note. Something to end my nightmare.

The manager lets me into the room. It's just the way we'd left it except the bed had been made, and my clothes are hung up in the closet.

No note. No scrape of paper in the wastebasket. No loving message written on the bathroom mirror. Nothing. Javier's cell phone is on the desk, along with my sack purse I'd left behind when we headed for Janitzio. I rummage through my purse. Everything is there. I grab a handful of pesos and bring them out. I search for the piece of paper where Carmen had written two phone numbers. Is this a time to call one of them? My cell phone is dead after almost a week without a charger. I toss it on the night table.

I stick the paper in my pocket, shove both phones in my purse and leave the room. When I ask the manager how to get to the police station, he gives me a puzzled look and asks if I'm all right. I tell him everything is fine, but I don't think he's convinced.

The Police station is on the plaza, tucked back under the covered arches in a small room. It is almost bare except for an old wooden counter, naked lightbulb hanging overhead from a cord, and several straight-back chairs along one wall. Behind the empty counter, an open door leads into a back room. It's from there a policeman comes out after a five-minute wait. Summoning my best Spanish, I ask him if he's had any reports of accidents. Any reports about Javier Ugalde

My Spanish marks me a *gringa*. He studies me for a long couple of moments, looking me up and down in a very uncomfortable and unprofessional way. He doesn't bother checking paperwork on the counter. "No," he says briskly. "Ugalde? No Ugalde."

"He's missing. Last night. On Janitzio. Can you find him?"

The man looks at me with raised eyebrows. A tall man, tending on the thin side, with light skin and a bald head, he is probably of the same *Purepecha* stock I am. He wears a pressed khaki uniform with a Sam Browne belt complete with holster large enough to hold a snub-nosed cannon, handcuffs and an assortment of other gear. His black-trimmed brown hat lies beside him, sweat stains making dark patterns on the brim. As he studies me, his expression changes. I can't identify it, but he seems to have come more alert when I mention the name Ugalde.

"We don't begin to count all who are missing on *Dia de los Muertos*. Drunks mostly," he says. "They turn up eventually, most of them anyway. Your man probably got drunk and wandered off."

"No," I insist, "that isn't it at all." I want him to know how serious Javier's disappearance is, but he is aloof and disinterested.

"*Norte Americana?*" he asks me with a sneer curling the corners of his mouth.

"I am," I tell him, "but Javier Ugalde is a Mexican national."

"I see." He pauses, grins. "Sorry. Nothing I can do."

"You have to do something! You have to find him." I'm standing over his desk now, in a frenzy, feeling my fear creeping back over me. I press my hands down on his desk.

He pushes back his chair and puts his hand on his pistol. "*Por favor*," he says, pointing at my hands. "Step back from the table, *Señorita*. If you do not, I will have to call for assistance."

"Please." I'm begging now. "Do something. He disappeared in the night. Vanished."

Again, I get a blank stare that seems to go on for minutes.

"Have a seat." He points to the chairs against the far wall. "I'll see what I can do for you. It may take some time."

After an hour, probably more, my body begins to ache from sitting in the straight-backed chair. The officer has vanished into the back room and hasn't reappeared. Activity on the promenade outside the door, and across the street in the *plaza*, picks up.

Sitting alone, obsessed by my thoughts of what might have happened last night, of Javier lying hurt and unnoticed somewhere on that island, occasionally, I hear voices in the back room, but I can't make out the words. Mostly I hear only deep, guttural laughter from the men I can't see.

When I get up and walk to the door to look out into the plaza, I see the sidewalk restaurants filling up for lunch. I look for a familiar face. Any sign. There is nothing. As I turn back, the officer comes from the back room, his hand on his belt, with two other men in uniform hurrying along behind him.

"Any word of Javier?" I ask, moving to block his way.

"You still here?" His look is flat, as if he is trying to remember me. "Excuse me," he says, brushing past and going out onto the promenade, still trailed by the other men. "We may know something when we return from lunch." He walks out of the office. I stand speechless, watching him go.

Dropping back down on a chair, I put my head in my hands, too numb to cry. I stay like that a long time, trying to sort through the events of the past twenty-four hours. Trying to make sense of what has happened, searching for a pattern. Nothing comes to me.

I dig in my purse until I find the paper on which Mama Gorda has written the phone numbers. I stare at it, turn it over, stick it back in my purse, pull it out again. Grabbing for Javier's cell phone, I punch out the number.

"Mama Gorda. It's me. Teresa Diaz..."

"In Patzcuaro..."

"No, I didn't go home. I came here with Javier..."

"He's disappeared..."

"Last night. We were in the cemetery on Janitzio..."

The phone goes silent on the other end. I wait.

"Are you there? Yes, I'm okay. Yes. I don't know what to do. No one will help me..."

"At the police station in Patzcuaro..."

The voice on the other end changes abruptly. It is no longer Mama Gorda's melodic voice. In an instant, it has morphed into a low growl. "Get out of the police station as fast as you can, Teresa. Right now! Find a place to hide. Do not let anyone see you. No one."

"It's Javier," I plead, "not me. I have to find him."

"Listen to me. You are in danger, Teresa. I'll get you some help, but you have to stay out of sight until I do. Understand?"

Absolutely I do not understand. I feel dizzy, overloaded, and now this. I hold the phone away from me and stare at it as if it were a scorpion. I want to throw it down on the floor and smash it with the heel of my shoe to make the craziness stop. But I hear Mama Gorda's voice calling out to me over the distance.

"Wait till you hear from me. Give me your phone number."

I tell her it is Javier's cell phone, and I don't know the number.

"Oh, God. Don't answer if it rings. Get rid of it. Throw it in the trash. Hurry Teresa. Do as I say. Hide. I'll get you help, but you are in danger. Get rid of the phone."

"But why—"

"Don't ask questions. I'll find a way to contact you."

The phone goes silent.

I look around the empty police station, panic rising in me. With each passing minute, my life is making less and less sense. Still holding the cell phone, I run out on the promenade and start toward the Villa. At the corner of the plaza, I stop and drop Javier's phone in a trash basket. I stare down at it lying there alongside an empty soft drink can, old, wet newspapers and dead flowers from last night. I can't do it. I can't throw him away like that. I grab the phone back and shove it into my purse.

"Teresa Maria," a voice calls out behind me. "Wait!'

Shocked, I spin around at the familiar voice, collapsing into papa's arms as he rushes up to me.

"Papa, oh my God, Papa," I cry, feeling my legs going weak. "How did you find me?"

CHAPTER 18

MY FATHER HOLDS me tight in his embrace. I cling to him, stunned. It's several moments before I regain control of my frayed emotions as people crowd past us on the sidewalk, casting quick looks in our direction then moving on.

Sobbing, still holding on tightly, I ask him, "How did you find me, Papa?"

"It's all right, Teresa Maria. You are here."

"No, Papa, it's not all right."

I push away from his chest, my pent-up frustration feeding my anger. He has a surprised look, as if he were expecting a different reaction from me. There's a new lightness to it, a new sparkle in his eyes. It's hard for me to find words.

"You left..."

"Come!" He takes my hand, almost brushing away my words. "I take you home."

"Our home is in Monte Vista."

"No *Paloma*. Our home is here now. In Uruapan."

I'm too wrung out to fight. I sag against my father again and let him lead me down several side streets to a white Toyota pickup truck.

* * * *

Climbing out of Patzcuaro in the pickup, heading toward the free road west, I have to talk; I can't stand our prickly silence. I ask him, "Where are you taking me?"

Matter-of-factly he says, "*Uruapan*. Home."

"Not my home." I twist in my seat and stare at him, as if I hadn't heard him. "Whose home? What's going on with you, Papa?"

"Our new home now," he says again. "Your home if you want it to be."

What's the point of talking? I slouch against the door, wiped out, confused, staring out the window. I'm riding with a stranger.

The free road winds across a high plateau where rugged pine-clad mountains crowd in on both sides. After a few miles the road drops off the plateau into a land of lush vegetation. We ride in silence for a while. Finally, he turns off the main road and weaves the Toyota through a series of narrow, cobbled streets in a middle-sized town.

"We're here, *M'hija*," he says when he pulls the car to a stop in front of a one-story house, partially hidden and uninviting behind a high stone wall.

He gets out and comes around to my side. A proud smile swells his face.

I can't describe what I'm feeling: angry, lost, afraid, but most of all scared. Every day I've searched for papa in Mexico, I've felt myself slipping further away from the life I wanted in California. My only purpose coming here was to find him, but now I've found him, I feel like a prisoner, just like I did at Mama Gorda's.

120

He opens the pickup's door and retakes my hand. I don't resist. I'm numb. But when he leads me toward the heavy wooden gate in the wall, I balk and shake off his hand.

"Where are we?" I'm not trying to hide my disrespectful tone. It's like I'm talking to a stranger.

"Our new home, *Teresa Maria*. We can all live here."

"Are you crazy?"

His face flushes, and his body stiffens. We can't communicate.

"I want to live in California with you and mama and Connie and Rico, not here in this shabby village. I want to go back to UCLA, maybe get an apartment near campus. What are you thinking, papa? Mama is worried sick, Connie and Rico are in trouble, I'm falling apart."

"I'm sorry about all that, but your mama shouldn't have worried. She knew the plan; we had talked about it. I had to be ready when the opportunity came."

"What plan? What did you talk about? What?" My pulse is racing, I can feel it throbbing at the base of my neck.

"Come inside, *M'hija*, I explain to you."

When he unlocks the gate and pushes it open, a dazzling new world opens up in front of me. A world of brightly colored flowers in a rainbow of hues. Birds of Paradise and low-growing shrubs with pastel pink flowers in beds bordering the *Casa*. Red and golden hibiscus, dahlias, geraniums in too many colors to count, bloom in hand-painted ceramic pots spotted about a brick patio.

Bougainvillea-covered stone columns and tiled arches extend over a long veranda, a small fountain bubbles in the center of the patio. The shaded veranda spreads along three sides of the house, looking cool in the mid-afternoon November heat. It all feels like a sanctuary, safely hidden behind the sturdy oak gate, with stone walls blocking the street.

The whole effect is breathtaking, like Mexican travel brochures I used to see in the windows along Peck Road. It reminds me of the courtyards of the villas Javier had taken me to. I push that memory away, and focus in what's in front of me, but I can't digest what I'm seeing; It is so not papa, I can't grasp it.

"You did this?"

He smiles at my reaction to his private paradise. "I tell you again, *Paloma*, this is our new home."

"Does mama know?"

He shrugs. "Yes and no. How could I tell her when the La Migra men would come? But she knew we wanted to return here. I've had people work on the house and garden so it would be ready when we come back."

"It's crazy."

"Perhaps." He shrugs again. "Let me get you a soda, and I'll tell the story, Teresa Maria."

"I need something stronger."

He looks at me for a moment, thinking something I can't fathom. "Such a beautiful girl you are," he says, then disappears through a door on the veranda.

* * * *

"Your mama and I went to California to give you a better life, *Paloma*."

Sipping the drink papa hands me, I can feel the warmth of the tequila in my stomach, calming me, but I've heard this story before.

"Mexico was in a very bad way back then," he goes on."

"How do you mean?"

"One day, the government changed the value of all our money. Overnight, it was almost worthless. We were poor again."

"I never heard of such a thing."

"Let me tell it. The government said it was for the good of the country, but that day we couldn't buy what we had bought the day before, it cost too much."

His forehead wrinkles into deep furrows as he describes what had happened. "When your mama got pregnant, we decided to leave. We wanted you to be born in the United States for a better life. Our families helped us. They gave us money so we could buy bus tickets."

The memory clouds papa's face as he talks. His brow wrinkles; his eyes narrow as he remembers the past.

"When the date was set for Rogelio to meet us, mama was within days of your birth. We boarded the bus in Uruapan, changing to another bus in Mexico City and again in Culiacán and finally one in Tijuana. The rides were hard on your mother. She was bounced around on the poor roads, slept sitting up, and ate only what we had brought along or could buy in the small villages along the way.

"We were climbing onto the bus from Tijuana to Tecate that runs close to the border when her water broke," he goes on, still with the vacant, faraway look in his eyes. "I knew it would be difficult for her to walk across the desert to Rogelio's car waiting in California, but mama wouldn't stop. '*Mi bebé*,' she kept saying."

"She didn't make it, did she?"

"Stop interrupting me what I try to tell you, *M'hija*. We would have made it across in time if the bus hadn't broken down outside Tecate," he continues, giving me a look to stay quiet, an old look from my childhood. "Her pains came on fast. After only four or five hours of labor, while the bus driver walked into Tecate for help. The women on the bus delivered you. After resting a few hours, she insisted on getting across the desert, so you could be taken to a hospital and examined. Wrapped in her *rebozo*, I carried you in my arms into California. '*Mi bebé*,' she kept saying as we walked across the desert."

"Were Lupe and Rogelio still waiting?"

Papa shrugs at my interruptions. "Lupe was waiting with Rogelio. They had almost given up hope and were about to leave. No hospital would take you without payment, but Lupe knew of a clinic in a barrio that treated illegals. There, we learned the newborn could only be given a birth certificate if we went back to Mexico. We couldn't go back, so you were a child with no citizenship."

"We lived with Rogelio and Lupe in their apartment for a while, I remember that... with Antonio," I remind him.

"*Que trieste*." He looks at me, shame written on his face. "Antonio was the start."

"Start of what?"

Papa stops for a few moments and only continues when he is able to talk.

"The gardening business was good. I thought Monte Vista would be good for us. I was wrong."

"I thought you and Uncle Rogelio did well."

"Well enough. But we were never treated with respect. The *gringos* paid well, but always looked down their noses at us. I invested some money in an avocado orchard here; the *Casa* came with it. When we sold the business I was ready."

"Papa, you always told me to make a life for myself in Monte Vista."

"What else could I say, *Paloma*?" He shrugs again, the sad look on his face deepening. His face holds an expression of helplessness, but behind it, his eyes smolder. "We wanted the best for you—schools, more opportunities than we had. No matter what you hear, always remember, *M'hija*, that everything I did in California was for you. Your mama and I talked about coming back often. After your trouble, I decided I wanted to live in Mexico to end my days. I saw that you might have a better future here."

"You knew?"

"We knew enough. By the way you acted. Hints we heard from the neighbors. You became such a lovely girl, Teresa Maria. Everyone saw it. How could we not guess? Boys started hanging around, sniffing like street dogs. I couldn't stand the thought. Here that never could have happened. In Monte Vista, there was no pride. Here you could be special. I wanted to kill those boys."

* * * *

Shadows dance across the walls of the *Casa* as my father talks into the twilight. The story he was telling was unbelievable. But the numbers don't add up. How could he buy this villa with an avocado orchard? Where had the money come from? It still doesn't add up, but I don't want to question my father. I don't know what to think.

"Mama knew all this?"

"No, I never spoke a lot about it, but she knew I wanted to come back."

Doubt invades me. I can't stop shivering. I feel alone, as if everything is lost. I think of Javier lost, too.

CHAPTER 19

AWAKE MOST OF the night, trying to understand what is happening to me. The last couple of weeks have changed me completely. I have no anchor, nothing to hold on to. I don't know who I am. My life in Monte Vista and UCLA comes into focus in my mind, but it's like they're a video being streamed over and over in my head that has lost all meaning. Not me anymore. Being surrounded by Veronica Estrada and her posse of gangbangers in the back alley, my dress ripped, and my bra pulled down, are vivid and terrifying but they don't seem like they happened to me. Losing Javier and lying in a fetal position overnight in a Mexican cemetery are a nightmare, not real.

It is well toward daylight that I'm overwhelmed by exhausted sleep, only to be awakened by church bells calling worshipers to Mass in the cathedral at 7am. Too numb to care, I dress in the same clothes I wore yesterday and the day before. I have no choice. Papa says he will send a man back to Patzcuaro for my other clothes. I tiptoe across the patio, peeking into the kitchen as I go. Papa is sitting at a table in the kitchen sipping coffee and talking on a cell phone I didn't know he had. I'm glad he doesn't see or try to intercept me. I slip out the wooden gate to the street, still wrestling with the question of how papa knew where to find me.

A couple of scrawny dogs patrol the empty street. One yawns as I go by, the other greets me by scratching his ear. The day is crisp and bright; the late fall sun promises a warm day later. I shiver a little, glad for the *rebozo* I bought in Morelia.

With no destination in mind, my purpose is just to stretch my legs and relieve my tension, trying to forget all the questions that crowd my mind. Every street looks the same, filled with walled houses only distinguished by their bright colors—orange, deep blue, yellow and an occasional pink. Turning right and left as I walk, I make a map in my head so I can find my way back. But as I go, I begin to fantasize about what might lie behind each wall and street door I pass. It helps me relax.

The aroma of fresh coffee catches my attention. Following my nose to a small bodega, I buy a cup and go back to the sidewalk. As I do, a group of school kids comes hurrying by, chattering to one another. They're involved with their friends, oblivious to the grownups around them.

A young girl in a blue pinafore school uniform, over a starched white blouse, with matching blue beret set at a jaunty angle, busily talking to a companion, bumps into me. Coffee jumps out of my cup, most of it splashing on the cobblestones. Startled, the girl looks at me. We make eye contact, and then she drops her head to stare down at the sidewalk.

"*Lo siento, Señorita,*" she mumbles.

Her schoolmates back away.

Dropping down on one knee, I wipe off an imaginary spot of coffee. "It's fine," I assure her.

The girl turns her round face up to me. Her hair is dark, but not severe. It hangs in little bangs on her forehead. Her eyes are equally dark, with heavy brows arching over them. Chubby in the cheeks, with little spot dimples that grow as she begins to smile, realizing she isn't going to be reprimanded.

How pretty, I think. Then, for an instant, staring into her innocent face, I remember the picture of Sophie Javier placed on his makeshift altar. Will I ever have a child as beautiful at this one standing in front of me? As sweet as Sophie? Who would the child's father be? I pull myself together and put my hand on the girl's shoulder. "Be careful," I scold her with a smile.

"*Lo siento*," she says again but doesn't stop looking at me. We stay smiling, our faces close to together a few more seconds. Then she jumps back and runs to catch up with her friends. "I want to be a beautiful lady like she is when I grow up," I hear her tell them, with a certainty about life only a child can have. It isn't that long ago I had that kind of confidence, but not now. Once, the girl turns back to me. She gives a little wave. I wave back and laugh.

It's the first I've laughed since we watched the dance of the little old men in Patzcuaro. It feels good.

$$* * * *$$

Kids didn't wear uniforms to my elementary school in Monte Vista. Kids wore hand-me-downs, mended, clean and well ironed, but hand-me-downs nevertheless.

In the second grade, when I was seven, the kids from my neighborhood were with me in the ESL class.

"It's important that you learn English. Everyone in California speaks English," our teacher told us. "If you don't you won't get a good

education, and that means you'll never get a good job. People will treat you like children all your lives. Do you understand that, Teresa?"

I did. I never again said a Spanish word in school or at home. I knew it was better to be silent than to speak Spanish. It wasn't long before I was no longer required to be in the ESL class.

By mid-morning, I'm at the edge of the city on a street leading up a hill past vendors' stalls, each displaying a different craft. The bright colors and fanciful designs lighten my mood. At one stall, I admire religious icons and ceramic figurines of Jesus and the Virgin of Guadalupe painted in brilliant colors. From an old woman with white hair that hangs in ropes around her face, I buy a small statuette of the Virgin for Connie. Papier-mâché lions and bears and other animals for children at the next stall bring a smile. I keep walking up the hill, and soon I'm in a park-like setting. The roadway fades off to my right, and I'm on a path through a wooded area. Trees and giant ferns are dense on both sides of the path. Wild orchids grow in the crotch of tree branches. The sounds of water are faint up ahead, swelling louder as I climb the path. Soon I'm alongside a small river crashing crazily down the hillside toward the town.

I realize I'm not alone. People are walking along the path behind and in front of me. The calmness I felt earlier fades. I start looking around, turning to see who's behind me, paying attention to the people I pass. They return my stares, adding to my nervousness. I think about turning around and leaving the park, but the sound of the rushing water pulls me forward. I can hear the river crashing over rocks up ahead. The dense foliage, dripping droplets of mist, finally gives way to a waterfall. It isn't a big one, maybe only twenty feet high, but it's the first waterfall I've ever seen.

I drop down on a bench just off the path to stare at the water, foaming white as it hurls itself off the rock ledges. The sight mesmerizes me. Momentarily I forget my uneasy feeling. The shallow river, only thirty yards wide at best, carves small channels between the larger rocks in the stream bed. Then they merge and leap headlong, recklessly into the air. The river flings itself on the rocks, frothing and foaming at the base of the falls, then spreading out, as if taking a breather to gather itself again before continuing its reckless rush down the hill. I'm hypnotized. I concentrate on the falls, trying to find a pattern in the way the water leaps into space and destroys itself on the rocks below, only to be reborn before continuing down the riverbed. There is no pattern. There is no pattern to the events of my life that brought me to this bench either. I am the river. Out of control. I come to the edge and throw myself recklessly over it. No path. No plan. Somewhere upstream, I've lost Javier.

Movement in the corner of my eye arouses me. I come alert when something off among the trees attracts my attention. When I turn to see what it is, I think a man is watching me. I'm not sure. He turns away, heading down the path toward the street just when I look at him. Even the quick glimpse I get tells me there is no mistaking what I saw. I jump off the bench and run after him, catching up with the balding, white-mustached man walking toward the street. Determined to confront him, coming up behind him, I put my hand on his shoulder.

"Why are you following me?"

He stops, dumb-faced.

"You are following me, aren't you?" I know he understands English.

He shrugs, looks down at the sidewalk.

"Where is Javier?" I demand, grabbing his shoulder and shaking him. "Who are you?"

He turns his face sideways so he can look at me. His eyes have a vague, frightened look. He seems almost trembling. "*No soy nada*," he says through his thick mustache. "I don't know anything you ask. Let me go."

He walks off. There is nothing more I can say to him. No way to stop him. So, trembling, I watch him disappear into the crowd near the marketplace.

Walking quickly back toward papa's *Casa*, I pass the craft stalls on the road again, with only a quick nod to the woman who had sold me the statuette. Retracing my steps past the school, I go back toward the little store where I'd bought my coffee. As I pass it, newspapers stacked on an orange crate on the sidewalk have a headline that screams at me: HEADLESS BODY FOUND IN MORELIA!

CHAPTER 20

THE DEAD MAN is not identified in the newspaper, but there's speculation the murder is the work of a drug cartel. The body was found on the outskirts of Morelia. As I scan the paper for details, I have a terrible feeling about Javier. I can't stop trembling. Don't let it be him, I beg the Virgin. How can I go back to papa's *Casa* and act normally? How can I tell him about Javier? I can't.

People are crowding the street now, talking loudly and gestering to one another, but no one shows any interest in me. The mustached man is nowhere in sight. Women go by, hefting their loaded plastic Frieda Kahlo shopping bags, on their way home from the market.

The cell phone rings in my purse.

I grabbed for it, not thinking. "Hello—*Bueno*..."

Silence. The call ends.

Looking at the dead phone, I think about Carmen telling me to throw it away. I hadn't. Who is trying to reach Javier? Or was the call for me?

* * * *

My clothes from Patzcuaro are laid out on my bed when I get back to papa's *Casa*. Some are still in the garment bags from the Morelia dress shop. I start to hang them in a wall closet, still thinking about the horrible newspaper account, asking myself if I regret making love with Javier?

I don't.

After a few minutes, I realize papa is standing behind me in the doorway, watching. I wonder if he can read my thoughts. When I turn to look at him, he has a heavy face.

"You went to Patzcuaro with a man," he says. There is no inflection in his voice, no question, no accusation, no reproach, nothing.

"That's right, Papa."

"Who was he? Why did he leave you?"

"I don't want to talk about it, okay? I'll tell you when I'm ready."

"These are expensive clothes."

"I said I don't want to talk about it."

He continues watching me. After another moment, he backs out the door. In a soft voice, he says, "You're a woman now, *Paloma*. I won't ask questions, but I'll listen when you want to tell me."

He stops again to say, "A woman came here looking for you this morning. A large woman with red hair. She says she met you in Tijuana." He stops talking and studies me, but I stay blank-faced. "She wants to see you. She's staying at *Mansion del Cupatitzio,* you should find her there."

The tidal wave of my emotions is overwhelming again. How can my father not see how unworthy I am to be his daughter? I want him to love me, but I'm ashamed of myself. Ashamed by how I've changed. I want to forget Mama Gorda, Morelia,

Patzcuaro, Day of the Dead, and be his little dove again. But I can't. My feelings for Javier are stronger than my shame. I need to know what Carmen knows. "Can you drive me there, papa?"

* * * *

Mansion del Cupatitzio is an inn in the national park, near the stream I'd walked earlier, but higher up. A two-story, L-shaped building surrounding two sides of a patio with overhanging palm trees. I don't have to look far for Mama Gorda. She's in the lobby bar, taking up an entire couch, holding a shot glass of tequila in one hand and a lime in the other. Her hair hangs down to her shoulders. She is a mass of talcum-powdered skin, from her forehead, down to a large expanse of chest just above her bosom. Her red-lipped smile greets me.

"Sit." She points to the deep chair next to her.

Without changing her stare, she downs the shot, takes the salt and lime, then blots her lips with a cocktail napkin. The napkin looks like it had lost a fight when she sets it down. Then she draws in a sharp breath and gives me another smile that shows all her teeth.

"You should've gone home when you had the chance," she says.

"I should've."

"What happened?"

"I don't know. It got kind of crazy, Mama Gorda."

"My name's Carmen. Carmen Madrazo. The girls in Tijuana call me Mama Gorda, you're not one of them." Her voice is terse and reprimanding, but she continues smiling. Her smile and the tone of her voice have me off guard. "Javier happened," she says.

"He did."

She laughs. "I didn't think you were his type."

"Where is he? Do you know?"

"You found your father?"

"He found me. Right after I called you. How did he know where to find me? Where is Javier?"

"Let me ask the questions. You threw the phone away?"

"No. Someone called it this morning. Whoever it was hung up. Tell me what this is about, Carmen? What's happened to Javier? How did my father know where to find me?"

Raising two fingers, Carmen motions to the barman. She looks at me without speaking until he comes from behind the bar with a tray holding two shot glasses, limes and a saltshaker. "Drink it," she points to one of the shot glasses. "Are you still a virgin?"

I don't know if she means sexually or drinking tequila shots. Either way, I don't answer her.

The tequila burns my throat. I throw salt from the back of my wrist and jam the lime into my mouth, all in a rush like I've seen men in Monte Vista do it. I've never done this before, and I don't do it very well. It brings on a coughing spell that lasts several minutes while my throat and stomach burn.

Carmen holds a Cheshire cat smile on her face while my struggle goes on. "Are you?"

"Am I what?

"Still a virgin?"

I look around the lobby.

She chuckles. "You still haven't answered my question, but I think I can guess your answer. What do you know about Javier?"

"I know I miss him. He was wonderful to me. But I don't really know much about him, do I?"

"Did he talk about his family?"

I tell her the conversations we'd had. She nods her head from time to time. Then she calls for another round. "You'll need this."

Her words are chilling.

I handle the tequila ritual a little better the second time, reducing the coughing jag to just a brief spell. I can feel my tummy warming and fuzziness creeping into my head. It feels good. It's numbing my desperate thoughts.

Carmen looks around the room, empty except for us. She lowers her voice anyway. "There's a lot you don't know." She stops again to look around. This time she almost whispers. "The Ugalde family is well known in Mexico. They've had trouble. His father doesn't know what's happened to Javier. He's coming from Morelia. He wants to meet you."

I give her an astonished look. Then I pass out.

* * * *

I come to on my bed in papa's *Casa*. The room is spinning as if I were on a carousel. I feel sick. I want to feel nothing.

When I roll over, I'm looking straight into Carmen's flaccid face. Seeing her sitting beside the bed is unreal. I start sobbing. Then my stomach starts retching. She grabs me by the hair and drags my face over a bowl on the floor. I puke up everything; I think I'm going to choke. When I stop throwing up, she wipes my mouth with a towel. Then she blots the sweat from my forehead.

I expect her to make a joke or a sarcastic comment, but she doesn't. Instead she reaches out to take my hand. "You'll be fine, *Chica*," she says. "In time."

There isn't any way I will ever be fine again. I think she knows that by the soft look she gives me.

"Did I pass out?"

"Yes."

"Is he dead?"

"Possibly."

137

I roll over with my face to the wall, too weak to cry. Carmen strokes my back slowly. She continues stroking and begins singing. Her voice is too soft for me to hear her words, but the sound has a soothing tone. She keeps on singing until I fall asleep.

It's dark when I awake again. My stomach hurts. My mouth still feels like cotton. I'm alone in the darkness, with only a sliver of moon looking over the far wall of the *Casa* into my room. I lie on my back, staring at it, focusing so hard to drive all other thoughts out of my head.

I hear footsteps on the veranda. The French doors open, and Carmen comes in carrying a bowl of warm broth.

"For you," she says. Sitting on the chair by the bed again, she holds the bowl in both hands. "Sit up."

I'm not capable of resisting or making decisions. I feel empty. I sit up, and she feeds me *Albondigas* soup with a spoon. It's the same soup mama would give me when I stayed home from school with a fever.

"You're a sight." Carmen grimaces. "Where's the virginal beauty I saw in Tijuana? Your eyes are raw red. You're white, all your color's gone. Your hair's a mess, too. We have our work to do in the morning to clean you up."

"In the morning?"

"I told you before. For Felix Ugalde."

"I don't want—"

"Never mind what you want. He wants you. Rest now. No one says no to Felix."

✳ ✳ ✳ ✳

A taxi brings Carmen to the *Casa* the next morning. Papa lets her in with a nod but then leaves us alone.

"You look better," she greets me. Dropping into a chair next to me, she takes a mango slice off my breakfast plate. "I wish to hell I could bounce back the way you young girls do after a bad night."

"Good morning to you, too, Carmen."

She looks at me for a moment, then laughs. "You're feeling better today."

"I guess."

"Too much tequila."

"Your fault."

"I was only trying to ease your pain. Sometimes my ways aren't as smooth or as gentle, as respectable folks. I just wanted to ease your pain is all."

I can't help smiling. And I can see she is trying to be a little more pulled together. She's wearing a pair of cavernous dark brown dress pants with a tan pullover top that covers her bulk as best it can be covered. They are the most subdued colors I've seen her wear, but her hair and makeup definitely are not subdued. She has too much blush on her cheeks and deep blue eye shadow. The orange-red lipstick is like a neon sign outside a bar.

"Thanks for all you did for me yesterday."

"I feel sad for you, Teresa. Sad and maybe responsible. If Hector hadn't brought you to my home and I hadn't introduced you to Javier, you wouldn't be involved in this."

The sound of Javier's name brings a lump to my throat. I look hard at Carmen. Something seems very strange when she lays it out that way. I can't put my finger on it, but it's twisted a little in my mind.

"Involved in what?"

"Things are different here than in California—"

"Yeah, I've heard all that before."

Carmen looks hurt. "If you lived here, you'd know the truth. We act from necessity."

"What's your necessity?" I try to say it as gently as I can, but it doesn't come out that way. "I think you all try to rationalize what you do as necessity."

"There's a lot to tell." She doesn't respond to my tone. Instead, her voice gets softer.

"Go ahead. Tell."

"Once I was like you," she starts. "You don't believe that now, but it's true. I was a beautiful young woman. I had a strong voice. Everything to live for before my own government shot me. I could have been a big entertainer."

"Shot you?"

"You see me limp. It was like the shootings in your country. We won't talk of that."

"So, what am I involved in?" I ask her.

"Felix wants to help you," she says.

"I want to see Javier again alive." I can't stop the tears misting my eyes. "I want to get away from this craziness. I want my life back."

CHAPTER 21

FELIX UGALDE PAUSES in the doorway of Carmen's suite to give me the once over before entering. "Nice, Carmen," he says by way of introduction. "My son has good taste."

"Where is he?" I blurt out.

Carmen squeezes my arm to silence me.

"You are Teresa Maria Diaz," Felix says, ignoring my outburst. It's a statement, not a question, as if he is naming me for the first time. He introduces himself with a forced smile and pulls a chair up beside the couch where Carmen and I sit.

Felix no more resembles his son than a mule resembles a thoroughbred. He's about as nondescript as they come. He could pass for a successful, mid-level Mexican businessman— insurance salesman, middle-level banker, or maybe, in a stretch, an ambulance-chasing attorney. Probably in his sixties, he is of medium height with a stocky build.

I study his square face, whose most prominent feature is a high forehead that merges into male-pattern baldness. He inspects me through dark, aviator-style sunglasses and wears a salt and pepper pencil mustache under his aquiline nose. From

141

the white Panama straw hat, which he takes off immediately on entering Carmen's suite, to his highly polished black shoes, his dress is immaculate. He wears a well-tailored dark blue suit, with a white shirt and conservative tie. His shirt cuffs sag under the weight of massive gold cufflinks.

I have no idea why I'm sitting here with him. Carmen says he's concerned about my welfare. Is he worried about it in a protective way? Or concerned his enemies might be lurking about? Or if I might be one of them? Carmen says I should know the height of his concern by the fact he's come to Uruapan from Morelia to meet me. This morning, she insisted I put on suitable clothes to meet him. Suitable meaning pantyhose, a dangerously tight, Mexican print skirt and plain, off-white scoop neck, sleeveless top, all his son's selections from the shop in Morelia.

He stares at me again for several more moments before speaking. I wonder if other young women are as sensitive as I am at being stared at. Some might think it's a compliment. I don't, but I'm used to it. Ever since high school, men have stared at me—teachers, storekeepers in Monte Vista, bus riders to and from UCLA, even a couple of priests at Our Lady of Guadalupe. I never thought of myself as particularly attractive until towards the end of high school. In fact, that's how I met Ryan at UCLA.

✳ ✳ ✳ ✳

He was staring at me in our Econ class. One day he approached me when class ended. "I was just struck by how pretty you are," he said.

Not a bad first line, I thought, but a bit over the top. I blushed and didn't say a word. The silence led to an invitation for an apologetic cup of coffee. At first, it was awkward. We sat across from each other at a small table in a coffee shop near campus. As usual, I didn't have much to say, and Ryan was fumbling for a follow up to his brilliant opening.

"*You have an exotic beauty, tall and graceful like a cat. Are you Mexican? Your English is perfect, but there's a wonderful lilt in your voice.*"

"*I grew up here,*" *I told him.*

"*I was hoping that you were Mexican,*" *he said after the pause.* "*I don't know any Latinas, and I was hoping you were one.*"

"*Why?*" *This was beginning to take an uncomfortable turn.*

He leaned forward and gripped the edge of the table. His eyes—a gorgeous shade of blue—narrowed. "*You're the future,*" *he said.* "*The Hispanic population will be a majority here soon. My father says it's inevitable. I need to know more about the Hispanic culture, so I'm taking Spanish and Latin American studies as well as econ.*"

"*Because your father says so?*"

"*He's right, you know. What is your background?*"

"*My parents are Mexican.*"

Ryan's face brightened noticeably, like a little boy on the trail of a treat. He even reached across the table to touch my arm. "*Were you born here?*" *he asked.*

"*Close.*"

"*Are you legal?*"

"*That really none of your business, is it?*"

He held his smile and didn't seem offended. "*How would you like to do something together with me this weekend? I'd like to get to know you better.*"

* * * *

"I can't tell you more about Javier," Felix Ugalde says because I don't know more yet. But soon, I will." He gives me a worried smile, and I can see the concern behind it. "He has disappeared."

"Have you heard from the police?" I ask.

"No police!" He and Carmen both say in unison.

"Police are not to be trusted."

"Was Javier in trouble?" I ask.

The two of them stiffen and look at each other again. Silent messages go back and forth between them. Clearly, I've struck a nerve.

"What do you know about us? Our family?" Felix asks.

"Javier told me a little, but not very much."

Once again, Carmen checks Felix for signs before saying. "There's always risk."

This was going nowhere. They are holding back. So, I take the initiative. "What's going on? Can someone please tell me?"

Carmen interrupts the silence that follows my question. "Some things don't need to be discussed."

"I think they do." I turn to Felix. "Your son has disappeared, *Señor* Ugalde..." Then I have trouble saying the rest. I wait to quiet my emotions. "I was with him. We were run off the road. He disappeared when we were sitting together on a blanket having a picnic. Gone. No warning; no explanation. I think I have a right to know what's going on."

Ugalde watches me again for several moments. "I see why Javier was fond of you. He told me he thought he loved you when he phoned a couple of days ago. I'm here to respect him by coming to help you. But do not take advantage of that, *Señorita* Diaz."

"Take advantage? What do you mean? Every day since I've been in Mexico, someone has taken advantage of me. You need to explain."

The room goes quiet. It isn't a large room, and the silence is oppressive.

"Enough of this." Felix interrupts the silence. He stands and paces to the window, turning his back on us. "None of this is any concern to you."

"Javier is."

He turned back abruptly, giving me a look that says how impertinent he thinks I am. "That's why I came. I want you to be safe."

I look at him. Then at Carmen. Each has an expression that tells me nothing. "Am I not safe?" I ask.

"*Señor* Ugalde's men are looking for Javier," Carmen says. "If he is alive, they'll find him. It's possible he's not... We have to be prepared. There is no business in Mexico anymore without terror."

I feel the emptiness in my chest again. The same emptiness I felt during the long night in the cemetery. It chills me like a blast of cold air. The memory of his kiss is a dull ache.

"What's done is done," Felix says, appearing to ignore Carmen's words. "If something's happened to Javier, people will pay." As he says it, a mean look flashes in his eyes that hadn't been there when he first entered the room. It frightens me. "I came to ask what we can do for you, *Señorita?*"

"Tell me why he wouldn't be alive."

Ugalde shows his impatience. He continues pacing the room and stops by the window again, staring out. "What is it you want?" He demands.

I slump back into the couch. I don't know what to answer. So finally, I tell him the first thing that comes into my mind. "I want to get far away from this craziness. I want to go home."

"That can be arranged," he says.

"Arranged? Like a truckload of porn videos? No thanks. I'll find a way to get home on my own. Not from a smuggler."

That was not the right thing to say.

He looks at me with dull eyes.

A soft tapping on the door interrupts my outburst. Felix moves away from the window. Ponderously, Carmen gets up from the couch. She stands for a minute while her bulk adjusts to her upright position. She pulls her top down over her bulging stomach, then limps to the door. Opening it only a crack, she speaks quietly to the man outside. He responds in words I barely make out. Through the narrow opening, I can see the man with the mustache who has been hovering around me since Morelia.

Carmen closed the door quickly and comes back into the room. "Some Federales are nearby. You should leave."

* * * *

Felix leaves hurriedly, putting on his hat and giving us a quick bow. Carmen looked at me after he's gone. There is an accusing tone in her voice. "Javier is Felix's whole life," she starts. "His wife is gone. After Sophie died, Javier was the only one left. Feliz vowed he'd never let anything happen to him. Now he's distraught. You disrespected him."

Tears form in my eyes. Coming to me, she hugs me to her large bosom, smothering me in the softness of her flesh.

"I know, I know," she whispers.

She rocks me back and forth for several minutes, then frees me and leads me to the couch.

"Felix wants to look out for you, Teresa. You were rude to him."

"If I was rude, it was because he didn't answer my questions. He treated me like a child or a servant."

"There's no need to insult him, he's just like the rest of us."

"And what is that?"

"Soiled. I know you think we are criminals."

"You are." I blot my tears and gave Carmen an unsympathetic look.

"You haven't lived here. You can't understand."

"Stop it, Carmen! I'm not a schoolgirl. All I've heard from you and...Javier is that you are all victims of life in Mexico. How did you get involved with the Ugaldes anyway?"

"Felix helped me. A long time ago."

I slouch on the couch, trying to comprehend the unfair world these people have concocted to justify what they do. "Tell me," I say.

She does over the next hour. She says she is the daughter of a government worker, born in Mexico City. When she was sixteen, she fell in love with a young college student.

"The students were demanding reforms because the government was so corrupt," she says. "I knew even my own father took bribes. Everyone did. Ramon was a leader of the students. I loved him so much I would have done anything he asked."

She says the government cracked down on the students. When soldiers occupied the university, the students staged a rally in Mexico City. Mexican soldiers fired on them. Many—no one ever knows how many—were killed. "I was shot in the hip. I couldn't believe the government my father worked for would let that happen. I never went home again. When I healed, Ramon and I fled to Oaxaca. I never wanted to see my family again."

Carmen starts the slow process of pushing herself up from the couch. "Come," she says when she is finally standing. "We'll have lunch by the pool."

* * * *

We sit at a sheltered patio table in the crook of the L-shaped building. Carmen orders tequila, I pass. She laughs, teasing me about yesterday. She orders lunch and eats it hungrily. I pick at my salad.

Continuing her story, amid the clatter of waiters and conversations of the guests, she says she and Ramon had gone to live in a commune in the Oaxaca jungle.

"I had a wonderful singing voice, until this took it away." She points at the shot glass. "I earned enough singing in some of the restaurants in Oaxaca for us to live on. At night we drank, smoked pot, and made love in the jungle. Do you know how wonderful it is to be with a man that you love with all your soul?"

I start to choke up.

She pays no attention but continues. "Men from Mexico City told me I had talent. They wanted me to go back to sing in night clubs there. Ramon didn't want to leave. I had to make a choice. I had to find out if I could make it. It was sad for me to leave him... but I had to try."

She stops talking and looks over the pool into the jungle of vegetation beyond. I see a vulnerability I haven't seen in Carmen before. When she resumes her story, she speeds it up, as if not wanting to dwell on it any longer. Without Ramon, she says, she drifted between a lot of men who said they would help her career, but usually only took her to bed.

Her career never went forward. But she says she learned about men, how corrupt they all were, and how powerful. "Some of them helped me when my singing stopped. Hard to believe now that I was a desirable woman in those days. Men wanted me. I was a mistress to several powerful men in government and other pursuits. I met Felix. He set me up in business in Tijuana."

I give her a long, hard stare. She doesn't go on, and I don't ask obvious questions.

"Enough about this," she says, abruptly bringing her story to a close. "Do you really want to go back to California?"

Same question, same uncertain answer. "I do, but everything's so different now. Papa wants us all to move here, live in his *Casa*. If I go back, I'll be alone."

"Why go?"

"I'm in college, remember? At least I was. Remember the cheerleader outfit you wanted me to wear? I was a communications career major, going to have a good job when I graduated. I want to work in the U.S., to live there. I want to have things my parents never had."

"It's a great costume, isn't it?" She laughs, giving me a wink. "You would have looked terrific in it." She turns serious again, holding her smile. "Such big dreams. I had big dreams once. You could achieve your dreams here, Teresa. In Mexico. I told you before, your looks are the kind men admire here. I am sure you could work in TV or movies if you wanted. I could help you get started."

"Are you serious?"

"I'll show you if you stay."

"If I stay?"

"If you don't? Felix could help you."

"I'll never ask him."

"So, how will you get back?"

"I'll get back."

CHAPTER 22

"WHY YOU DON'T stay, M'hija?"

Papa looks hurt, maybe a little angry, too. In the deepening twilight, I see it in his eyes. While collecting my thoughts and packing my things, I've avoided him, but our talk is inevitable.

"I'm sorry, Papa. I can't live here. I tried so hard to make something of myself in California. I wanted you to be proud."

"I *am* proud. And I would be even prouder if you stayed."

"I need to go back. I want my college degree."

"You could get a degree here. Plenty of schools here."

The conversation is pointless.

I take a deep breath. "Was it all just talk when I was growing up, Papa? You used to tell me how much you wanted for me in America. Were those just words?"

He gives me another sad smile—there have been a lot of sad smiles over the last few days—and shifts in his chair. "Maybe so," he says, "I don't know anymore. I believed them when I said them. But it didn't turn out the way I thought. When Antonio died, our lives changed. Rogelio blamed me... We couldn't work together anymore."

"Blamed you? Why?"

"*No importa* now..."

Papa stops. His hands ball up into fists, tiny, old man fists, clenched tightly. When he starts talking again, there's a harshness in his voice. Part of it is anger, but what I hear most is defiance. "I wanted respect for you. For me, too. People treated us like we weren't human. I wanted more. I looked for ways. Made my choices. I started thinking about coming home years ago."

His gaze drifts off over the *Casa* wall into the gathering dusk. He speaks distantly, no longer looking at me, looking instead into a place only he can see. "You were my hope, *Paloma*, my bright star. I thought all the hard work and disrespect might be worth it to see you become something you couldn't be in Mexico. But now I see you can be more in Mexico than you ever could be there."

"Like what, Papa? What are you talking about?" He was beginning to sound like Carmen.

"You would make me proud. You were always achieving what I never could, but I felt important just being your papa. We can both have the respect we deserve here."

"Papa, I don't understand. What are you saying? Tell me!"

"I always tell you to accept the life God gives you. Do not fight it."

He stops again and seems to think about what he's just said for a moment before dismissing it. "Go back. Finish what you started. Maybe then you understand."

"I'll miss you, Papa."

"I love you Teresa Maria. How will you cross?"

"I don't know yet."

"You have no ID. I can get you some, take a few days."

"You?"

"I know people."

It takes a moment for me to understand what he has just said. I can't believe what I hear. "You, too, papa?" My mouth drops open. "Is that the life God gave you to live?"

I get up from the chair, kneel at his feet, hug his legs, and cry with my head on his knees. I hardly feel his gentle touch on my hair. His fingers trace through it.

"We take the life God gives us for good or bad. I just want you to be safe."

"Safe? Huh. I have no ID. I'm not American and not Mexican. Am I safe, Papa? What am I?"

"You're my beautiful *niña*... We should have registered you before we crossed. I'm sorry for that."

"It's not that, Papa. You worked so hard. Mama did too. Now you talk of fake ID. Where is the dignity in that?"

"You could stay here, then."

We both go silent. I stay kneeling at his feet, hugging his knees. He sits almost rigid, his hands brushing through my hair and stroking my face.

"Don't worry, I'll get across. I'll find a way," I tell him, rising to my feet and heading for my room.

"Be very careful, *Paloma*," Papa calls after me.

✳ ✳ ✳ ✳

I meet Carmen at the Uruapan airport the next morning for the three-and-a-half-hour flight to Tijuana via Mexico City. My last goodbye with papa is stiff. We each struggle to hide our emotions. Neither of us wants to think it might be our last time together.

The planes we take are 737s, like the ones that fly low over Monte Vista toward LAX. I'm disappointed with them. They're cramped and dingy, not like Javier's King Air 350, but we get to

Tijuana in half the time. It's only a week since Javier and I flew to Morelia. I'd started to love him in that short time, but even now, his image is blurred.

The little elf man who works for Carmen meets us when we arrive. She calls him *El Pelon* because of his hairless scalp. He takes our bags and shuffles off into the parking lot, reappearing a few minutes later behind the wheel of an aging mud-brown SUV. Carmen gets in back and motions me to sit beside her.

"I want to go to the American Consulate's office," I tell her. "Can you take me there?"

"No, no," she wags her finger at me. "You come to my house first. When you're ready, *El Pelon* will drive you and stay with you. Don't be deceived, he will protect you very well. Young women do not walk around Tijuana alone."

Now back to being called Mama Gorda again in her house with her porno girls, Carmen, protests when I tell her I want *El Pelon* to take me right away. "You go tomorrow," she says with finality.

"No, I have to get home. I have to go there now!"

"Please don't leave," Vivian pleads. She's been standing in the front hall with us since we arrived, urging me to stay.

Mama Gordo gives me a dismissive flip of her head when she sees my mind is made up. She calls for *El Pelon* again. Smiling shyly, he drives me back to Tijuana. It's just past 3:30 when he pulls up by concrete car barriers in front of two-story American Consul General's office.

When I open the SUV door, it groans a metal-on-metal grinding sound. The ancient vehicle is more rust than paint, slightly out of line judging from the sound the door makes. *El Pelon* gives me a cautionary look. "Don't come out till you see SUV," he warns me.

Pushing past a line of people stretching down the street for half a block, I hurry up the steps into the front hallway.

"Hold it right there, *Señorita*."

A swarthy uniformed young guard, with hair as black as tar and just as sticky-looking, blocks my way. He reeks of the gunk he's plastered his hair with.

"I want to apply for a visa," I tell him.

He looks me up and down. It isn't a warm look. "Not today, you don't, *Chava*. Come back tomorrow."

Holding my breath against his bad smell, I take a step, putting my face close to his. "The sign on the door says open till four-thirty. I've still got time."

"If all your papers are filled out, you can get in line with the others." He put his hand on my shoulder and pushes me back out the door.

"Get your hand off me! What papers do I need?"

He backs up a step but still holds me in his stare. "You won't get in today. Why a beautiful *mujer* like you want to leave Mexico, anyway? Stay in Tijuana, I show you the sites, *Chava*."

"Not in your best dream. Show me where to get the forms."

Anger rises in greaseball's face. Hurt anger. He looks at me for several moments with narrowing eyes and compressed lips. He points to a far desk in the big room behind him and moves aside. "I won't forget you," he hisses. As I brush past him, I feel his hand reach for my thigh and slap it away.

The American behind the desk is polite when I approach him. "How can I help you today, *Señorita*?" It's almost a purr. He sits luxuriously in his deep leather chair, like a cat surveying all the human activity in the large room around him. "It's almost closing, I don't have much time." He doesn't encourage me to sit in the chair next to his desk, so I stand across it from him, very quickly explaining that I have to get home to Monte Vista.

"Home, you say. Do you live there? Are you a citizen?"

I shake my head.

He shakes his head. "I see."

Of middle age, he has a very slight build and fine blond hair, thinning and maybe on its way to white, with wire-frame bifocals. As much as he tries to stay passive, I can hear a hint of ridicule in his voice, but ignore it.

"I've lived there all my life. My family is there, and I have to get back to them."

"You're not a U.S. citizen, is that correct?" His voice is flat. The unctuous warmth has left him. His eyes jump back and forth from my face to my breasts and lower.

"Yes."

"So, you were born here? You are a Mexican national?"

"*Soy Americana*," I protest. We are both surprised by my outburst.

"*No es Americana*," he replies smiling. "*Pero es Mexicana*."

"Only in your eyes."

"*Señorita*, it is not a question of my eyes. In the eyes of the United States government, you are a foreigner. The fact you have been living in California all your life doesn't change that. You are an illegal immigrant. A Dreamer staying unnoticed under the surface, hoping my government will bestow citizenship on you. Might I ask why you don't request a visitor's visa?"

I explain about papa moving back to Mexico, and that I am going to California to arrange for my mother and brother and sister to move back with him.

The man looks skeptical but nods understanding. "So, you'll move back to Mexico, too? When your family moves?"

"I will." I lie.

"Well then, you can apply for your visa with your Mexican citizenship."

"How long does it take to get a visa?"

"Four to five weeks," he says.

"I can't wait that long. I have to get back to my mother."

He opens a desk drawer and pulls out a packet of papers. "Fill these out. Call for an appointment—which could take two or three days to set up—and come back with your proof of Mexican citizenship. It's time for me to close up now."

Desperation comes into my voice, and I try to hide it. "I don't have a birth certificate. I was born just before my parents took me across the border."

"You will have to show a valid Mexican birth certificate or some other proof of your nationality."

"How do I go about doing that?"

"I don't know, *Señorita*. You should talk to your own government about that."

He lets his shoulders sag into his suit jacket. He sets his pen down and puts one hand on top of the other on the desktop. He almost yawns, but it turns into a purr again.

"Let me see if I understand," he says in his most formal quiet voice. "You are not a U.S. citizen, and you can't prove Mexican citizenship. Is that correct? You are, in fact, a woman with no citizenship—a woman without a country as it were."

With that, he allows himself a smirk.

I have to pass the greaser again, leaving the building. Pausing momentarily in the doorway, I look down the street for *El Pelon*. The guard leers at me again. "How 'bout it, *Chica? A noche?*"

That's enough. I rush past him onto the sidewalk, searching up and down the street for a sign of the SUV. When the guard shuts and locks the door, people lined up in front of the Consulate, trying to get out of Mexico, dissolve into the side streets like smoke from a match. In a matter of minutes, the sidewalk is deserted, and I'm alone. The guard is still glaring at me through the glass of the massive front door.

Tijuana scares me. I feel alone and very vulnerable. No matter what the Consulate man says, I am not a Mexicana. The land where papa lives is insanely beautiful, most of the people are friendly, but I can sense a sinister atmosphere hanging over it. I have to get back to Monte Vista—to mama, Connie and Rico—quickly, before something bad happens.

I climb into the front seat alongside *El Pelon* when he finally pulls up. He looks at me but doesn't say a word as he drives away from the barriers.

El Pelon is off in his own thoughts, and I'm playing mind games about what I should do next as we head toward the beach. The task of getting a Mexican birth certificate sounds complicated and time-consuming, but possible; the idea of getting a visa is out of the question now. Buying a forged one would be easier if I knew how to go about it, but what if it's discovered a fake at the border? What would they do to me? And what would that make me?

When we reach the beach road approaching Mama Gorda's house, I ask *El Pelon* to stop the car. He looks pained but pulls off onto a sandy apron of blacktop.

I stare straight out the window at the ocean for several moments, thinking, gathering courage, not looking at him. Finally, I face him.

"Do you know how I can get across the border?"

His look is blank. He stays dumb.

"Well, do you?" I insist. I realize he needs to be commanded and not asked for his opinions."

"*Si*." He avoids looking at me.

"How?"

He shifted in the driver's seat, his hands locked on the steering wheel, refusing to look at me. When he realizes the question isn't going away, and I am still staring at him and not going away either, he drops his shoulders. One hand leaves the steering wheel to reach for security in his lap. "Mama Gorda no—"

"Never mind Mama Gorda. She's not to know. *Comprende*?" I level him with my stare.

He nods his head. "*Comprendo.*" A wan smile parts his lips. He tells me he has heard of men—*rateros*, he calls them—who take people across the border at night at secret places in the desert. When I push him harder, he allows that he might know a couple of men who can arrange to get me across.

"Not good *hombres*." He shakes his head vigorously. "Maybe okay, but maybe not safe for you."

"You must take me to these *rateros* and never speak of this with Mama Gorda. Never! Understand?"

"*Si, es possible mañana por la noche*," he whispers. Then under his breath, he muttered, "*Los rateros son malos... Muy malos.*"

CHAPTER 23

EL PELON STOPS the rusted SUV near a shack painted a vivid blue, like a thousand other hovels dotting Tijuana's hillsides. It looks as if it was built of old garage doors and scrap lumber, with cinder blocks thrown in here and there. It's near the Otay crossing, close to the border, and surrounded by slums and *maquiladora* factories.

I'm wearing a pair of jeans, a heavy dark sweatshirt and a pair of no-name running shoes I bought on the way from Mama Gorda's house and changed into at the store. My hair is pulled back into a ponytail. My gold chain is tucked inside my bra next to my heart.

My elfin friend looks at the shopping bag on the back seat as if it were a rattlesnake that might strike him dead. It contains the silk blouse and dress pants and flats I wore when I told Carmen I wanted to go shopping in Tijuana. *El Pelon's* job is to sneak those clothes back to the upstairs closet with all my other clothes. I'm only taking what I wear plus a change of socks and underwear in my purse.

A shadow appears from behind the blue shack. A man approaches to within a dozen yards and silently beckons me to follow him. Behind the shack, he points to an old Chevy van parked out of sight. He motions me toward it.

"*Dinero*," he snaps.

I have the agreed amount in my purse. I let him see there is no other money in there, hoping it will chill any desire he has for more. The remainder of my money is safely hidden away under the removable insert soles of my new running shoes.

When I open the van door, I'm startled to see two young men already inside. Their hands are clenched around paper sacks. They stare straight ahead as if I'm not there. I climb in over them and sit in the far back seat.

Within half an hour, the van is full. Eight men and women are crammed into the two back seats. Their clothes are clean but old. Like the two young men and me, the others hold something on their laps, purses, or athletic bags or plastic sacks containing everything to start a new life in California. Everyone stares straight ahead, reluctant to make eye contact with anyone else. Like the first two men, they all stare into the night, stone-faced, with the barking of dogs, distant church bells and car horns the only sounds. The van smells of a mixture of despair and poverty.

The man who took my money opens the front door, startling everyone alert, and pulls himself up into the passenger seat. Ten minutes pass. The tension and fear fill the van as if they are physical substances. I feel as if a spider is on my back. Another man comes from the shadows of the shack and climbs in the driver's seat. He looks at the fluorescent dial on his watch and slams the door.

He starts the van, and keeping the headlights off, pulls onto the road, brightly illuminated by a three-quarter moon rising large and orange on the eastern horizon. The van doesn't miss any rut or pothole in Tijuana's streets as we leave the city.

Heading east, I think we must be paralleling the border. Bright lights from California subdivisions blaze on our left, but on the right, only an occasional light pierces the darkness. Soon all lights disappear. We ride into the desert like a bullet fired that can never be recalled.

After an hour, the van turns off the highway. It inches along the desert floor, dodging vague shapes of creosote bushes and yucca plants that materialize out of the blackness and vanish again behind us just as quickly. Joshua trees stand guard, silhouetted against the moon like armed assassins. It's an alien land. A forboding place.

A mile or so off the highway, the van stops. The man in the passenger seat opens the sliding door and gestures all of us out. The night air is cold, but I'm sweating. The clear sky is very far away, holding more shimmering stars than I ever thought possible. I have never felt such profound silence. The spider keeps moving.

The *rateros* line us up at the head of a shallow ravine leading north. Looking into it is like looking into an open grave. We move to the edge and stare blankly north into the blackness. Everyone seems regretful of the decision they've made. The two *rateros* watch us for a couple of minutes, talking quietly to each other. Then they signal us to come close around them.

In low voices, they tell us to get moving, following the trail through the ravine, keeping the moon to our right. They assure us we will come out on a highway in California where other men will find us and take us to LA. They tell us we're on our own and there is no water.

"*Largarme de aquí!*" the driver hisses. "Get going!"

For a minute, the group mills around. No one wants to be first. The two young men with their paper sacks look at each other. They each give a shoulder shrug, stumble down the slope, and disappear. The rest follow in small groups.

A hand reaches out and takes my arm. "*Un momento, chica.*"

The others are absorbed into the darkness. I squirm to get free, afraid of being left behind. I would never be able to find my way alone. But the man grabs both my shoulders and spins me around. "Not so fast, *Mujer.*"

His partner comes in front of me. He glares into my face while the other pins my arms behind my back. I struggle, scream, "Please, I have to get home." A hand claps over my mouth.

"You are Ugalde's *mujer*," the *ratero* growls.

It isn't a question, and they don't expect an answer. My mouth goes dry. I struggle to get away. I kick at them, but they hold me securely. I'm helpless, a child lost in the darkness. The spider is crawling up my back.

The van driver forces me to the ground, throwing me on my back. I hit the pebbly sand with a hard thump. The other one straddles me, one hand already groping under my sweatshirt while his other hand pulls at the zipper on my jeans. The first man kneels at my head, holding his hand over my mouth, even though there is no one in miles to hear my scream. I try to bite him. He pushes down hard, so my lips press against my teeth.

Whimpering at the pain, I beg them to let me go, but no sound came from my mouth because his hand is pushing my head into the hard ground. He leans over to grope at my body. His smell is overpowering, like something inside of him is rotting. The other man, who is straddling me now, has my jeans unzipped and is tugging them off. He grunts animal noises and pants like a beast as he tugs. I can feel the damp sand on my bare legs, scratching my skin like needle points when I try to squirm free.

I feel him pulling my panties off. Then he stands and looks down at my nakedness. Grinning, he loosens his belt. All I can do is divert my eyes, trying to look at the millions of stars beyond the brute holding my head. The first man let his pants fall to the ground. My mind goes blank. My body is numb. This is not happening I tell myself. It can't be.

"*Yo primero, su proximo,*" the man laughs to the other man.

He starts lowering himself onto me. Oh, God, no, the voice in my head screams. No! Please, God, no. No sound comes out. I wait for the horror I am about to feel, trying not to feel anything.

He begins to penetrate me. I hear two popping sounds. The man lurches forward on top of me. Smothering me. His partner lets go of my head and starts to run. Another pop. He falls over.

It takes a few seconds before I realize I can move. Then I begin to cry. I push the man sprawled across my stomach off me and crawl, crab-like, away from him. Both men are lying with their faces pressed in the ground. Blood puddles around them and stains my blouse, merely dark shapes in the moonlight. I feel warm blood on my stomach, and I want to vomit; I'm sobbing out of control. A shape starts toward me out of the darkness. My first thought is that he will continue where the other two left off.

The shape stops a few yards off. "*Vestirse, Señorita.*" He waits, coming forward only after I pull on my panties and jeans, and button my blouse. I barely can make out this new figure, only a shadow in the moonlight. He pays no attention to the two men on the ground.

"They would have killed you when they were done." His voice comes out of the darkness. "And searched for your money afterward."

"Why me?"

"You are foolish to cross alone. They knew."

"Who are you? What did they know? How did you know I was here?"

He doesn't speak again, only pointing with his handgun into the ravine. He starts down the slope, and I follow him. For an instant, I hesitate. Maybe he is still going to do something worse. What choice do I have?

I grab his sleeve. "Who...?"

He presses his finger to my lips.

I start to speak again. I don't know what I would have said— "Thank you for shooting those men?" But he presses his whole hand across my mouth and motions me forward. I don't talk again.

We walk through the ravine. Then he leads me along a trail I can barely see in the waning light of the moon. He never falters, and he never speaks. He guides me along the trail for two hours, but we never see the others who were ahead of me. Then he veers off to the left and walks parallel to a road where occasionally I see headlights flash by. We walk for another mile until a faint light blinks up ahead. A car is parked on the shoulder. He points to it but doesn't climb the embankment with me.

"You're safe. That car will take you home."

"But how..."

"You have friends."

When I get in the car, I begin shaking out of control. The driver puts me in the backseat and covers me with a blanket. I shrivel up under it, shaking all the way north. The horror keeps replaying over and over in my head.

CHAPTER 24

WATER SO HOT my skin burns pours over me. I soap my body from head to foot, then rinse off and soap all over again. I still feel dirty. I let the water beat on my chest and my back. The spider still grips me. No matter how hard I scrub, I still don't feel clean. Toweling off, I examine myself in the mirror. I guess I knew growing up, I was pretty, but it wasn't until those few days with Javier that I felt desirable. When I close my eyes, I can still see us together in Patzcuaro.

No longer a virgin. And not a naïve young girl anymore either, Mexico has changed me. In the mirror, I try to see what Javier saw. What Mama Gorda's video cameras had seen. What is it others see in me?

I let my eyes inspect my body in the mirror. I'm not what anyone would describe as built. Nice breasts—but not large. The chain with its gold cross nestles between them, but it doesn't get lost. My body is firm. Good hips. Tight butt. I let my hand stroke down over my tummy and touch myself. Shuddering as the images of the men in the desert darkness descending on me comes back, I think about my period. It seems like it's due. Did my fear of being raped have an effect on that? I don't know. Sex is a frightening subject my mother never talked about. How could I tell her what happened? I can't.

She taps on the bathroom door and calls out. "Teresa Maria, a telephone call."

Quickly, I finish drying. Wrapping a towel around my head and belting my robe, when I open the door, Mama is hovering in the hall, holding our house phone. She has a frightened look on her face. "Who calls for you?" She asks.

The minute I say hello, Carmen fires a barrage of questions at me. Mama's face holds a reproachful look when she hears me respond. I wish she'd leave the room, but she only retreats to the head of the stairs and still listens, her hands planted on hips. She might have stayed there for the whole conversation if the teapot on the stove hadn't started screaming for attention downstairs.

Carmen's voice is excited. "I heard!" she almost cried. "I heard. I was so worried. Are you all right? *El Pelon* is crazy..."

"I'm okay."

"I was crazy with worry, Teresa." Her words gush out. "When he came back without you, I almost killed him with a kitchen knife."

"I'm fine, Carmen," I tell her, feeling a little confused adjusting to the conversation. Sitting in Monte Vista, talking to Carmen in Tijuana. The clash of my worlds. "How did you get this number?"

"Hector tracked it down for me."

"He never gave my mother the money you gave him. He abandoned me."

"He's going to make it right, Teresa. I gave him a good scolding. He'll give you the money for her." She waits a minute before

168

continuing. I can picture her face going tense as she considers her words. "I'm glad he brought you here, brought us together."

"The only reason I let Hector take me across the border was because he said he could find out about my father. He promised me documents that would get me back home. He lied. Do you know how angry that makes me?"

"I know," she says again. "I know." Then another lull in the conversation. I wait, wondering what's going on. I try to picture the house on the beach with the porno girls. Funny, I miss Vivian.

"Teresa," she finally breaks the silence, "I've got some news for you."

"Javier?"

"Listen to me."

I hold my breath, feeling myself go rigid. Looking around the room, I make sure mama isn't listening.

"It wasn't him."

"Wasn't him?" The words rattle around in my head. I try to hear them again. "What do you mean?"

"The body—the headless body wasn't Javier."

"Is he alive?"

"We don't say yet, but the body wasn't his. That's all."

"What's going on?"

"I can't explain."

"Can't or won't."

Silence again.

"Come back, Teresa. You can live here with me."

"And make sex movies?"

"No, I promise. We'd find other things for you. Movies or telenovelas."

"Tempting. I had such a great time there." I don't know if Carmen knows if I'm being sarcastic or not. "I'm going to finish college here. Just a couple more quarters. My father will let me live in the house."

"I miss you. No fooling." Carmen stops talking again. "What should I do with your clothes?"

"I dunno. Keep 'em."

"Give them to the other girls?"

"Sure. I guess. Why not? Give them to Vivian and the others."

"You looked so beautiful in them in Uruapan. Vivian can't stop talking about you."

"A lifetime ago."

"I guess... I'd better go. Hector will get in touch. I made him promise." Carmen stops talking but doesn't hang up.

"Carmen," I say.

"Well?"

"I think *El Pelon is* playing for both teams if you know what I mean."

"Teams?"

"You know what I mean. Watch him."

"I'll take care of *El Pelon.* Don't worry. Come down whenever you can, Teresa. Even to visit. But be very careful."

"Wait, Carmen..."

The phone goes dead.

✳ ✳ ✳ ✳

When I explain to mama how papa is living and what he has told me, she seems relieved and not very surprised. "He talk about going back, but I never know if he was serious." She tells me. Then she quickly starts making plans to take Connie to Uruapan after Christmas. I don't think Connie really understands what's happening, but she's excited about seeing papa again. I tell her about the flower gardens in his *Casa* and the mountains, and the butterflies. I tell her about the children I saw going to school. She prances around the house like a little princess and demands to be treated like one, behaving like a normal self-absorbed nine-year-old.

Rico wants to stay in Monte Vista, to go to school, he tells mama. It's the worst thing I've ever heard, probably a lie to boot, so I tell him what I think.

"You can't stay here on your own. You don't have a job."

He shrugs it off. "I'll get one."

"How will you stay in high school if you're working?"

"No big deal."

"How will you eat? You don't even know how to cook."

"That's what you're for."

I slap his face. His disdainful attitude tries my patience. "What's come over you, Rico? I used to have a brother I could talk to. Remember? Now you're... you're turning into one of those gangbangers."

"I just got smart is all. Some *chavos* wised me up. They told me how the world really works."

He starts for the door, but I won't let him go. Grabbing him by the shoulder and spinning him around, I almost shout in his face, "You're my brother. I care what happens to you. Do the *chavos* care?"

No answer. Before I can say anything more, he turns away from me and is out of the room, slamming the front door behind him.

I argue with mama to take Rico with her. It's hopeless. "You know what will happen if he stays here alone," I plead with her.

She won't make eye contact with me. Staring down at the floor, she hunches her tiny shoulders defensively. "*No se*. What can I do? He's almost 18. He refuse to go. He say he run away if I force him. If his papa were here..."

"Papa isn't here. You have to make him go. If he stays, he's headed for trouble."

"Maybe he changes his mind after we go. I pray for that. *No se.*" She shakes her head as if she is shaking the problem away like she shakes dirt off a rug. Then she looks back at me with anger in her dark eyes.

"You go away. Two weeks you go, Teresa Maria. You don't know. Rico, not Rico, no more. The street gets him. Papa and I see it happen all the time. We hear other parents talk. Their boys give up. Rico giving up. I would do anything to save him, stay here, take him with me. You don't know my heart, so don't speak to me about that. You don't see my tears. I lose my son, and you say I don't try. Shame on you. You should respect your mama more."

✳ ✳ ✳ ✳

Tension grows in my stomach, waiting outside Professor Jacobsen's office in Bunche Hall. I haven't been on the UCLA campus in well over a month. The knot in my stomach gets worse when the door opens and old, tobacco-smelly Jacobsen blocks entry into his cubicle. Behind him, his desk buckles under the weight of his books. They cover the floor and all but hide his windows. Professor Jacobsen studies me for several moments through his thick reading glasses for what feels like a long time.

"Miss Diaz," he says slowly, reaching up to fondle his beard between thumb and forefinger. "Miss Diaz," he repeats my name, this time with a note of cynical recognition in his voice. "I remember you. How was your vacation?"

This isn't a good start. Still, I launch into the little speech I've prepared on my three bus rides to campus. I tell him I'm sorry

I've missed so much of his class, but I'm ready to take whatever makeup exams I've missed.

"Missed class," he laughs. "Miss Diaz, you've missed most of the quarter."

"I know. I'm sorry, Professor Jacobsen. I've had family problems that kept me away from campus, but now I'm back and ready to make up the work."

"Miss Diaz, I'm sorry. After you skipped the mid-term, I assumed you'd dropped my course. I wasn't surprised. It's a tough course, especially for someone who hasn't a basic grasp of American economic history. A lot of Hispanics start my course, but not very many finish." He says this last as if he's proud of the fact.

"Won't you let me explain? Let me make up the work? I need the credits."

The smell of ancient tobacco embalmed in his old office sweater is reaching out to me with the unpleasant but familiar aroma of Earl Jacobsen's American Economic Theory lecture hall.

"No, I won't," he says matter-of-factly. "That's not my problem. *You're* not my problem. I suppose you can sign up for my class again next fall. If the Dean lets you back into school."

"If I were Anglo, you'd let me back in," I tell him.

Jacobsen slams his door.

I race over to the dean's office and sit for an hour trying to get in to see her. When she finally beckons me into her office, she seems friendlier and more solicitous of my situation than Jacobsen. But no more helpful.

"We're sorry, Theresa. We had no word from you, so we naturally assumed you weren't coming back."

Staring out the window behind her at the traffic moving along Hilgard Avenue, I try to understand why UCLA has deserted me. Each of my professors has parroted something like Earl

Jacobsen's Life-is-Tough-and-You're-Not-My-Problem speech. The Dean is a long shot.

How stupid of me not to alert anyone I was going to Mexico. But then, why would I? I was only going to Tijuana on a Saturday. It never entered my mind to tell them I needed some time off after papa was deported. It never dawned on me that after three years, the University wouldn't work with me.

"It's too late to apply for readmission during the winter and spring quarters, but you have plenty of time to apply for next fall," the dean explains. "With your record, I'm sure you'll be readmitted."

"I've almost finished my junior year. I only need a few more credits to graduate. I need to finish as quickly as I can. I'll lose my scholarships if I'm out till next fall. Isn't there anything you can do, even for the spring quarter?"

"I'm sorry." Her face is stern but solicitous. "You should have thought of that before you left. It's out of my hands now."

She sits back in her swivel chair, crossing one skinny, gabardined leg over the other, and folding her hands in her lap. It's her way of telling me there is no hope, and the interview is over. She takes a deep breath.

"Try to see this from our point of view, Teresa. You're an AB540 student."

"You mean I'm illegal, don't you?"

"Well, yes. As a matter of fact. Very few AB540 students finish here. They stay for a while, till their scholarship money runs out or their families move on. We had no word of your whereabouts or your plans so naturally, we assumed..."

"You assumed I'd been deported because I'm what you call a Dreamer, didn't you?"

"Well... something. Wouldn't you in our place? I'm pleased you're still here, of course. We'll be happy to welcome you back next fall. Just follow the admissions process, and it'll all work out."

I wondered how the Dean assigned to Dreamer AB540 students could be so confident *it would all work out*. My head talk is a tirade against her insensitivity and a crushing indictment of my own stupidity as I go down the stairs and out of Melnitz Hall. I pass several students I know by sight but hardly acknowledge them. I go out into the Sculpture Garden, my head down, oblivious to the triumphs of creative expression dotting the lawns and tucked under the trees. The most celebrated works of the greatest sculptors our world has known, like Alexander Calder's *Button Flower* and Auguste Rodin's *Walking Man*, stand about me, one of the University's finest treasures. But absorbed in my anger and self-pity, alternating like a neon store sign, I don't notice.

At one time, the Sculpture Garden had been the favorite meeting place for Ryan and me. When there was time, or after class in the spring, when the Jacaranda trees were spilling puddles of purple flowers on the walks, Ryan and I would stroll among the magnificent sculptures. We pretended to appreciate their genius but really trying to appreciate each other. Were we a fit? It was always top of my mind. I was never sure. Ryan's interest in me seemed less romantic and shorter-term than my interest. It always seemed to boil down to would this Latina girl put out? And would she be good for my career? During those walks, I had decided to be cautious.

But it isn't Spring now. And I'm not as cautious. It's mid-November, the Jacaranda trees' purple magic faded months ago. The firs and eucalyptus trees cast deepening shadows as the sun loses intensity. The bus stop is a good way off, so I pull my jacket collar closer around my neck and start to walk. As I do, I notice two men off to the side of the garden, partially hidden by a few trees next to Marck's statue *Maja*.

I pay no attention to the men in the distance, but notice one take off toward the street when I glance in that direction. For a moment, I think he looks like the driver who had brought me home from the border. I quicken my pace, trying to catch up. After a couple of minutes, convinced I'm being followed, and still very jumpy, I stop short and turn around quickly. Knobhead is standing twenty yards behind me. Caught, unable to hide, he comes toward me with a sheepish grin.

"What are you doing here?"

"Looking for you."

"Go Away."

"Mama Gorda said to find you."

"How did you know I was here?"

"Rico."

"Where'd you see Rico?"

"I didn't. I texted him. Here's your money." Knobhead reaches in his trousers and takes out a wad of bills. He peels off five one-hundreds, holds them out to me, then stuffs the rest of the wad back in his pants.

"Money for my mother."

"Yeah, I should've kept it for all the trouble you caused me, but Mama Gorda gave me hell."

I look at his hissing snake with a new understanding. I pity him, but that doesn't lessen my fear. Taking the bills as if I were taking a dangerous toy away from a kid, I stuff them in my shoulder purse.

"You left me in Tijuana with no way to get home." Venting my anger is useless, but it comes out anyway, and I don't try to soften it.

Knobhead just stands there. He deflects the abuse I heap on him with a shrug, like he's used to abuse. When I don't say more, he slowly raises his head till his eyes find mine. They are tough, pinpoint eyes. Vague eyes. "Sorry," he says. Then, after another pause, "I'll look out for you in Monte Vista from now on, Teri. Like I told you before."

"Who was the other guy with you?"

He shrugs. "Just a *cabron*."

"Is he looking out for me too?"

Knobhead doesn't respond.

"Teri," a voice called out from across the garden.

I see Ryan heading in my direction from the north campus student center. Giving him a weak wave, I turn back to Knobhead. He seems to get the message instantly. Without a word, he hustles away from Ryan, who is cautiously approaching me.

"Where have you been? I thought you'd dropped out when I didn't see you in Old Man Jacobsen's class."

"He thought so, too, I guess. I'm out of school till next fall."

"How come?"

"Long story. Family problems."

"You're okay now?"

"Sure. Did you miss me?"

"Well..." Ryan pauses.

The expression on his face tells the whole story.

The door of the student center opens again, and Jen, the IRS girl, burst out and hurries toward Ryan, calling his name. "Wait for me, Ry," she shouts.

The look on Ryan's face is pained. His words come awkwardly. "I didn't know if I'd ever see you again. I called your cell phone. No one answered. I didn't know what had happened. Thought you were ghosting me."

Jen catches up to us now, breathless, grabbing Ryan by the arm and pulling him closer. "Hi, Teri," she says with a kind of smirk hanging around her mouth.

I looked at her mascara-rimmed blue eyes. I don't know whether to laugh or cry. "Looks like you and Ryan are a couple," is all I can say.

"Oh... well..." Jen's smirk gets more obvious, as wide as her face.

"How are things at the IRS?" A stupid question.

"We're growing. More and more people are worried about border security. People are clamoring for more walls."

"Our borders aren't safe," I say, knowing Jen doesn't have a clue.

Ryan is uncomfortable, standing between us.

I smile. "Good for you guys. Maybe your IRS group should build its own wall." I start to turn away.

"Teri," Ryan's voice stops me.

"What?"

He hesitates. Looks at Jen. Then looks back at me. "I was wondering if I could get the money back I lent you."

All manner of nasty responses races through my brain. Mindless stuff like kids say on the playground. But I don't share them. Instead, I reach in my purse for the $500 Knobhead has just given me for mama and shove a hundred dollar bill at Ryan. When he doesn't take it immediately and just stands there, I let it flutter from my hand to the ground. I walk on to the bus stop.

CHAPTER 25

I NEED TO earn some money if I'm going to get back into UCLA next fall. So, I answer a newspaper ad after the holidays. A small insurance company within walking distance on Peck Road is looking for a receptionist. The pay seems decent, and without any commuting, I can be home enough to keep an eye on Rico. I call for an interview.

The man who meets me at the door, with the small *Seguros Mexicanos* sign above it, reminds me of Felix Ugalde. He has the same middle-class Mexican look but is nothing like Felix. His clothes aren't hand tailored. In fact, he looks like he hasn't had a new suit in ten years. Probably in his fifties, younger-looking than Felix, he is already going bald. What little hair he has is plastered across his scalp to make it look like more hair than it really is.

Like Felix, Ernesto Ayala looks me over very carefully. His is a different look. Right away, he makes me feel comfortable. I guess he finds me acceptable because he smiles and leads me into his office.

"Habla Español, Senorita?" They are the first words out of Ernesto's mouth when I sit down in the chair he points to. "If you don't speak Spanish, you're no good to me."

"I can," I tell him, hoping I can get by,

"*Bueno*." Ernesto's smile stretches across his face and makes me feel comfortable. He looks around his small office as if to apologize. "We were closed for the holidays. My family comes from all over California, some from Mexico. Lots of kids and grandchildren, so everyone gets time off." He laughs. "We went to Disneyland, had our own *Posada*, lots of Masses. A good time with family. You have a family?"

I tell him I live at home with my mother and two siblings. I don't say mama and Connie have already left for Mexico.

"We can use a lovely young woman like you," he says. "Our business is all Mexican. From Monte Vista and other nearby communities. Our customers are families that can't qualify for other insurance—for healthcare or life. Each week they bring in their money. Mostly cash. A few dollars at a time to pay for their policies. We keep records on all of them and pay out when they have a claim. Of course, we keep a little from each family for ourselves, no?" He laughs. It isn't a greedy laugh. Ernesto seemed a happy, simple man.

"If I hire you, you will be in our front office," he continues. "When people come in to pay, you take their money and give a receipt. Soon you get to know them. Nice people. Hard-working people. Another girl works in the back room. She has a new baby. Sometimes she brings him to work with her. She takes the money and handles the banking."

Ernesto adjusts his tie and looks at me in an innocent, fatherly kind of way. "So," he says after a pause. "What you think? I pay fifteen dollars an hour."

What I think is that sounds too good to be true. "Just three of us work here?"

"*Sì*. The last girl left to have a baby. I'm always losing girls to have babies. Are you married, Teresa?"

I tell him no. "Do we speak Spanish in the office?" I ask him.

"Only if customers need us to," he assures me. "Rest of time, we speak English." He looks me over one more time. I wait, not sure what else is on his mind. "You're a pretty girl, Teresa. I think you will be good for my business. After you get to know the ropes, maybe you can come sell with me. A pretty girl is always good. I could give you a commission on what you sell."

"We'll see," I tell Ernesto, not wanting to turn him off. Not wanting to sell insurance either.

✳ ✳ ✳ ✳

Ernesto is waiting for me in the front office on my first day. I'm late because I've had to make sure Rico was going to school before leaving the house. Looking more skeptical than he had during our interview, he shows me my desk, and hovers over my shoulder, anxious to know if I understand my responsibilities. He shows me how to write a receipt and where to put the cash and checks. How tough can this be? You take the money, write a receipt in the book, give the top copy to the customer and clip the second copy to the money and put it in the drawer. I get it.

When Ernesto is satisfied, he goes into his office, leaving me alone. I'm busy exploring all the desk drawers when I hear a gravelly voice in the doorway say, "Oh, shit."

Looking up, I see a heavy, shapeless young woman standing there, a small baby on her hip. Her hair is all a tangle of frizzy black curls, and the look on her face is pure mean. How could I ever forget the familiar voice? I can't.

"Veronica?"

"Yeah, me. Never thought I'd see you again."

181

"What are you doing here?"

"Whaddaya think I'm doin'? I work here."

"Me too, I just started." I gulp for a breath. It feels stupid the way I say it.

"Shit," she says again. Still carrying the baby on her hip, she goes into the back room.

No time to reflect. My first customer, a gray-haired, middle-aged woman, already pulling bills out of her purse, comes through the door and slaps them down on the desk in front of me.

She is followed during the morning, by a steady stream of older men and women, each with a few dollars to pay on their weekly insurance policies. Almost all payments are cash, and I'm careful to fill out a receipt for each one of them. But I don't want to make any mistakes. Some of the people want to chat, especially the old men who are shy, but happy to see a new girl. They sneak quick looks at me as I write their receipts. The women generally want to get rid of their payment and get back home as fast as they can.

A radio in the back room blasts Norteño music throughout the morning. There are no other sounds, Just the chatter of the customers and music from the back room, not even a whimper from Veronica's baby, just the incessant music of Pedro Infante, Jose Alfredo Jimenez and others. At noon it stops. Veronica comes out of the backroom with the kid still on her hip and looms over my desk. She hasn't aged well. She has gained a lot of weight over all of her body, especially her copious breasts, likely swollen with milk. She wears no makeup, no jewelry, and her curly hair is a stranger to a hairbrush.

"If we gotta work together, we better talk," she snaps at me. "Come on." Turning and going out the door, she hangs a "CLOSED" sign on it, without bothering to check if I am coming.

I follow her for no good reason I can think of. She doesn't wait for me, and I don't hurry to catch up. Shifting the baby to her other beefy hip, she goes into a little taqueria. She's already sitting at a table with the baby on her breast when I come through the door.

"Look," she says before I am barely seated, "I'm sorry about the thing back in high school?"

"The thing? Is that what you call it?"

"I'm sorry. It got outta hand. We only wanted to scare you."

I keep silent. The baby's arms flail, grabbing at her blouse, at her large bare breast, and at her face with his pudgy hands.

"Really," she says, brushing the child's hands away. Her dark, tired eyes look intense as she stares at me. They seem to pry, looking for some response. I stay blank.

"What have ya been doin' since high school?" She asks, ducking the subject.

"College," I tell her. "UCLA."

"Figures. You were always the brainy one. You had all the looks, too, but you never bothered with the guys. I thought you were a lezzie. I'll never forget our *Quinceañeras.*"

* * * *

Who could forget? My Quinceañera ranks very high on my list of the worst times in my life. I didn't want a celebration. I stomped my feet in a typical fourteen-year-old pout whenever my father brought up the subject. "It's coming soon," he said. "We have to make plans."

"Don't make me do it, Papa."

"It's our tradition, Paloma. Respect that. I have the money."

"This is not for you, Teresa Maria, my mother told me, "this is for your papá. Obey him. You break his heart if you don't do this."

In the end, we compromised. Papa and I agreed to talk to our priest.

183

We waited for Father Miguel to finish Mass one Sunday. Then went into his office and explained our differences.

The priest's face lit into a smile, almost becoming a laugh. "Unusual," he said. "Most girls want a big celebration, Teresa Maria. Your father wants to give you the best one he can. Why do you resist him?"

It was hard to explain. I told him I was more interested in getting good grades and going to college than in meeting boys.

"I see," he smiled again. "That will change. But Teresa Maria, a Quinceañera, is not just about boys. It's a time for you to renew your vows before God. And for your parents to give thanks to their saint."

"M'hija, it's a time for your mama and me to present you to our friends. We want to celebrate your womanhood."

My womanhood? How could he say that in front of the priest? Besides, we didn't have that many friends. Not since Antonio was killed. My tears started. I didn't want the two most important men in my life to see me crying. I cried anyway.

"What it is, M'hija?" Papa asked.

How could I tell him I wasn't a popular girl? That I didn't have any girlfriends to be my damas? That no boy would dance with me?

Father Miguel's solution was like Solomon's, he tried to satisfy everyone and succeeded with no one. He said some of the other girls in the parish came from families that couldn't afford a Quinceañera, so why didn't we combine them and have one ceremony for all of us. In the end, papa paid all the costs so the other families could be proud.

✳ ✳ ✳ ✳

"It was like a cattle auction," Veronica laughs huskily. "All of us parading in those silly organza dresses our mothers made. A bunch of black heads, wrapped in pink and white gauze, looking like matchsticks, thinking we were all hot. Except for you, Teri. You tried to hide behind everyone else when it came time to dance."

I had to ask Sergio Sanchez to be my escort. He was the only one tall enough to stand with me. He wasn't eager to do it, but he was polite, more than I had any right to expect. Still, I was so happy when it was over. Papa and mama were pleased.

Veronica's baby has been whimpering. Now he starts to cry. "Come on, we havta order at the counter." She jumps up from the table, and chasing him off her breast, mounts him on her hip again. "We only get forty-five minutes."

I change the subject when we're seated again eating fish tacos. Veronica eats with one hand and with the other opens her blouse again and shoves the baby back on her nipple. I keep my eyes on the tacos. They are not like the squid tacos I ate with Javier in Tijuana, just plain whitefish, more like what papa what caught in Long Beach. I don't want to talk with Veronica about anything, but I can't eat in silence. I sneak peeks at the child with his face buried in her breast to make sure he isn't suffocating. "How old is your baby?" I ask her.

"Three months," Veronica tells me. "Roselia's in childcare at the community center, but this one is still too young for that. My mother usually watches him during the morning, and I go home to feed him at noon. I can't afford a sitter. Today, she had to take my father to the doctor."

"How long have you been married?"

"Married?" She answers in a mocking tone. "Married? Pepe don't want to get married. He just wants to keep banging me. It's okay though, I love him. I got pregnant before graduation. He lives at home. So do I. He thinks we should find a place together, but he don't work much. He wants me to pay for it, but I can't afford a place. I'm always short on money, and this job sucks, but he don't seem to care."

"Pepe?" I stopped for a moment watching the ugly memory play out in my head one more time. "He was the one..."

"Look, like I said, it got outta hand, and I'm sorry. Can't we just move on from all that high school crap?"

✳ ✳ ✳ ✳

When I get home, Rico is sleeping. I change into jeans and a sweatshirt then kneel by the bed before going downstairs to start dinner. I ask the Virgin to forgive me for still not trusting Veronica. And I pray for guidance with Rico.

He comes into the kitchen, rubbing his eyes when I call up to him for supper. Looking at his plate, his face lets me know what he thinks about the food. Then his mouth does. "This crap again. Why can't we have steak?" He gets up from the kitchen table and starts out of the room.

"Because I'm the one buying the food," I fire back and follow him out into the hall. "Whenever you feel like kicking in, I'll be glad to buy us a steak."

"Tell papa to send money. He can afford it."

I let that go as just being Rico's lousy attitude. "Mama's been gone two weeks, and all you do is hang out. You're hardly home, and when you are, all you do is lie around the house. Get yourself a job if you want to eat steak."

"I don't need this. I'm going out."

I dart around him to block the front door. "What's going on with you, Rico? What happened to the brother I used to have?"

"Get outta my way, Teri. I'm old enough to do what I want."

"You're seventeen. What exactly *do* you want?"

"I'm doin' it. Goin' out."

"Hanging out on street corners? Is that what you want?"

"How'd you know?"

"Don't be stupid, Rico. Of course, I know. You're not going to school. I never see you doing any homework. People tell me."

He gives me a dead-eyed look, the kind of lost look you see all the time on the buses. "You call that *cabron* your friend? Let me go."

When I continue to block the door, he presses in close. He thrusts his face into mine.

"So, what is it you think I should be doing, big sister? You think I should go down under the freeway where the unemployed *chavos* hang out waiting for day jobs? Is that what you want me to do?"

"If you stayed in school, you'd have a better chance at a decent job. I'll buy the food, maybe even a steak now and then, if you go back to school until graduation."

"Get serious, Teri. School's for losers. The street's where it's happening. Papa knew that—"

"What is that supposed to mean?"

"The only jobs anyone around here gets are the under-the-freeway day jobs. You make enough to buy a pack of smokes and a *cerveza*, then you're broke until the next gringo boss drives up and points to you. Staying in school doesn't make the jobs any better."

"I got a job. Because I had some education."

"Tell me you went to college so you could take money away from the poor people in the barrio. That's what you do, isn't it? They come in and give you a few dollars they'll never see again just so they can feel like they got some security. They don't got security, Teri. It's just some Mexican guy you're workin' for with a scam to rip off other Mexicans. It's like he's robbing his own people. That's what this place is all about, everybody robbing Mexicans. Get outta my way now so I can go out."

I don't budge. "What would your papa say if he heard you? He and mama busted their backs to give us a decent life. Just like those people who pay for their insurance each week."

"Oh, yeah? Sure. Look at papa." Rico lets out a mean laugh. "You're a fool. Where's papa now? He saw it was all a big joke, Teri. He figured it out. He split. He's gone." Rico is almost shouting his meanness at me, but he pulls himself back. He stops abruptly and just stares at me. Continuing in a lower voice, he says, "He saw California was all a big scam. He saw we were never going to get anything with hard work. He got smart. He did what he had to."

"How can you say that about papa?" I slap Rico hard across the mouth—I've never done that before.

He rubs his face, and his voice became a snarl. "Look around, Teri. Do you see papa? Get outta my way now. I'm goin' out. Don't wait up."

"What street corner are you going to hang out on tonight?"

"*Chava*, you sound like my mother."

With his hand, he pushes me away from the door and opens it. As he goes past me, I can see the handle of a knife tucked down in his shoe, almost out of sight.

"What are you doing with a knife, Rico?" For the first time, I'm seriously scared.

"Some black dudes wanna horn into our neighborhood. We're gonna have a talk with them. We gotta keep what little we still got."

He saunters down the front walk and turns up to the corner. I shut the door, standing there for several minutes with my back pressed against it. "Holy Mother protect us," I say to the Virgin on the wall.

* * * *

188

Knobhead jumps out at me from a doorway a couple of days later as I head to work up Peck Road. He scares me enough that I pull back from him. In one hand he has a paper coffee cup and a bakery bag in the other. He gives me a smile, but his chipped teeth make it look like he is leering at me.

"For you," he says, thrusting cup and bag at me.

"I look at him, surprised. "What are you doing?" I almost laugh. "You trying to be my friend now?"

"Yeah, Teri. We should be friends. Here, have a donut."

I can't read him. Is this a joke? "Thanks." Cautiously, I open the bag and take out a donut and hand the bag back to him. "You have the other one, Hector."

He smiles. "Call me *El Niño*," he mumbles, biting into the donut.

"Not in your lifetime. I'm more comfortable with Hector."

"Suit yourself."

He walks with me toward the insurance office. When we get there, I start to open the door. He puts his hand on my shoulder and stops me.

"Mama Gorda told me to watch out for you."

"Thanks. I don't need anyone watching out for me."

"She says you're special."

Coming from Carmen, the word confuses me. Try as I might, I can't figure out why I'm important to her. "I'm not special, and I don't need you or anyone else to watch out for me. I'm doing fine."

Knobhead ignores my words. "But you have trouble."

"What trouble?"

"Your brother's trouble. Be careful for him. He could have more trouble than he can handle soon."

CHAPTER 26

APPROACHING THE OFFICE, the following Monday, a crowd milling about on the sidewalk stops me dead. Yellow tape stretches across the entrance to *Segueros Mexicanos.* Two cops stand guard in the doorway, holding back the crowd I try to get past into the office.

"I know you," an old, hunched over woman in a green housedress shouts at me. "I want my money."

I give her a confused look.

"We've been robbed," she shouts. "You stole all our money."

I'm stunned speechless.

The police are stone-faced, determined to keep the old Latinos away from the door, blocking my way inside, too. "Move back," one of them orders me. "You can't come in."

"I work here," I tell him. He keeps his hand on his hip just above his holster as he gives me the once over. He looks at his partner, who nods and lifts the tape for me to get under. "You'd better go in, Miss. They'll want to talk to you."

Inside, men are crawling all over my desk like ants, opening drawers, and rifling through papers. Others, in black jackets with

191

"Police," stenciled in white on the back swarm over the rest of the office. Ernesto sits in a corner looking pale, twisting a linen handkerchief in his hand.

A heavyset man in a shiny blue suit coat and scuffed up shoes with crepe soles scuttles across the room to me. "Who are you?"

"Teresa Diaz."

Ernesto jumps off his perch in the corner and rushes to the man's side. "She's new here. She has a key. She could've —"

"Step back, Sir. Let me talk to the woman, would ya?"

"What's this about?"

The burly man acts as if he hasn't heard my question. "I'm detective Lopez." He says it with a sneer in his voice as if he wants me to know that being detective Lopez is a very special thing to be. "Please come with me."

He leads me through the maze of cops into Ernesto's office in the back.

Seating himself in the worn leather chair behind Ernesto's desk, he motions for me to sit in an equally old side chair. "What time did you leave here on Friday?"

I tell him. He follows up with a barrage of questions, all of which I answer. "What is this about?" I ask for a second time.

"I'll ask the questions. Your office was robbed over the weekend."

"I didn't know."

"How long have you worked here?"

"A couple of weeks."

"You handle the money?"

"Yes."

"Tell me."

"I take it from the customers and give them a receipt."

"Then what?"

"The money goes in the desk drawer until Veronica takes it in the back to do the entries and makes out a deposit."

"Who's Veronica?"

 "The other girl who works here."

"Where is she?"

"I have no clue."

"Don't get smart. You two hang out together?"

His questions come one after another, like a hammer driving a nail. I keep answering, and he keeps throwing new ones at me.

"Did this Veronica go to the bank with the money Friday?"

"I don't know. That's not my job. She left early Friday. Her baby was sick."

"Did you and she conspire to leave the money here over the weekend so one of you could come back and steal it? That's possible, isn't it?"

"Possible? I suppose it is. But I had nothing to do with it."

Lopez relaxes his grip on the desk. He slouches back in the chair and looks at me for several moments with a kind of smug, I-know-you're-the-perp-and-I'm-going-to-nail-your-ass look.

"We gonna find your prints on the desk?"

It is all I can do to keep my cool. "It's my desk. I'm sure you'll find my fingerprints there."

"You steal the money? You and the other girl?"

I notice his eyes are green as he stares at me. He makes me feel squirmy. Maybe that's what he wants.

"I told you I didn't steal the money," I keep my voice as under control as I can.

"I think we need you to come to the station to answer some more questions." Detective Lopez rises from the desk. Taking my upper arm, he pulls me from the chair and leads me toward the door.

He continues firing questions at me when we get to the Monte Vista police station. He keeps asking the same ones over and over, hoping to trip me up at some point, I guess. While he fires away, I keep thinking about one of my psych instructors who said that doing the same thing over and over and expecting a different result is a sign of insanity. I don't think that was an original thought with her, but it makes me look at officer Lopez in a different light. Is Lopez insane? I don't tell him what the professor said, but he seems crazy to me.

Then he takes a different tack. "Let me see your driver's license," he demands.

"I don't drive."

"Don't drive? Everyone drives. Did you take the money to buy a car?"

"I've told you I didn't steal the money. Why do you keep asking?"

"Don't get hot with me, Missy. You start playin' games, and I can lock you up for a day or two 'til you cool off."

He pauses for a few seconds to make sure I get his message. Then he gets up from the chair and walks over to talk with another cop for a few minutes, pouring himself a cup of coffee. When he comes back, he stands looking over my shoulder.

"Maybe there's another reason you don't have a driver's license," he starts. "Where were you born?"

It's the question I've been dreading. I feel as if a trap has been sprung on me. Lying might be the worst thing I can do but telling the truth doesn't seem much better.

Lopez reacts to my silence. "I figured you for a Dreamer—an illegal alien from the start." Sitting back down at the desk, he stretches his hand across it as if he is reaching out to touch me. "I'm pretty convinced you didn't do the robbery, Miss Diaz, but

I think you know something about it. I don't want to jam you up here, but if you aren't going to cooperate, I'll turn you over to the Border Patrol people. Understand? *Comprende?*"

Of course, I comprende-ed. I meet his stare and don't let go. As firmly as I can, without losing my composure, I tell him I have told him everything I know. I tell him Veronica and I had gone to school together, and that we had sort of reconnected since I've been working for Ernesto. Beyond that, I know nothing about where she lives or what she does."

"Okay," he says. "We already picked up Veronica Estrada. She's in the other room with another detective. She says you're the one who did the robbery. We think she's lying, but we need your help to nail her butt. Refuse, and you'll get a ride in the Tijuana taxi."

It sounds to me like Detective Lopez has watched too much bad television.

Just then, the door swings open and Rico charges through it, followed by Knobhead, moving more slowly. Rico goes right to the desk sergeant and loudly demands to see me, like he'd been watching bad TV too.

This can't be good.

It isn't. Rico starts right away, giving loud attitude to the cop behind the front desk. Knobhead tries to calm him, but Rico shoves him aside and charges straight for Detective Lopez, who sees him coming and gets on his feet in time to meet him.

"Stop right there, Mister." His voice halts Rico.

"What are you doing to my sister? You got no right to hold her."

"Kid, I got every right in the world to do whatever I damn well want to do with your sister. I got the right to do the same to your ass if you start making a fuss."

"Fuckin' cops...!"

That's all Rico gets out of his mouth before Lopez and three of his pals throw him down, pinning him to the floor. He makes another mistake struggling, so one of the uniform cops rolls him over and handcuffs him.

Knobhead stands off to the side. He watches Rico getting dragged down without interfering. Without saying a word, his eyes stay focused on me.

"That's my brother. He's hasn't done anything. Let him up," I plead with Lopez. "Please. Take the handcuffs off him."

"Your brother, eh? He's a gangbanger we've been watching. He a Dreamer too?"

"Goddamn it, let me go," Rico's voice now lacks the aggressive tone he'd come through the door with. He even sounds a little scared.

"Get him out of here," Lopez snaps at the uniformed cop. Then he turns to confront Hector. "You want the same? Get outta here before I have ya locked up."

Knobhead gives the cop a slight smile. "Look, Detective," he starts. "I haven't done nothin'. I just came in here with my friend to see about his sister. You can't do nothin' to me for that." He pauses and focuses directly on Lopez before asking. "Is this woman under arrest? Can she go? What's goin' on?"

"What business is it of yours?" Lopez demands.

"I'm makin' it my business because this young woman is a friend of mine; I'm makin' it my business because I know how carried away you guys can get when somethin' goes down in our hood, especially with a Latina. I don't want no trouble, officer. Just tell me what's going on, or I'll have an attorney in here faster than you can eat a donut."

That last wasn't a good thing to say, but it brings a smile to my face. Knobhead grins at his own cleverness. I shoot him a quick look, but he ignores me. Some of the other cops in the room chuckle, but Lopez stands frozen-faced.

"All right," he concedes, "she can go. But don't go far, Miss Diaz."

"What about her brother? When you gonna let him go?"

"We'll kick him in an hour. When he cools off. But I'm telling ya, warn your guys in the street we won't put up with shit from any of you. If one of you did this robbery, we'll nail em."

✳ ✳ ✳ ✳

It's mid-afternoon when Rico comes home.

"Are you okay?" I greet him at the door, hug him, happy to see he hasn't been roughed up. "That wasn't so smart."

"I guess not. Yeah, I'm okay. They wanted to work me over, but some gringo came into the station, and right away, they let me go. I think he might have been an attorney."

"Attorney? What's going on? We don't have an attorney. You were just stupid, and the cops were just doing their job with me, even if Lopez was a bit over the top. We don't need an attorney, do we?"

Something is happening I don't understand. Too many new people are in my life, and I don't know why. I feel unsettled.

"I was gonna ask you."

"I'm okay, Rico, but we have to talk. Sit down."

He gives me a don't-give-me-orders look but flops on the living room sofa. I pull the little side chair close to him.

"Are you in trouble? Hector says you might be."

"Nothin' I can't handle."

"Look, Rico. Stop with the tough guy stuff. We're alone here, and we've got to stay together. Got to be smart. Just tell me, do you have a problem with the cops? Is that why they threw you down?"

"Like I said, Teri, nothin' I can't handle. Don't ask anymore."

"Hector seems to know what's going on on the street."

"What about you? You're the one they hauled down to the police station. You're the one Hector is hanging around. You in any trouble?"

"I don't know. Maybe. I didn't steal that money."

"I know that. But ever since you came back from Mexico, you seem kinda messed up, Teri. Look, I gotta meet some guys. I'm going back out."

Rico starts to get up from the couch, but I grab his sleeve. "Wait. I'm not finished."

He gives me one of his impatient, rolling his eyes, tough guy looks but sits back down.

"Hector says we should go to Mexico."

"Fuck that! I ain't goin' nowhere."

"Shut up and listen to me! And don't ever talk that way around me again! He says the cops will report me to ICE."

"So?"

"So that leaves you here alone. I can't live with that. We have to go back to papa and mama."

Rico's face flushes. Sitting on the edge of the couch, he starts to speak, then catches himself. "It's weird," he says finally, "I'm an American citizen, and you're not because of where each of us was born. It isn't fair. We're both from the same family."

"Not fair, maybe, but real for me. If I go to Mexico again, I don't know if I could come back."

"You meet a guy?"

"Maybe."

He looked at me in a different way, and smiles. "With forged papers, you could go back and forth. I can get 'em for you."

"Seems like everyone but me breaks the law. Hector can get them too."

"What's with this Hector? It's Hector says this, and Hector says that. Since when did he get so important?"

"I don't like him, Rico. He scares me. But he's street smart, and I'm not. He knows people, and he knows how to survive. Look, you have a birth certificate, so you can come back. I want you to come with me if I decide to go."

Rico goes silent again. His face scrunches up as if he were trying to figure out some solution to a problem.

"You know what the *chavos* I hang with call themselves, Teri? *Hijos de la chingada*. Maybe I have a birth certificate, but I don't belong anywhere, just like you. Doesn't matter where we were born, we're nothing. Look at you, Teri. You've got it all, brains, good looks, and a drive to get ahead. You're a good sister. But really, you've got nothing. Like me."

I start to protest, but Rico won't let me interrupt. "The cops came right to the Mexicans, didn't they? There was no question you or the other girl did it. The University did the same. They figured it wasn't worth saving a place for a Mexican girl. You might as well go to Mexico, there's nothing here worth staying for."

"Come with me then. You're in the same situation."

"I am. *Hijo de la chingada*. Fucked."

CHAPTER 27

I'M BACK IN Tijuana a week later. Not because I want to be here. Because the Tijuana taxi gave me a free ride thanks to Detective Lopez. Knobhead warned me the night before it happened, but I didn't believe him. He came by the house. When I wouldn't let him come in, we spoke through the screen door.

"You gotta be ready. They're coming for you."

"How do you know?" Ever since papa has been deported, Knobhead or Hector—whatever he's called, but definitely not *El Niño*—has been an unsettling presence in my life. His round, hairless face, with scaring around his mouth, scares me. He has no eyebrows, also victims of his street life in Mexico City, I guess. But his eyes are fierce. As black as obsidian, they probe and penetrate rather than see.

"I know. I have contacts. They tell me." He says.

"About me?"

"We keep an eye on you. The guy who got Rico sprung told me Lopez was after Rico because he acted stupid."

"Who is the guy?" Who are all the people who have come into my life since my father's deportation? Everywhere I turn, it seems someone is watching me.

Knobhead stays silent.

"I'm going to stay here," I tell him. "I have to work. Get back in school. Watch out for Rico...please."

"He'll drag ya down."

"He's my brother. I've got to look out for him."

"He's already draggin' you down."

"What do you mean?"

"They're lookin' at him for the robbery. They figure if they put you across the border, it will be tougher on him."

＊ ＊ ＊ ＊

I can't believe my eyes when the rusting SUV pulls up at the detention center minutes after the ICE men let me go. Carmen is wedged behind the steering wheel. Her trademark hair and ear-to-ear smile greet me like a *Dia de los Muertos* mask. Laughing, she rolls down the window and calls to me.

"How did you know?" I call back. My voice reflects my surprise.

"Hector alerted me."

I can't stop myself. Seeing her here is too much. Way too much. I burst into tears. Squatting down on the sidewalk, my head in my lap. My knees splay out to either side, my skirt hikes up on my thighs. I must look like some poor homeless woman. I don't care how I look. I'm losing control again. Actually, I've never had control.

Carmen kills the engine and squeezes out from behind the steering wheel. She limps to my side and squats beside me.

"Gotta move that car, *Señora*," a man's voice call out. "No parking here."

"*Un momento!*" She reaches down to touch my hair. "What's wrong, *M'hija?*"

I'm startled at the way she speaks to me. I'm not her daughter. But I see the concern in her face.

She takes my hand. I pull it away from her.

"*Niña* come. Get in the car. We havta go." She reaches for my hand again. This time I let her take it because I feel so lost I don't know what else to do. In a strange sort of way, I'm happy to see her smiling face, but I'm freaked out that everyone seems to know my every move before I do. I feel as if my life no longer belongs to me.

On the ride out to the beach house, I dry my tears, and try to collect myself. When we get there, Carmen stops the SUV but doesn't make any move to get out. Pinned behind the wheel, she can only twist her head to look at me.

"So, what is this? I drive to *La Migra* when I hear you are there, and this is how you treat me? With tears and silence? What gratitude is that?"

"What's going on, Carmen? Please don't play pity games. Be honest with me. I don't know what's happening to me. I'm losing my mind."

"You have friends here now, Teresa Maria. We look out for you."

"It all started in Patzcuaro."

"*Sì.*" She nods her head.

"Is it Felix?"

"You are a special girl," is all she says.

✳ ✳ ✳ ✳

The porn girls are excited to see me. When I go into the house, they crowd around, all talking at once, asking all sorts of questions.

"Are you coming back to make more videos with us?" Vivian purrs. Her long blond hair cascades down to the top of her signature bustier. She's wearing a thigh-high skirt and smiling sweetly at me. I hug her.

Carmen shoos the girls away. They go into the *sala*, curling up on couches to watch a noisy telenovela. She leads me upstairs to the same room I'd slept in before and drops into the chair by the window to catch her breath. My clothes still hang in the closet.

"You have to stop pouting all the time," she says.

"Pouting?" I look at her face, surprised by her words and her anger. In that moment, when we lock eyes, I see resolve in her face. Her penciled brows flat line scornfully. But staring at her, I can faintly see her underlying beauty. Her well-structured face, sagging with flesh now, was probably strikingly beautiful when she stood on a stage in front of an audience all those years ago. It doesn't take a map to understand the road her face, and the rest of her body have taken. It comes clear to me at that moment that I have to stop being a victim. Carmen has never allowed herself to be a victim, and it's time for me to take charge of my life, too, regardless of what's going on around me, just as she has.

"What makes you think I'm back?"

"You don't need me to lay it out for you. You have no choice, Teresa. There is nothing to go back to California for. And if you don't mind my saying, there was never much that was real for you there in the first place. You were just pretending. You were playing at being an American college girl. But you're not. Not since..."

"Not since Javier?" I interrupt her silence.

"Well, yes, that, and your papa's deportation."

"But Javier's disappeared."

"That doesn't matter."

"Felix?"

"Yes."

"I don't get it, Carmen. I only spent three days with Javier. One night."

"Like I said, it doesn't matter. Javier is all Felix has left. He told Felix he loved you, so Felix is determined to look out for you."

"Even in Monte Vista?"

"Some. Felix isn't the Wizard of Oz, you know? He isn't pulling strings. Just asking his people to look out for your best interests."

"Mine or his?"

"Perhaps they're the same."

"How do you know all this?"

"Felix and I go way back together."

"I don't want him looking out for me, Carmen."

"Don't you understand, Teresa?" Carmen has an exasperated look constricting her face "It is no longer your choice."

* * * *

I call mama and papa on my new cell phone to tell them what has happened. Right away, mama asks about Rico. I keep it brief, trying not to frighten her too much. Papa wants to know when I'm coming to Uruapan. He's excited about me living in the *Casa*. "Oh, *Paloma*, so much better than your old room. I miss you, *M'hija*."

I tell him I might be there in a few days, but I need some time to myself. He doesn't understand, but lets it go without pinning me down.

I figure Rico already knows where I am, but I text him anyway. To my surprise, he responds immediately, telling me Hector is driving him to Tijuana on Saturday to see me. I ask him to bring as many of my clothes as he can cram into a couple of suitcases.

On Saturday, Mama Gorda's girls greet Hector as an old friend. Then they swarmed around Rico like hummingbirds on the hibiscus flowers growing in front of the house. Rico's eyes grow large at the female flesh jiggling around him. He keeps stealing looks at Vivian. There's no doubt about his excitement.

Carmen is being called Mama Gorda again. She plays the role of brood hen, clucking at her girls, and shooing us out to the veranda overlooking the ocean. Hector follows along, acting hurt by all the attention the girls are lavishing on Rico. His face takes on a sullen expression, his lump-of-coal eyes burn.

"*Donde esta El Pelon?*" he asks Mama Gorda.

She darts a quick glance at me, then a look of unbridled anger crosses her face. "Gone!" Is her only answer.

Rico sits on the edge of a chaise. Vivian and two other girls gather around, almost smothering him. They use their best English when they realize Rico understands only minimal Spanish. Hector leans against the veranda railing in back of Vivian, trying to lure her attention away from Rico. No matter which way he tries to strike up a conversation, Vivian only occasionally nods her head and smiles weakly at some of his remarks. Finally, showing his frustration, he suggests we all go down to Rosarito Beach for a few beers.

It's hard to miss Rico and Hector vying for Vivian's attention. After a couple of rounds of beers, Rico remembers I'm there.

"This isn't what I expected Mexico to be like, Teri," he says, still having trouble taking his eyes off Vivian. She's now wearing a halter top with tight shorts even in the chilly January afternoon. His eyes flit from her breasts to her thighs, where her shorts are riding up her crotch.

"Better than you expected?" I ask him. "What a surprise. Your buddy, Hector, can explain how all this happened on the ride home. This isn't the real Mexico."

"It is," Hector interrupts, taking my words as some kind of slur on Vivian. "Vivian comes from Sinaloa. Down south. Mama Gorda is sending her to school."

The other girls giggle.

He puts his hand on her bare shoulder. She flinches, but smiles at him, letting it rest there for a few minutes.

"So, what do you do?" Rico asks her.

I interrupt quickly before she has a chance to speak, "Vivian's an actress. I met her when I was here before. She lives with the other girls and makes movies."

"Movies." Rico's face lights up.

"All in Spanish, so they're nothing you've ever seen."

Vivian flashes me a "thank you" look.

"She's terrific," Hector interjects, still touching her shoulder. "I've never seen her movies, but I come down here as often as I can just to see her."

Rico goes blank.

The conversation moves on. The sun begins falling into the ocean, casting long, spidery shadows across the terrace from the tall palm trees along the beach. The beers have taken their toll; everyone is subdued. A Mariachi band comes from inside the bar to our table playing *Para Siempre*. Hector jumps up and hands the lead guitarist a few pesos, asking him to play *Besome Mucho* for Vivian. Rico gives me a lost look, so I dip into my purse and slip some money to him under the table. When the song is finished, he looks hesitantly at the leader, then thrust the money at him. "Play it again," he pleads. Turning to Vivian, he adds, "I hope you might take me to see one of your movies next time I'm down here."

By the time we get back to Mama Gorda's, it's too many beers later for Knobhead and Rico to drive back to Monte Vista. Carmen shows them a room to sleep in well away from the studio and the girls' quarters.

Vivian knocks softly on my door and comes quietly into my room. She has a shy smile on her face, and I can't help thinking how bizarre it is that this beautiful, almost doll-like girl performs sex acts in front of a camera. "He's a wonderful guy," she tells me, settling down on the edge of the bed.

"You mean Hector?" It was a hopeful, stupid question. I know who she's talking about.

"Your brother. Does he have a woman in California?"

"Not that I know of. I'm glad you like him, Vivian, but he's young, hardly eighteen."

"*Sì.*" Her face darkens, her head bobs up and down, making her curls bounce off her shoulders. "He might not like me, but I like him. He says he has the money to buy a car."

I smile at that. But it sets off an alarm in my head. I let it go. "Hector likes you."

"*Sì,* he does. I know. But he's strange." She looks at me. "Is that the right word in English—strange? He scares me, Teresa. Sometimes he's happy, but most of the time he broods, like a dog searching the street for scraps of food, always ready to fight for them. I hope your brother comes back to see me again."

The next morning, I get Rico's take on Vivian. A beautiful girl, he says it over and over. He seems to be in a lover's daze. There isn't anything I can do to shake him.

"She's not right for you, Rico. Maybe too street smart. She's lovely to look at, but I think you need to find a girl closer to home."

"I'm old enough so don't tell me. We spent a lot of time talking last night. We hit it off great. She wants me to come back whenever I can."

"Talking last night?"

Rico blushes.

"Little brother, you'd better be very careful..." I don't know what else to say. He looks at me like a cock rooster, all puffed up and proud. I shudder at the picture in my mind. I have a panicked feeling in my stomach. The only thought that calms me even a little is knowing Carmen takes the girls for checkups often. Finally, all I can manage is, "Watch out for Hector. He has his eye on Vivian, too."

Carmen and I stand in the doorway surrounded by the beautiful young women as Hector and Rico get in the black Expedition to head back to Monte Vista. From the looks on their faces, and the distance they kept from each other, I think it will be a long, quiet ride home. Vivian stands at the front of the group, waving a headscarf and calling "*adios*" long after the SUV disappears down the road. When she finally gives up, she turns to me. "What a fine brother to have, Teresa Maria. *Qué chico! Muy macho.* Please don't object." I think Vivian has guessed what I'm thinking.

Carmen takes me by the arm, steering me away from the others, out to the veranda. We sit in chairs at the far end facing each other. The cook brings out cups of strong black coffee and *Bolillos* and jam, setting them on a table between us.

"Your brother will stay in California?" Carmen asks.

"For a while, I guess. But he can't stay by himself for long. He doesn't have any money. ...I don't know what he'll do."

"Not good for him to be alone. He can live here and work for me."

Startled, I give her a look so aggressive it might peel paint off the side of her house. Realizing what she's said, she laughs. "Don't worry. And you?"

She turned to look out over the ocean as she asks the question, watching a line of pelicans flying south in formation, low on the water, just above the wave tops. The sun is climbing steadily in the sky, casting millions of sparkles off the waves, too dazzling to look at for long. She avoids looking at me while I struggled for an answer.

"I'll go see my mother and father in Uruapan. Then, I don't know. I thought about what you said on the phone the other day, Carmen. In a lot of ways, you're right. There isn't much for me to go back for anymore, even if I could go legally."

"If you want to go back, it's no problem. But I think you see staying here with me might not be your best choice. You can go to the University in Mexico City if you want. But you have other choices here too. I've told you before, I think you could have a career in modeling or TV."

Carmen is patient. She goes quiet and waits in silence while I spread the jam on my *bolillo* and take a couple of bites. The sounds of *Paloma Querida*, another Jose Alfredo Jimenez song I recognize, drifts from one of the girls' upstairs window. Without thinking about it, I pick up the beat with my toes. It's time to be honest, but I'm still not sure what honesty means for me. Finally, setting my coffee cup down and looking directly at Carmen, I say, "In Monte Vista, I wanted a way out of the barrio. I thought if I studied hard and went to college, I'd stop being an immigrant. I'd be accepted. But even at UCLA, the other kids looked at me like I was different. They were polite most of the time, but no one ever wanted to get too close or be my friend. I went back and forth between Monte Vista and school, going from one world to the other, trying to figure where I could fit in. Carmen, I didn't fit in either place."

"*This* is your country." She reaches across the table to take my hand. "You belong with us."

"I guess when I was with Javier, I thought so, too. He is a wonderful man. I miss him so much, Carmen."

"And so do I."

Her hand squeezes my arm, her face holds a bittersweet smile. We both dab at the corners of our eyes. "I pray he's still alive."

After that, we grow absorbed in our own thoughts for what seems like a long time. The breeze is cool but soothing. How easy this could all be, I think, but then I have to come back to reality.

"I don't see any point in going to the University," I tell her. "At least not for a while. I need time to learn about Mexico."

"This could be a good time for you. Perhaps you could do some modeling while you're thinking about it. If you want, I can introduce you to some people. You could also audition for TV." Carmen pauses. "You are so lovely to look at, Teresa Maria," she continues after a few moments. "Your beautiful hair is dark, but not too dark, and your light skin is in fashion in Mexico these days. Your look is so innocent I can see you on TV or anything you set your sights on."

"Thanks, Carmen, but I'm not that pretty."

She stops talking to look at me sharply. "Pretty enough. Are you pregnant, Teresa?"

I blush. My worry had been short-lived, and I've been very regular since. "No," I assure her.

"Sure?"

"Sure."

"You need to lose a few pounds then."

I'm offended. I had always prided myself on staying trim. The thought of TV has a strange appeal. It was what I was working towards in California, but I always assumed I'd be speaking English, not Spanish. "Where would I start?"

"I know exactly how to go about it. I still have lots of contacts. If you let me, I can make it happen for you. But to start you need to get more comfortable speaking Spanish."

The thought is sinking in that Carmen is serious about helping, not just making talk.

"Yes," she muses. "I can do that. The first step is to get you settled—not here, of course. Then we need some publicity and after that, the *Mexicana Belleza* Pageant. That would be perfect for you. But we don't have a lot of time."

"A beauty pageant?"

"*Sí, Mexicana Belleza,* The Miss Mexico contest."

CHAPTER 28

I CAN'T SEE myself in a beauty contest. I've seen those girls on TV, and I've never fantasized about being one. I'm happy with my looks, but don't see myself on that level. And why would I want to prance around a stage so men can gawk at me? I don't think I can compete with females whose whole life is so focused on their looks.

Besides, how can Carmen think I have a chance? She does though. It's like she is possessed. She even takes a break from directing Vivian and the other porn girls to spend hours making phone calls to people she knows all over Mexico.

I begin thinking this is only her fantasy, a way of reliving the life she'd once had. But one evening, a week after Rico and Knobhead have gone back to Monte Vista, she comes into the *sala* where I'm watching TV with the other girls. As if she's won a lottery, she says, "I think we have something, Teresa. My photographer friend in Guanajuato just called. He's willing to take you on as an assistant."

I feel faint. Maybe this isn't a fantasy after all. It's beginning to scare me. I can see her getting me into a situation where

I'm bound to fail. "Carmen, I don't know anything about photography," I tell her.

"Don't worry about that," she replies. "César knows that. He knows my plan. He'll teach you."

"That's it?" My panic turns into indignation. "Do I have any say at all in this?"

Frowning, she says, "Not if you want to win the *Mexicana Belleza* Pageant. I know what's best for you."

Vivian jumps up from the sofa and rushes over to me. "*Aì, Teresa, qué fantastico,*" she bubbles, kneeling down beside my chair. She looks up into my face and puts her hand on my knee, softly, like a dove landing on a tree branch. I can't help feeling a kinship with her. She's a younger sister who needs my protection, like Connie only older.

"Maybe when I find a place to live, you could come to visit me, Vivian. I'd like that. Would you?"

"Of course. I would come any time I could... if Mama Gorda lets me."

Carmen gives her a parental frown. "We'll see, Vivian. We'll see."

＊ ＊ ＊ ＊

César Cordova is a solidly built man I guess to be in his early forties. When I go to his studio after arriving in Guanajuato, I'm greeted by his muscled back, narrow waist and tight rear end because he's standing at a bench cleaning his equipment with his back to me. He doesn't bother turning around.

"Stand over there, will you?" he says. "Stay out of my light till I'm finished here."

He's wearing tight-fitting black pants and a black T-shirt with sleeves rolled up over his shoulders. First impressions are funny, because only ten seconds inside his studio I know he's a difficult man.

Ten minutes of silence later, he finishes and turns to look at me. There is no doubt he's handsome. His hair flows down over his shoulders in soft dark brown waves and his eyes are large and bright.

"So, you're Carmen's girl," he says. As he looks at me, I see he has a neutral face, but his eyes take their time going from the top of my head all the way down my blouse and jeans to my sandaled toes, scanning slowly, with a photographer's eye, not concealing that he is appraising my assets.

"Not exactly. I don't do porn."

"Really? What do you do?"

At that, I'm stuck. What do I do? I'm too embarrassed to tell him Carmen is trying to arrange a career for me. But that's the fact. Maybe he knows. "She thinks I might have a shot at modeling."

"Oh, for God's sake." He lets out an exasperated huff. Slamming his hands down hard on his hips, he looks at me sideways. "The dear woman has lost her mind. Look at you, for God's sake. No posture, no poise. Your style is all wrong. Your hair! What has she sent me? A lump of clay I'm supposed to make into a goddess? My advice to you, whatever your name is, is to get back on the bus to Tijuana and do porn."

I don't bother to answer. I start toward the door.

"Where are you going?" he calls out. "For God's sake, get back here."

"My name is Teresa Maria Diaz. No one talks like that to me."

"Well, sorry, dear. Don't be offended for God's sake, and don't take it personally. If you want to learn to be beautiful in front of a camera, you'll just have to put up with me. Is that what you want? Yes or no? Don't waste my time."

I can't believe how squeaky my voice sounds when I tell him yes.

"Here's how it works then. First, I'm the boss. You do whatever I tell you to do and never complain. Second, you do all the grunt work here: carry the lights, set up the shoots, work with the models, go for the lunch, anything I say. Third, there's an apartment upstairs you can live in. From time to time, I may give you a little spending money, but it won't be much and don't ever count on it. I pay for all the expenses when we travel. Yes or no?"

Something takes possession of me, he's a *bruja* maybe, or some devil, because I look him square in the eye and tell him it's a deal. I'm not going to let this overbearing man get the better of me. He has no idea how tough I can be.

"Let's get started then." He turns back to the bench.

"Now?"

"Of course, now. What did you expect?"

"Can I unpack first?"

"For God's sake, Carmen is going to owe me big time."

I do my best to thank César for enslaving me and wonder if Carmen has a life of my servitude in mind? He points me toward the staircase leading to the apartment. Halfway up, he calls out from the studio.

"One more thing, Sweetheart. Whenever I call you come running. There are no hours in this job. You belong to me from now on."

✳ ✳ ✳ ✳

The next morning, I find out César isn't kidding. He has a fashion shoot scheduled, so the studio is chaos as he assembles his equipment.

"Run down to the *panaderia* for coffee and *pan dulce*," he calls out to me as I come down the stairs from the apartment. "Money's on the table there. Hurry!"

Standing for a moment in the doorway, I'm undecided which way to turn. The studio is on *Calle Positos*, just down the block from Diego Rivera's birthplace, and close to the center of Guanajuato. It's a coin toss, so I head toward the University on *Calzona de Guadalupe*, where I find a bakery, order coffee, and start to pick out a sweet pastry.

The young girl behind the counter calls out to me, "*No Señorita*, no touch. Please use tongs and trays."

"*Lo siento,*" I mutter, embarrassed. "*Esta bueno.*" The girl has a nice face, but her smile shows a gap in her front teeth. Going to the counter, I ask what I owe. Studying me while making change, the girl says in her best English, "You are a Norte Americana, no?"

I'm stunned she can tell.

"This coffee is awful," César howls when I return to the studio, spitting it into the sink. "For God's sake, dearie, what *panaderia* did you go to? Go get me more coffee—I can't work without it."

This time he gives me directions, and I use the stainless-steel tongs to make my selection. It doesn't feel like the day is off to a good start.

After we load all of his equipment into the back of his white Cadillac Escalade, César dons a floppy gray felt hat with red and green rooster feathers stuck in the band. I climb in the front seat beside him.

"In the back." He jerks his thumb over his shoulder. "Front seat is for our model. Only sit in the front seat when I tell you."

✳ ✳ ✳ ✳

He uses the tunnels under the streets of Guanajuato to whip around the city, picking up the young model, then doubling back along *Calle Positos* to *Cinco de Mayo* and heading out of town. We climb steadily through several neighborhoods until we reach *La Valenciana* on the road over the mountains. Pulling into a parking lot, he tells me to get the equipment up to the church just above us on the hillside.

A collection of small stalls surrounds the parking lot, displaying icons, rosaries and votive candles. A few sell folk art for tourists. There are three or four ancient old women, wrinkled and twisted in frayed white cotton dresses close to rags, sitting on the ground at intervals near the stalls. Each one looks closer to death than the one next to her. They all keep their eyes downcast, staring at clasped hands upturned to catch any coin a passerby might drop their way.

As I climb the steps, I get my first glimpse of *La Valenciana*. The mid-morning sun is just beginning to illuminate the rose-colored stones of the old church. I see why César wants to capture the special light reflecting off the front façade. Stone carvings over the door look as if someone had dripped liquid sugar from the roof that hardened as it trickled down into magnificent designs.

It takes four trips to carry all the gear up the steep steps to the forecourt. By then, I'm panting for breath in the thin mountain air. César is already setting up his spot flashes. Pointing to a large reflector, he shouts, "You'll hold that one where I tell you." He fusses and fumes his way through every step of the setup, then struts around, hands on hips, feathers in his hat bobbing up and down, like a cock rooster, making sure it's the way he wants it. In about half an hour, he's ready to shoot.

The model sits off to the side the whole time, under the shade of an umbrella, out of the breeze. Her hair is perfect when César is ready. But he isn't pleased.

"For God's sake, get the brush and fix her hair, will you," he shouts at me.

The girl, about my age I guess, gives me a distant smile that barely cracks her face. She has nothing to say, sitting motionless like a show horse being groomed before being led to the judging arena or auction ring.

I study her features while I brush her hair. I can't see how I could possibly compete with her or other beautiful young women in a beauty pageant. Her skin is flawless, she definitely has *mestiza* features but is not too dark. Her skin glows when the light reflecting off the church illuminates her.

Looking more closely, I see she is not so delicately featured. Her nose is a bit too prominent on her face, her cheeks are full in a typically Mexican way. But all her features work together to make her the attractive Mexican *Señorita* next door, which is exactly what the clothing manufacturer is paying for. Her simple outfit consists of a pair of tan casual pants that hug her hips, and a chocolate brown, scoop-neck T with tiny straps over an off-white T showing just enough cleavage. It's nice enough, like what you might buy at a Ross store in Monte Vista. When I finish brushing her hair, she sweeps it all off to one side, leaving the right side of her face uncovered.

César takes about a hundred shots, moving around and alternating between barking orders at the girl and cooing over how good she looks. She moves well enough, tossing her mane so the sun highlights it as it swirls around her face. She runs through a series of well-rehearsed expressions, from sultry to sensual to seductive, with César cooing the whole time. I feel completely out of my element. I could never compete with a girl like this, and I'm not even sure I want to. What was Carmen thinking?

When he has enough shots, César hollers out to me to pack everything back in the car and meet him and the girl in the restaurant across the street from the church.

Lugging the equipment back down to the Escalade, I have to pass the beggar women again. One sits close enough to the SUV that I almost brush against her ragged cotton skirt each time I walk by. Seeing her wretchedness makes me uncomfortable, so I keep my eyes on the ground.

On my final load, the crone slowly reaches out and touches my leg with her fingertips. An electric jolt runs through me as if the hand of death has touched me. I freeze. When I look down to see what she's doing, she reaches her hand up to me. I think she wants a contribution, so I act like I have no money. Her gnarled, withered hand holds a small piece of paper. Feebly she thrusts it at me. I think probably it's a religious piece she's using to beg with. I start to move on. But her frail hand is insistent, poking her fingers into my leg. Tiny, weak, translucent, wrinkled like a worn glove, her hand seems to block my way, begging me to take what she offers. I take it without looking and keep moving. Hurrying to the car, I shove the paper in my pocket. She murmurs her gratitude.

A couple of mangy little dogs patrol in front of the restaurant, hidden behind a white stucco wall. The street looks poor and tired. Ragged children run around the stalls where their mothers sell icons and votive candles. Stepping through the carved wooden doorway of the restaurant, I'm transported to another world, where the glamour of colonial Mexico shuts out the blight on the street.

Our young model brushes past me into the outside courtyard as I come through the door. Out on the street, a young man leans against a large motorcycle holding a pair of helmets. She hops on, stuffing all her hair up inside the helmet he hands her. They roar back down the hill to the city.

César sits alone at a patio table under an orange umbrella, surrounded by massive green palms, pink bougainvillea, and gurgling stone fountains. He sips on a bottle of Barrillto.

"What happened?" I ask.

"They don't stay. Always a man comes to pick them up. Offering lunch is only a formality." He looked into my face. "Still want to be a model?"

I'm embarrassed by his question. "Am I hopeless? I couldn't do what that girl did in front of the camera."

"You'd be surprised what *I* can do for *you*, Princess. You'll see."

After eating the lunch he orders for me, César leads me back across the street. Grabbing a digital Nikon with a flash from the Escalade, he takes me back up the stairs to *La Valenciana*'s forecourt.

"Nothing fancy," he says, stopping in front of the main entrance to check the light. "I'll just take a couple of pictures so I can see how much work I'll have to do on you. Stand up close beside the main entrance in the shadow and try not to look as wooden as the door."

I feel wooden as he moves around me, snapping pictures.

"Get used to this! In a few months it'll be happening to you all the time. Relax for God's sake. Smile at the camera. Make the camera your friend, your lover. Let it know how much you care."

I gasp.

When he finishes shooting, his face breaks into a grin that morphs into a smirk. "I'm not supposed to do this but come inside with me. I think we can get a couple of good shots in there."

If the façade of *La Valenciana* seems ornate to me, the gold altar inside makes it look drab by comparison. It takes my breath away. Everywhere I look, the spectacle overwhelms me. The hand carvings in wood and stone of Christ on the cross, the Virgin of Guadalupe and more saints than I can name or count, embody the same indigenous art I've seen in the stalls outside. Still, at the same time, the magnificence of their piety is stunning.

César heads straight for the pulpit of dark hand-carved wood, inlaid with ivory and gemstones. A curving staircase, sensuous in the way the wood had been shaped and smoothed and inlaid with lighter colored woods, leads up to it. The pulpit leans out over the nave like the prow of a ship. Behind the altar of gold, three *retablos* set with masterful gold statues looks down on us.

"Blessed Virgin," I gasp again. "This magnificent church set amid the poverty I saw outside... I can't... Why here?"

César's face shows surprise or maybe even shock. Holding the Nikon, he puts his other hand on the railing and stares at me with dark eyes seeming to burn into me.

"You don't know about *La Valenciana?*" His hand slaps the railing, then he slams it down on his hip. "For God's sake, you expect to be Miss Guanajuato, and you don't even know our history?" He sighs, as if to himself. "This job may be even too big for me. Hundreds, maybe thousands of Indians died for this church, Teresa!" The way he tells me makes me feel responsible for their deaths. It makes me want to curl up in a ball.

I catch my breath. "Building it?"

"Not building it, paying for it. Don Antonio Obregòn built *La Valenciana* with the enormous wealth his mine gave him. It was the richest silver and gold mine in Mexico. Don Antonio worked his Indians to death digging rock and hauling it up the steep, narrow steps through the smoke, from the guts of the earth into the clear light of day in straw baskets. Year after year. For a long time, most of the world's silver came from *La Valenciana*. Then Don Antonio, the cheap son of a bitch, tried to make his peace with his God by building this church. He even asked his workers to contribute some of their wages to build it. I hope he is rotting in Hell to this day. I could show you the mine shaft, it's just outside a ways, but the sight would make you weep at the brutality of that man and for the souls of the dead. It would ruin your makeup. So come, climb into the pulpit and let me take some shots. Then we go."

La Valenciana sobers me. I stay subdued as we rocket down the hill to the studio. César never does anything slowly, it seems, and driving through the crowded streets is like a challenge to him to see how close he can pass other cars at high speed. I am too distracted to be scared, absorbed in the tale he had just told me, feeling stupid for not knowing more Mexican history. Had papa tried to teach us, and we'd paid no attention? I really don't know.

After carrying the equipment back into the studio when we arrive, and cleaning it all before putting it away, I am free for the rest of the day, César says.

The small apartment is really quite cozy for me. It has a little balcony where I can look out all the way to the University and the apricot-colored Basilica at the head of Plaza de la Paz, blazing in the failing light. I change into jeans and a sweatshirt. As I hang up the pants I'd been wearing, the sliver of paper the beggar had thrust at me falls on the floor. I'd completely forgotten about it, but my curiosity prevents me from throwing it in the trash basket. I take it over to the window where there's light to read it. By then, the sun is just clipping the edge of the mountains ringing the city. I unfold the fragile paper slowly. My hands tremble as the words appear. My chest pounds. I feel so weak I have to sit down on the bed. Looking at the few simple, hand-scrawled words, I fight for breath.

As if some instinct warns me, I crumple the paper in my hand again. I sit staring out to nowhere. The afternoon sounds of the street traffic fade as my mind drifts off. I'm too scared to look at the paper again, but after a few minutes, when my pulse has calmed, and my thoughts are no longer racing through my head, I smooth it out and slowly let my eyes look down at the words again.

"Meet me at *Mercado* Hidalgo this evening. I love you. J."

CHAPTER 29

AN EVENING CHILL drifts down from the mountains as I make the short walk to *Mercado* Hidalgo. At Avenida Juarez, where *Mercado* Hidalgo stands, the street opens into a small plaza dominated by a church. In too much of a hurry, and too excited, I bow my head when I pass. I make the sign of the cross and ask the Virgin for divine guidance in finding Javier alive and healthy, and keep on going.

Farther down Avenida Juarez, the *Mercado* looms in the darkness. A gigantic building with a curved roof arching over its entire length, it throws a long, dark presence over the street. On one side, a tower rises above the roof. The illuminated clock on its face says it's almost eight o'clock. Hurrying along, I curse César for demanding I run out to fetch his dinner, keeping me chained in servitude until well after seven.

When I enter the market, a lump forms in my throat. Shoppers swarm over the stalls and scurry up and down aisles, more aisles than I can count, reaching to the far end of the building. The arched ceiling soars high overhead supported by a delicate latticework of steel. Everywhere I look there are people three deep.

Frozen where I stand, not knowing which way to turn or where to start, a riot of smells overwhelms me. Motor oil, wood for heating, incense, perfume and, most pungently, the smell of people all going in different directions on the floor of the *Mercado* invades my nose. I try to map out a plan.

With so much movement coming at me from all directions, it's hard to stay focused. My eyes want to explore the incredible assortment of goods for sale, but I fight the urge. Scanning the people I pass, I'm anxious to spot a handsome, lean-bodied man with dark brown hair and a strong nose in front of me. I keep moving up one aisle and down the next, searching for him. At times, I have to push my way through the crowd. A loudspeaker announcing the *Mercado* will close at nine, adds urgency.

I make it all the way to the far end of the building without spotting him, but it takes a long time. Every conceivable item I can think of, and many I can't even imagine, are here for sale. I pass brightly decorated stalls selling dead rooster legs, electrical parts, toys, cosmetics, children's clothing, fresh fruit and vegetables. Shrimp, live birds, lingerie, you name it, all with shoppers flocking around them. I chide myself each time my eyes drift to a passing display.

I go back to the center staircase. The sound of my shoes clanging on the solid steel steps gives off a hollow echo as I climb to the balcony. It sounds like a metronome clicking off the minutes until closing. Fewer stalls are on the upper level, but I have to circle the entire perimeter of the building, checking each stall and the people shopping.

The hands on an inside clock are ticking off the minutes till closing. I'm beginning to feel panic deep in my stomach that I won't find Javier. It's the kind of panic you feel in a dream when you're lost, and no one will help. No one cares.

Then I spot him! Below me, near the entrance. I shout, "Javier," but my voice is drowned out by the buzz of the crowd. I rush to the stairs, clattering back down to the main floor. People jostle and shove me as I push against the flow, heedless of their insults. The whole *Mercado* is an uproar of sounds beating in my ears. I push through a knot of people. I'm out of breath, my heart pounds. When I get to the aisle where I'd seen him, he's gone.

My panic grows. What should I do? I run down the aisle toward the entrance, looking in each direction, moving as fast as I can, almost tripping in my urgency. Nothing. I turn back toward the center of the building. Where else could he be? I'm not thinking straight now. I have to find him. He's here if only I can get to him.

I get to the far end of the building again, just as the clock chimes nine. A metallic voice over a loudspeaker is telling everyone it's time to leave. I can't leave. I have to find Javier.

I race back to the front door. For the first time, I can see there are two other entrances to the building. People are streaming out of them. How can I check them all? I can't. I think what if Javier has been going up one aisle while I was going down the next. It's my nightmare. Always in front of me, never in sight. My eyes cloud with tears.

Thinking I see him walking out into the night, I run after him. Dodging people, I mumble lame apologies, but push past them just the same. He is walking down Avenida Juarez. His solid build is familiar. I run up to him and reach out for his shoulder.

"Oh... *lo siento.*"

The man smiles at me. "Can I help you, *Señorita?* Are you all right? You look pale."

I'm not all right. I'm desperate. No way to get back into the building, the doors are closed now. I haven't found Javier. "*Lo siento*," I tell the man again and turn away, tears streaming down my cheeks.

I'm desperate. I've known all along one reason I've come back to Mexico is a blind hope I'd find Javier, that he is alive and looking for me. Now, I know he's alive. He wants me. But I've lost him again. I go back into the plaza, stumbling through my grief, paying no attention to people gathered in bunches around the church. I climb the steps to the door, go in and flop down in a pew near the entrance. I can't think of anything else to do.

Kneeling on the footrail, I begin a prayer to the Virgin. Help me, Mary, I pray. Comfort me. Help me find him and never lose him again. I stay kneeling, looking at the cross on the altar. Numb. There is no feeling in my arms or legs, only heaviness. My chest feels crushed. I stare at the cross until I feel a hand touch my shoulder.

Has the Virgin heard me? When I turn around will I see Javier's beautiful face? My heart races again.

It's not Javier.

"Don't turn around," a familiar voice commands, keeping his hand firmly on my shoulder.

It's the man with the bushy white mustache. "You're Felix's man," I say.

"Javier's man."

"You followed me in Morelia and Uruapan."

He ignores that. "I'm Triny. Listen. He was waiting. He needed to meet you in a crowded place, but he couldn't stay. Others look for him. He had to run. Told me to say don't give up. He find a way soon. Have faith. He say for me to tell you he love you much. Wants you to win pageant."

CHAPTER 30

I MAKE UP my mind to put all my effort into getting ready for the local pageant. The thought that Javier knows and is encouraging me, that he might even be there is all the motivation I need.

César continues to build my portfolio, taking pictures of me whenever we're on location for other shoots. He coaches me on posing, how to smile or look serious or sexy, in his usual sarcastic fashion. "For God's sake, Sweetheart, can't you look any more seductive than that?" For God's sake this and for God's sake that. Always preening, walking around with his hands on his hips, goading me with his insults and exasperations, rooster feathers fly back and forth on his hat. Every so often, a smile breaks out. "You're a natural beauty, Princess. You make my camera happy. When you look like that, the whole world lights up."

One morning, as we're getting ready for another fashion shoot, he mounts the stairs to my apartment and taps on the door.

"Here, put this on and wear something over it," he says when he comes into the room shoving a bikini bra and bottom at me. "We're going up to *Pipila*."

"Going where?"

"You'll see."

The bikini is brand new. It looks expensive. White and very skimpy. What would papa think? I shudder as I strip off my jeans and top. Mama would never have let me out of the house in this.

* * * *

Mama never approved of the way young women dressed in Monte Vista. In my junior year in high school, Sergio Sanchez asked me to the school prom. I knew he had a crush on me by the way he seemed always to be hanging around my locker, but he was so shy about asking me. Who could blame him after the way I treated him in junior high and then used him for my Quinceañera escort?

I took the bus to the shopping malls in Whittier and Pasadena on Saturdays, searching for something special. I found a dress. A slinky black dress that clung to my figure and showed off my skin. When I told papa the price, he grimaced but didn't say no.

Mama said no. "We can't afford a dress like that," she scolded. "Papa work too hard for us. I sew you a dress."

She made me take her to the mall to show her what I wanted. I thought she would faint when I did.

"You want everyone to see your breasts? You want to disgrace papa and me? Only bad girls show everything. No, no, Teresa Maria. I make you a dress for the dance. A modest dress."

Modest it was. It fit perfectly, but I looked like I'd been wrapped in a garbage bag. When Sergio arrived at our front door, I saw him take one look at me and gulp.

The boys at the dance stared at me. The girls smirked but kept their distance—all but Veronica Estrada. She sauntered over, her boobs trying to escape over the top of her dress and her large butt tightly wrapped in cloth. "You look like the Bride of Frankenstein," she said, then stalked off.

Sergio was great. He didn't leave my side, and we danced a couple of dances. "Let's go outside," I whispered in his ear during one slow dance.

On the dark terrace, we could still hear the music from inside and rocked back and forth in each other's arms.

"What's wrong with you, Teri? Are you crying?" Sergio said in my ear.

I pulled away from his shoulder and dabbed at my eyes with my lace sleeves. "I don't know... I mean we're not Mexicans, and we're not Americans. It's like we're trapped on the border between two different worlds. Look at me. This is how my mother thinks girls should dress in Monte Vista."

"Yeah, I know," he said, "Sometimes I get so confused. I don't know who I am. It makes me crazy. It's like we're kinda lost, isn't it? But we'll make it, we're together."

With that, he pulled me closer, and we had a very awkward first kiss. I could feel myself tremble.

✳ ✳ ✳ ✳

Putting on the bikini out of César's sight, I asked myself what Javier would think of it? That brought a smile. It fit perfectly, accentuating the narrowness of my waist. My breasts and hips looked just right, and it seemed to set off my long legs and rear end. Then I studied myself in the mirror. There is a problem. A big problem. Reluctantly, I put my jeans back on.

"For God's sake, why aren't you ready?" César almost shouts when he comes upstairs.

"I can't wear this bikini without a wax."

He throws up his hands, shakes his head, making me feel terrible. "You're screwing up our schedule. I'll make an appointment for you. Do I have to do everything?"

Several days later, we finally go to *El Pipila*, the gigantic statue of a man standing on a hill overlooking Guanajuato. His stone torso is twisted, and he carries a torch high over his head. I think César is going for a kind of beauty and the beast photo.

El Pipila is a very popular spot, usually crowded with tourists getting their first view of the colorful city spread out below them. Postcard sellers, tour guides, and the usual vendors of fruits and corn on the cob and ice cream are scattered around the plaza. The beggar crones in their rags are there, too.

"Who are those old women?"

César laughs, then gives a shrug of his shoulders. "They're at all the tourist spots. Just ignore them."

"Where do they come from?" I persist.

"They're *camposinas*, old Indian women from the surrounding villages. Begging is almost a family tradition for them. They do it generation after generation. It's all organized, Teresa. They are moved around in vans from one tourist place to the next every few hours."

He stops to stare hard at me. "Are you wasting my time, Princess? Take off your clothes so we can take these shots before the sun goes down tonight, for God's sake."

"Here? In front of all these people?" The idea terrifies me. What would mama think?

"Exactly. What did you think? That we'd shoo them all away for a while?"

"But—"

"No buts. It's time you got used to people looking at you. Be brave. Like *Pipila* up there."

"He's stone. Why do you call him brave? I don't feel brave."

"I can't believe it," César throws up his hands. "You truly amaze me. You are going to be in the Miss Guanajuato pageant in a month, and you still don't know a damn thing about Guanajuato. You will lose the contest if you don't pay attention. You're pretty enough to win, but that won't do it, for God's sake."

With his hands on his hips, he gives me a very scornful look. The rooster feathers wag disparagingly at me. Several tourists stop. They look at César and me as if we were about to fight. When they hear him start talking, they came closer. He's pleased to have an audience.

"*Pipila* is one of our great heroes of the first revolution," he starts, "the revolution against Spain. It started in 1810, just on the other side of the mountains in a village called Dolores. When the fighting came to Guanajuato, the Spaniards barricaded themselves in that large, fort-like building you can see down there." He points, and all the tourists' heads snap around in unison to see the stone building below in the city.

"The rebels wanted to capture that building because it had weapons and money inside, and they wanted to kill the Spanish soldiers. Each time they got close, the Spaniards on the roof with rifles drove them off."

Now César turns to the statue and looks up at *Pipila*, getting ready for his finale. "*Pipila* was a giant of a man. He picked up a huge slab of stone and put it on his back. Then he lit a torch and walked hunched over to the gates of the building. The Spanish soldiers couldn't hurt him with their guns, the bullets bounced off the rock. With his torch, he burned down the gates to the building so the rest of the rebels could charge inside."

The tourists gasp in amazement. They gather around César, applauding and thrusting pesos at him.

"And now," he addresses them directly, with a wicked smile creeping over his face, "This young woman is going to take off most of her clothes so I can take pictures of her. She'd like everyone here to turn their backs for a moment while she undresses, but I would prefer you watch her do it."

No one turned their back except me. The men around me seem to move closer, while the women look at each other with hesitant expressions.

Praying the wax job has been adequate, I very slowly unbutton my jeans, thinking I want to get very small in any case, or vanish altogether.

César continues coaching me for the Pageant. It still seemed unreal, but I am now committed to following his instructions, learning what to expect when the Pageant starts.

"The first thing you must do is show them your birth certificate," he says. "To show your age." He stops, seeing the stricken look on my face.

"You don't have one, do you, Dear?" he groans. "We've got to do something about that. You don't have to have been born here, but they will want to know you're a Mexicana."

"I am," I tell him. "Just barely. I was born in the back of a bus before my parents crossed to California."

"Not good enough." It's the only time I've ever seen César at a loss. He pauses for a few minutes, hemming and hawing about what to do. Finally, he tells me to go to the state office and ask them what I should do.

"It's a problem," the middle-aged woman behind the counter says after I've waited in line over an hour to speak with her. "Nothing I can do. If there was no midwife and you weren't reported to a hospital, we have no way to verify your birth." She stops talking to stare at me. She drums on the counter with the eraser tip of her pencil. She continues to stare, waiting as if expecting me to do something. Drumming again. When I don't answer, she says, "Of course there might be ways to get around that."

"What ways?"

"Sometimes, there are special things that can be done. If you're willing."

"Like how?"

The woman's face contracts. Her eyes narrow, and she purses her lips. "Sorry, *Señorita*," she says after waiting for my response, "nothing I can do. Please move on, there are people behind you. Perhaps you will think of something, then you can come back to see me."

I leave the government office in a bleak mood. All Carmen's plans for me gone, just like that, in a bureaucratic dead end.

César roars with laughter when I tell him what happened. "You are such a gringa, I don't know if we can ever change you." He pauses and stares at me with mocking eyes. "*Mordida!* The bite!" He exclaims. The woman was asking for a bribe to get you a birth certificate. You didn't understand, so she shooed you away. You are too naïve, Sweetheart. Whatever will I do with you?" He says, throwing up his hand in mock despair.

The next day I go back to the government office and wait another hour before seeing the woman again. She isn't happy when she looks up from the counter and recognizes my face. "Well, did you think of something?" She says.

"How can we solve this problem?" I say and slip an envelope across the counter to her.

"One moment," she says, looking at the envelope. Then she steps away from the counter, taking the envelope with her. She goes to a distant corner of the room and counts the money. Coming back smiling, she says. "You said you were born in

Tecate, no? Is okay. You come back tomorrow. I will have a birth certificate ready for you."

When I got back to the studio, César is busy at his bench, but he calls over his shoulder, "You have a visitor. I told her to wait upstairs."

"Who is she?"

"How should I know?" He gives me an icy look. I'm not your social secretary," he says, turning back to the bench.

I climb the stairs, my curiosity gnawing at me. Carmen? Mama Gorda? I can't think of anyone else who knows where I am. No one in the city knows me. When I open the door, I'm surprised to see Vivian sitting on the edge of my bed. She's wearing a long cotton skirt and a high-necked sweater blouse and twisting a handkerchief in her hands.

She jumps off the bed and rushes at me with her arms outspread. She embraces me, hugging me tightly.

"It is so good to see you, Teresa Maria, but not so good."

Holding her at arm's length, I try to interpret her words. I look deep into her face. Her cheeks are pale. Without any mascara or eyeliner her eyes seem to retreat back in her head. Even so, she's still beautiful. Her golden hair glistens in the light coming in the window from the street.

"I'm glad to see you, Vivian. I was getting lonely here and thinking about you. Has Rico come to see you? Where did you get those clothes?"

"Mama Gorda got them. She didn't want me coming here on the bus in my own clothes."

"So, tell me what is the news?"

Vivian's tears start immediately when I ask her about Rico. They come on in a flood, rolling down her cheeks. I hug her, afraid I've said something to upset her. I get a tissue for her, then lead her back to sit on the edge of the bed.

"I don't know how to say," she begins. "All the way here... I try to think how to tell you, but I still don't know."

"Just say, Vivian. Whatever it is, I'll understand."

"I don't think you will." She takes a big breath. "Rico is in jail."

I look at her, not comprehending. What is she talking about?

"In jail?" It comes out weakly, almost just a catch in my throat.

"Yes. *El Niño* called to tell me Rico was arrested two days ago. He was gloating. Where you used to live, he held up a bodega as it was closing. *El Niño* said he pretended to have a gun and made the cashier hand over all the money. He said Rico wanted the money to buy a car."

I look past her out the window into the distance, trying to see all the way to Monte Vista.

"I'm sorry to be one to tell you."

I'm in shock, with nothing to say. But in a way, I've been expecting something like this ever since papa left.

"There's more, Teresa Maria." Vivian pauses to let her words sink in. Her face still dominated by a forlorn look. "When he was arrested, they fingerprinted him. His prints match from another robbery of a little insurance company. *El Niño* said you would know about that."

✳ ✳ ✳ ✳

Vivian and I stay close together the rest of the afternoon. We only speak a few words here and there to console each other. She tells me how fond she is of Rico. Rico is special, she says. I tell her stories about him. I wonder now if any of them had really happened.

The light coming in the balcony window fades, but we don't pay much attention. Vivian moves over from looking out the window at the gathering darkness to sit beside me on the bed again. She puts her arms around me, and we cry off and on. The room grows dark, but no one moves off the bed. After one long silent spell, she leans over and kisses my cheek. Her hair brushing against my face is soft. It has a pure, innocent smell.

We fix a simple meal in my tiny kitchen, but we eat without much enthusiasm or conversation. Sitting together, well into the evening, we are finally able to talk about Rico, and what we expect will happen. We cry again, exhausted from our sorrow. Down in César's studio I find an extra-long T-shirt for her with Cerveza Barrillto printed on it and two round-shaped bottles stenciled over the breasts.

In the darkness we get into bed. Lying there awake for a while, feeling her just barely beside me, I try to sort out what to do next. I'll have a birth certificate tomorrow, but it could take too long for a visa. What will happen to Rico in the meantime? Going back could mean giving up the Miss Guanajuato Pageant. I'm used to my plans falling apart, but then I think about not seeing Javier. His image never leaves me. What chance of seeing him again would I have if I go back? And then I think about Rico.

I sob silently, just little catches in my throat. I sense that Vivian is awake too, wrestling with her own thoughts of Rico. She reaches out her hand to touch mine. It's comforting. I roll over and give her a hug.

"You're coming with me to Monte Vista," I whisper to her.

CHAPTER 31

I DIAL THE number on the slip of paper crumpled in the bottom of my purse. Not Carmen's number, the one she said was only for an emergency. I'm surprised how quickly the call is answered. I explain the situation and plead for help. We agree on time and place, and that's the end of it. All very professional, very quick.

I dread making the next call. I tell papa about Rico then quickly say I'm going back to Monte Vista.

"Absolutely not," he almost shouts over the phone. "Let me take care of Rico."

I tell him there's no choice. It's safer for me to get across than for him. He still argues.

It's the first time I've ever hung up the phone on my father.

* * * *

The same King Air that Javier flew me to Morelia in at the start of our relationship is now piloted by a man I've never seen before. He keeps silent, intent on his job, while Vivian and I sit behind him, abandoned to our own thoughts.

Mine are desperate. I feel to blame for what has happened to Rico. If I could somehow get him out of jail, I'd still have to get him away from Monte Vista. How that is going to happen, I have no idea, but it's up to me. I keep trying to figure it out. Over the Sea of Cortez, I run out of possibilities, and I can't stop my thoughts from drifting back to Javier.

"Don't trust anyone in Mexico, not even me," he had said at the start of our relationship. "In Mexico, nothing is as it seems."

Was he serious? To me, it was just conversation, just words a naïve girl flying across Mexico with a handsome man pays no attention to. Now? Now, it seems to me I've been too trusting of everyone. Even now, I'm trusting them to get me back to Monte Vista.

The runway of the General Abelardo L. Rodríguez International Airport, not more than a football field away from the border wall, stretches ahead of us, perpendicular to it. As the plane drops to a landing, the fence doesn't look so imposing, nothing that couldn't be surmounted if your motivation was strong enough. But the thought of what lies ahead makes a giant lump in the back of my throat.

* * * *

Vivian and I are hustled into a non-descript black SUV with heavily tinted windows that make the middle of the day look like twilight. The driver gives me a strained smile, and holds the door open for us to climb in the back seat. Then he slips behind the wheel and drives off in silence.

We follow a route from the airport out of Tijuana to the East. It's the same road *El Pelon's* buddies had taken me into the desert, but we turn onto another road on the outskirts of town. In a few minutes, we stop in front of a familiar, large stucco house. The house I slept in the night before Javier and I flew to Morelia.

"Stay here," the driver commands when we stop. This time he isn't smiling. He's all business.

"I'm frightened," Vivian whispers when we're alone. "I should have gone back to Mama Gorda's house from the airport."

"You still can. But if you want to see Rico, this is the only way I could think of."

She nods and slumps back in the seat.

The driver returns after a few minutes. He opens the door and beckons to me. "Please follow," he says. Pointing to Vivian, he adds, "Remain in the car for now, *Señorita*."

She gives me a panicked look. I try to reassure her with a smile, although it's weak.

When the driver opens the front door of the house, a world of white greets me. I'd paid no attention to the last time with Javier. Stepping into the foyer of white marble and alabaster walls is like walking into a blizzard. The driver steers me down a long hallway, knocks on a closed door and we wait. When the signal comes, he opens it and gently pushes me inside. Felix Ugalde sits behind a massive desk in a room paneled from floor to ceiling with beautiful mahogany. In contrast to the whiteness of the entry, this room is dark, almost as dark as the look on Felix's face that greets me.

Buenas tardes, Señorita Diaz. A pleasure to see you again. I hear you are preparing for Miss Guanajuato."

"*Buenos Tardes, Señor* Ugalde. How did you know?"

"I know things." He dismisses the question with a sweep of his hand. Then points me to a chair alongside his desk. "What brings you to my home?"

"I need your help. You told me if I ever needed it, I could call you."

"I remember. And I remember you telling me you would never accept my help. So why are you here?"

"Vivian and I need to get to California quickly. I hope you can do that for us."

"Vivian? Is she one of Carmen's girls?"

"Yes. She's wants to see Rico,"

Felix drums his fingers against the blotter on his desk. Then he picks up a letter opener shaped like a medieval sword and studies its blade. All without talking. Smiling, silently, he looks at me for several seconds, then asks, "You think I can get you across the border?"

"I do. I think you are in that business." I might have gone too far with that, but I hope he will respect me for it.

"You call me a smuggler, *Señorita* Diaz. I prefer to think of myself as a businessman. I fill a need for which people pay me well."

"He's alive, you know. Javier's alive. He contacted me." It blurts out, maybe just to calm my nerves.

"Of course, I know."

"I think you knew in Uruapan but didn't tell me."

He set the letter opener down and leans forward in his chair closer to the desk and me. His face, as always, is blank. No hint of friendship in his eyes. "*Señorita* Diaz," he starts, "you are my impetuous son's lover. That does not give you the right to know my business. Had you known Javier's whereabouts it would have been beaten out of you when you tried to sneak across the desert."

"It was your man who saved me?"

I get another dismissive wave of his hand. He leans forward and shoots the cuffs of his shirt from his European-tailored suit sleeves, so his gold cufflinks break free. Then he picks at an invisible speck of lint on his right cuff.

I watch his face soften. The look he gives me is less condescending. "These are challenging times for me, *Señorita* Diaz—may I call you Teresa? We have competitors who would stop at nothing to destroy us. Nothing! I know you read the papers; murders are happening all over Mexico. I'm an old man. My wife died a long time ago, my little daughter died. Javier is all I have left, and I will do everything in my power to protect him and those he loves. Right now, that includes you, but there are no guarantees that will last. You understand? But, of course, I would like to have grandchildren before I die."

"Why not quit, get out of this terrible business."

"I wouldn't last a day. Neither would Javier."

He looks quizzically at me, picking up the sword again, and turning it over in his hand, running his fingers along the blade. He sets it aside. "So, you want to cross the border, is that right? You want me to get you a safe passage to California? Why do you want that, Teresa Maria?"

"My brother's in jail. I've got to get him out if I can."

Felix shakes his head. "I see," he says, looking straight at me. "Family is important to us all, isn't it? Perhaps someday you will have a smuggler for a father-in-law. Or a husband. Family." A little laugh escapes his lips. Then he turns stone-faced again. "My man will get you across the border. *Via con Dios, Señorita* Diaz. I hope we will see you in the *Mexicana Belleza* Pageant in Mexico City."

I get up and go to the door where the man is waiting on the other side. Felix calls out, "*Señorita* Diaz, one more thing."

His face is stern when I look back at him, but somewhere behind his eyes, there is a tiny spark of humanity. His hands are folded across his suit coat.

"We'll do our best for your brother, but don't expect miracles. He may have to do some jail time... but we can try."

243

His words stun me. I shiver, looking at him with hundreds of questions racing through my head, unable to form any of them into coherent words. "You?" the word stumbles out. "In California?"

"Don't expect miracles," he says again. "We do our best to take care of family, but who can say about Rico? *Vaya con Dios, Señorita*."

* * * *

Vivian is all aquiver when I get back to the SUV. She takes my hand, but I signal her to stay quiet. With Felix's man driving again, we ride in silence back into Tijuana, near the airport. We wind through a maze of deeply rutted dirt streets in a modest neighborhood near the border. We roll and pitch, as the SUV avoids the biggest potholes. Definitely the kind of street you wouldn't pick unless you knew what you were looking for. We hold on to the door handles to keep from bouncing off the seat. With our other hands we hold onto each other.

We stop in front of a ramshackle house, one of at least a dozen look-alikes on the street that's no different than all the other streets we've passed. The driver pulls the SUV around to the back and stops. He tells us to follow him inside.

The house is minimally furnished. A folding table and a couple of chairs are in what should have been a kitchen but has a bare spot on the wall where a sink used to be, and pipes protrude uselessly.

The driver rushes us into a back room. He opens a closet door and takes out three jumpsuits, handing one to Vivian and another to me.

"Put these on," he orders, stepping into the remaining one. "No time to waste."

We look at each other, unsure what comes next.

"What for?" Vivian asks.

"Just do it, *Mujeres*! You will see."

We pull them up over our jeans and sweatshirts. When Vivian zippers hers all the way up, I see it has a crest on the left breast pocket that says, "San Diego Gas & Electric." So, does mine. Written across the back, it says, "Maintenance."

"Hurry now. And absolutely no talking." He hands each of us an SDG&E baseball cap to wear. Then he opens a door at the back of the room. A rough-cut wooden stairway, little more than a ladder, but not by much, leads down into a dark, damp, foul-smelling tunnel. He goes first.

When I step off the last rung, I feel water seeping into my shoes. I start to panic. The stench of raw sewage attacks my nose. It overpowers me for a few seconds. I think I might vomit.

Already Felix's man is disappearing into the darkness. Vivian is waiting on the step just above me. I swallow hard to keep from adding the contents of my stomach to the witch's brew flowing past me and grab a breath. I can't see where I'm walking. Still, I imagine the swill contains a concoction of human feces, dead animal parts, and poisonous chemicals. I cover my nose and mouth with my hand and start after him. I hear Vivian's gasp for air as she enters the swill.

We walk in the darkness through the sewage, at times just a trickle and other times more of a shallow stream. The tunnel is blacker than any blackness I've ever experienced. We are marching like dead souls in a circle of Dante's Hell. I try to make the sign of the cross, but I can't even see if my hands have moved. I beseech the Virgin to protect us.

In front of me, our leader has no form or shadow. I can hear his breathing, a Darth Vader sound. That's all. There is no way to make out the sides of the tunnel. I could walk with my eyes closed and not know the difference. Like a dead woman, I walk on, trusting the man ahead. That thought strikes me as if I've been hit in the back with a broom handle. Here I am trusting someone else I don't know again.

The tunnel echoes with small sounds. I guess the scratching sounds are rats running ahead of us on the dry ledges of the tunnel floor. I clench my shoulders, trying to make myself small so no rat will touch me. Still, I feel an involuntary shiver. I can't identify the sounds I hear. I march along, seemingly without an ending, concentrating on the sounds, lost in a black world. The blindness assaults my eyes. I don't know if they are open or closed. I'm sure I will never see daylight again.

I scream. The sound reverberated up and down the tunnel, growing stronger as it bounces from wall to wall. I fling out my hand to clutch at my hat. Nothing is there. But something had been there. The disembodied voice materializes out of the blackness, telling me to keep quiet. "Only bats," he says, "they won't hurt you." I'm not reassured. I keep my hands on top of my cap as we trudge onward through the void.

Time and distance cease to exist.

It's endless. Minutes, hours, days, no way of telling what time passes. We walk slowly so not to slip in the muck that swirls at our feet. Occasionally, my shoe is bumped by something floating by faster than we are walking, my imagination flares. My stomach starts to rise into my throat again.

Once, I reach out and feel the side of the tunnel, slimy, wet, rough stones, or concrete. I pull my hand back immediately to cover my head again.

Then I start to giggle, quietly at first, but as the image grows stronger in my mind, the laugh escapes my lips. I can't control it.

Our leader schussed me, but I can still see myself standing with other young women in our most elegant ball gowns competing for the Miss Mexico crown in this sewer system. Standing in ankle-deep scum, smiling as cameras click away, and a large rat runs across the stage.

And then the man calls out in a low growl to stop. I hear knocking, a few more whispered words, and then a light intrudes into our tomb, blinding me. Forcing me backward with the strength of its brilliance. I stagger back into Vivian and almost fall. She catches me. Together we slump against the wall. We don't fall but cling to each other desperate to keep our balance. The light is an open door above us. Our guide is already halfway up. I quickly mount the steps after him, with Vivian holding on to my jumpsuit.

"*Bienvenidos a California,*" the man says.

CHAPTER 32

WE CHECK INTO a motel on Peck Road, the kind of ordinary, uncomfortable, cheap chain motel that makes people feel invisible. But it's close to the police station.

Vivian thinks it's wonderful. She bounces on the edge of the bed then prances around the room as if she were staying at a five-star hotel. I tell her it's not very good, but she won't hear it.

"Not nice? *Qué bueno!* For me, it's a fine place. I will be very happy here." Vivian comes over to where I'm sitting and kneels down beside me. She sweeps her blond curls off to one side of her face and gives me a sad, thoughtful look that dims the brightness in her eyes and causes tight creases on her forehead.

"Teresa Maria," she says, reaching up for my hand, "you are such a good friend. But you don't know about me. This room is the size of our family house in Culiacán, where I was born. It was made of wood scraps and cardboard. My mother stuffed newspaper in the cracks to keep out the cold. Here we have water and heat and a bed for each of us. In my house, three older sisters slept in the bed with me. They tried to fool me, saying,

249

'Vivian, please run and get this or get that for us.' When I came back, they had taken up all the space."

Squeezing her hand, I can't help thinking of her like a sister, not a little girl sister like Connie, but a beautiful teenager who it is my responsibility to care for. My other hand gently stroked through her golden curls.

"Do not be sorry," she adds. "Mama Gorda take good care of me."

"But what you do..." My voice trails off, remembering the studio, the lights, the men... "How can you...?"

I can't finish my sentence. I keep stroking her hair and looking across the room, so I don't have to make eye contact with her.

"We all do what we have to, don't we Teresa Maria? Maybe someday you will have to do something unpleasant, too. For me making sex videos is what I have to do. I don't mind, it has brought a better life for me than what I would have had in Culiacán."

"But Vivian—"

"You will never understand what can happen to a poor girl in Mexico. A man could take her for his mistress and beat her whenever he chooses and throw her out when she has a baby, or her breasts start to sag. Or she could be kidnapped and sent around Mexico or across the border, a slave to have sex with whoever will pay the men who own her. What I do is not so bad compared to what it might be. You are lucky your parents brought you here."

I don't want Vivian to see my tears, but I can't stop them. I turn my head. "When I get settled in Mexico, with a job and a place to live, I want you to come live with me. I'll talk to Carmen. I think she'll let you leave if I ask her."

"That would be wonderful, Teresa Maria. When Rico gets out of jail, I think he would like me better if I don't do porno."

Early next morning, we walk to a *panaderia* on Peck Road. Vivian has given up her modest look in favor of a tight-fitting sweater blouse, cut low enough to cause a riot when she bends over. Walking under the freeway, where the cacophony of traffic is so loud we can't talk, she grabs my hand and stays close. Exhaust fumes spill down from the traffic on the highway above us, gagging us for a moment. We move across the street, away from the men hoping for day jobs, and keep going toward Valley Boulevard. Vivian is mesmerized by the posters of All-American Breakfasts in the window as we walk past a Denny's. "*Qué padre!*" she exclaimed. "*Ai*, so much food."

In ways, her childlike pleasure at each storefront we passed reminds me of Connie. A *joyeria* captivates her for several minutes while she studies the jewelry with wide eyes.

"I've never seen anything like this in Mexico," she tells me.

"I saw beautiful jewelry in Morelia and Guanajuato, Vivian. Better than this. All the stores along Peck Road are trying to attract the Latinas who've moved here."

"But so beautiful."

"I should take you to the shops in Pasadena or Westwood to see truly beautiful things. This is only a town for middle class people."

"Can we go?"

"What about Rico?"

"Oh... I forgot."

Detective Lopez is on duty at the police station. He glowers at me when we come through the door. Then he checks out Vivian.

The other cops don't hide the way they look us over either. César has taught me to get used to men's stares. Even so, I want to walk over and slap Officer Nuñez in the face.

Lopez outdoes all the others, smirking in a very nasty way as he gets up from the wooden swivel chair at his desk. He gives Vivian an aggressive strip search with his eyes, then focuses his attention on me. He presses in way too close, making me very uncomfortable. I back up a step, but he presses forward.

"Told you I would find out who did the insurance job, didn't I? Turns out it *is* someone you know very well. I still think you had something to do with it, *chica*, and when I find some evidence, I'll nail your precious butt to the wall."

"Get away from me, you idiot," I tell him in a voice loud enough for the whole room to hear. "This is the cop who called the Border Patrol and had me picked up. A standup guy, huh, Vivian?"

Lopez backs off, looking around the squad room to see if his buddies have heard me put him down. They're busy looking down at the floor or off in some other direction.

"Who's the bimbo?"

"None of your business, Lopez. I want to see my brother."

Regaining his composure, he presses into my face again. "I don't have to do anything for you. You greasers are all the same." His face is way too close; his morning breath scorches me. "You screw up this country for the rest of us," he snaps. "We can't build walls fast enough or high enough to keep all of you out, in my opinion. How'd you get back?"

"I want to see my brother!" I ignore his insults. "If you don't take me to him right now, I'll call a lawyer.

* * * *

The small jail at the rear of the police station is out of sight down a long hallway. Officer Nuñez leads us into a big room with a couple of tables in it. It isn't like the visiting rooms I've seen on TV. No window separates the visitors from the prisoners. No telephone connection. Just a crummy old green-painted metal table with metal folding chairs.

Veronica Estrada, seated at the other table, taunts me as we enter the room. "Goddamn, it's like a high school reunion here."

"What brings you here, Veronica?"

"Visiting Pepe. It's getting to be our usual meeting place."

Across from her, Pepe looks a lot less fearsome than he had that afternoon in the alley back of the high school. Seeing him now still sends a shiver up my spine and a flashback memory. I walk past Veronica without saying a word. She doesn't scare me anymore.

Pointing at Rico coming into the room, she crows, "You're down on our level now, *chica*."

Rico is cuffed, wearing an orange jumpsuit, like the kind you see on TV.

Vivian sees him coming to the table and starts to rush toward him, but the guard steps between them.

Rico smiles sheepishly, then waits until the guard has seated him at the table before speaking, and then only in a low monotone so no one around him can hear.

"Thank you for coming. Both of you." He nods to me, but his eyes are big and bright for Vivian. He tries to keep eye contact with her but can't stop himself from dropping his eyes to her breasts.

"How did you get here?" he asks her. Then, "You look beautiful."

She giggles and jiggles a little. Looking around to see if people are listening, she says, "We walked."

"I wish I could walk back with you."

"What are they doing to you?" I'm impatient to ask. "How long have you been here? Will there be a trial? When? My God, Rico, what did you do? Why?" My questions gush out in a torrent, bringing my frustrations with them.

In a matter-of-fact voice, he tells us the story of his arrest.

"You stole to buy a car to come see me?" Vivian asks. She has a kind of exalted look on her face, not a smile, more like a display of pride.

He nods, yes. "I had to see you again."

"And Ernesto's insurance business?" My voice is tinged with anger. "How could you? That money belonged to all those old people."

"Yeah." Veronica's shrewish voice comes from the next table, "they tried to pin that on me."

"Shut up. You tried to pin it on me."

Rico has a forlorn look. "I'm sorry I got you jammed up. I didn't think."

"But you thought about the other one?"

He sits there, blank-faced. I can see he's lost.

Vivian stays silent during the exchange, looking down into her lap, twisting the hem of her bright print miniskirt. Her face looks heavy with sadness. When Rico stops talking, she looks up and smiles at him.

"I miss you so much. What will happen to you?" It seems as if it is an effort for her to get the words out.

Rico's eyes moisten. It's his first sign of emotion since we sat down. I would like to leave them alone, but I don't know what would happen if I got up from the chair.

"There'll be a hearing tomorrow," he says. "The court will get me a lawyer.

"Jail?" Vivian looks scared.

"County jail, I guess. I don't have money for bail."

Vivian looks at me with a question.

"I don't have much money. Maybe papa—"

"Not papa. I do this on my own," Rico snaps. "I don't want him doing anything for me. Ever again."

His angry words hurt me. There's nothing more I can say. We silently look at him across the table until Vivian reaches her hand out to him.

"I can wait for you," she says wistfully. "Come to Mexico when you get out. Please..."

Rico takes her hand. The guard jumps off his chair and rushes over to us. "No touching. Your time's up anyway. C'mon, Diaz, back to your cell."

* * * *

It's a sad Vivian who walks back down Valley Blvd with me. After a long silence, she looks at me the way Connie used to when she was frightened.

"What will happen to him?" She almost whispers.

"I'm scared for him," I tell her. "If he stays in Monte Vista, he'll get in trouble again—I can feel it. He's angry. Maybe do something worse. He might get off easy this time, but if he's caught again... I think they'll put him in prison for a long time. There's no remorse in him, Just anger."

She looked at me with tearful eyes. "I think I love him."

All I can do is nod and squeeze her hand a little tighter, then wipe a tear from my eye. How have we become so entwined? A beautiful waif-like sex actress and a girl who doesn't know where she belongs. Both of us living upside-down lives.

We stop at a small restaurant on Peck Road, actually more of a glorified *taquiera* than a restaurant. We have no appetite but need to sit and talk, trying to deal with the jail visit. The waiter, a Latino teenager, shows his disappointment when we only order cokes but enjoys standing over Vivian's shoulder, peeking down her sweater.

"Rico doesn't deserve to be in jail," Vivian says after the kid leaves the table.

"Yes, he does." I'm quick to jump on her words. "I love my brother, but something's happened to him. He's going to have to pay for what he's done. I wish he didn't."

She nods grudging agreement but stays quiet. Her eyes roam around the room and out to Peck Road. When she looks back, she has an expression I can't interpret that darkens her eyes and tightens her face.

"It's funny." She starts, then trails off before starting again. "We're alike, you and I, aren't we? I love Rico, but he's in jail, and I can't be with him. You love Javier, but you can't be with him either. We're both lonely and sad without our men, Teresa Maria. What will happen to us?"

Caught off guard, I wonder what does Vivian know? I guess Carmen has said something about Javier to her. No harm, I suppose.

"I don't know if I'll ever see him again. I was only with him for a short time. Who knows? Maybe he doesn't care anymore."

"Oh, he does care. Yes, of course, he does," Vivian says emphatically. "Mama Gorda says he does. She says he can't wait to see you again."

"Really? How does she know?"

Vivian looks surprised. "She talks to him almost every day. She says he talks about you all the time."

Strange. Carmen has never mentioned speaking with Javier to me. The fact she hasn't makes me uncomfortable.

"For a long time, I didn't even know if he was alive."

"Mama Gorda said that was the way it had to be to protect you."

"Really?" Where was this conversation going? I look away from her, so my face doesn't give my thoughts away. "Tell me, Vivian, why does she talk so often to Javier?"

Vivian sets her empty coke can down abruptly. "You don't know?" A shadow of surprise darkens her face. Her eyes narrow, losing all their sparkle. Her jaw stiffens. I can see she is suddenly wrestling with something.

Finally, she resolves whatever conflict she's been struggling with. Looking straight at me, smiling weakly, she says, "You don't know? Javier is Carmen's son."

CHAPTER 33

WE'RE ALMOST BACK at the motel when Knobhead's black SUV pulls up to the curb in front of us, and he jumps out.

Almost shouting, he calls, "Vivian... I'm surprised... What are you doing here?"

"I'm with Teresa Maria, *El Niño*," she replies in her softest of little girl voices.

Hector looks from one of us to the other, speechless. He searches our faces, seeking an explanation. My face is blank, but Vivian's deer-in-the-headlights look tells him what he doesn't want to know—that she didn't come to Monte Vista to see him.

"Your brother's in jail," Hector says to me, his excitement vanished.

"We just saw him."

He processes that information with a grimace as if it's difficult for him to put all the facts together. The tiny burn scars around his mouth grow redder, angrier and hurt, as he puzzles through it. The muscles on his arms flex, straining against his T-shirt. The snake seems to come alive. One of Hector's large hand reaches up to rub his bald head. Finally, as it all sinks in, he aims his anger at Vivian.

"Mama Gorda didn't let me know you were coming. She was keeping it from me."

Vivian takes a small forward step. "I went to Guanajuato to tell Teresa Maria about Rico. She brought me here to see him."

"...but she didn't let me know," he says again slowly. "You told her not to, didn't you?" Then he gives me a mean look.

There's no need for an answer.

"We've had some good times, haven't we, Vivian?" He waits and says again, "Haven't we?" As he takes a step toward her, the snake bares its fangs.

She shifts from one foot to the other on the sidewalk but doesn't back away. "I'm sorry."

He takes another step toward her. "Why Rico?"

I start to move in between them, but without any warning, he wheels around and storms back to his Expedition. His tires scream as he races away, leaving us alone on the sidewalk, choking on the smell of burnt rubber and exhaust smoke.

✳ ✳ ✳ ✳

The next morning, with the thought of walking through the tunnel again sitting heavy on both of us, we wait for the car to take us back to the border. Vivian is lost in her thoughts. She hasn't spoken much since Knobhead's sudden departure yesterday.

Instead of a car, a van pulls up and two figures get out. I stop short, frozen to the sidewalk. My eyes not believing what they see. "Rico, what are you doing here?" The shock of seeing him in street clothes leaves me speechless.

Vivian rushes to him, throwing her arms around his neck, almost hanging on him. She kisses his cheeks and face. Finally, their lips come together before he can say a word.

The other man with him, dressed in an expensive-looking tailored brown suit doesn't move. He stands still on the sidewalk until I look at him.

Javier!

I don't trust my eyes. For an instant I continue to stare at him. He stares back. He's still as handsome as I remember. Even more. His eyes are soft and beckoning. His smile takes over his face, showing his even teeth. My pulse quickens.

"I want to see if you are as beautiful as I remember," he says. "More beautiful now, I think."

It takes time for it to sink in it is really him. Then I run into his arms.

He embraces me tightly. I look up into his face, reassuring myself he is not an image conjured up by my months of waiting and longing for our reunion. "It's you! Really you." My words rush out.

"It is me," he says. Then he leans down to kiss me on my lips. The feeling that runs through me is electric. But we're standing on a sidewalk on one of the busiest streets in Monte Vista, and for all that I want to stand here in his arms forever, after several more moments of kissing, I step back.

"Your brother was arraigned in court this morning," Javier says, still holding me by my shoulders. "One count of burglary and one of attempted armed robbery. His trial date is set for next month in municipal court. He could get five to ten years in prison if he's convicted. That's the best we were able to do."

Rico has Vivian nearly bent over the hood of the car, and the driver behind the wheel is trying to become invisible, not sure which couple to keep his eyes away from.

"He's out on bail." Javier says. "So, I brought him to you."

261

"Can you take us back to Mexico?" I ask him, my voice still trembling from my shock.

"The plane's at the airport."

"Get in the car," I order Rico and Vivian. "In the back." Javier and I slide into the middle seat, still in each other's arms.

"Get us to the airport," Javier tells the driver.

∗ ∗ ∗ ∗

In Tijuana, Vivian and Rico go on to Mama Gorda's. Javier and I fly on to Guanajuato. The drone of the propellers limits our conversation to small talk, so I sit back and let my mind drift to the memory of my first flight with him on the way to Morelia.

He stops the King Air on the tarmac outside the private arrivals building, turns off the engines, looks over at me and smiles. "It is so good to finally be with you again, Teresa," he says. "I've thought about you every day."

"I've thought about you a lot, too," I say. "Flying here I was thinking about our flight to Morelia, and the wonderful time we had together in Michoacán. That was a magical fantasy for me... until it stopped."

"And I want it to continue now." He says, reaching over from the pilot's seat to embrace me. "Should I get us a hotel room for tonight? We can have a private dinner."

"You're going too fast."

"Teresa, I love you. I've spent these past months remembering our night together."

I pull away from his embrace. "That seems like a lifetime ago, Javier."

"And I've dreamed of the time we'd be together again."

"It might be best if I just take a taxi back to the studio. I have an apartment there."

262

"Can we be private there? I have to fly back to Morelia in the morning."

"No. I think you should fly on now."

The look on Javier's face is one of great surprise and disappointment. "But I thought...I love you Teresa, I thought you loved me."

"I do love you."

"Then let's be together tonight.

"No," I tell him again. "I'm not the kind of girl who can make love with you once every six months or so. I need more." My emotions start overwhelming me. I'm doing my best to hold it together.

"What do you mean by, 'need more' Teresa?"

"It's hard for me to feel loved by the way I've been treated—"

"It is love, Teresa. I swear it. I told you about me in Morelia."

"You did. But you and your family have used me, Javier. I don't get it. Why? For what purpose? When we flew to Morelia, I was very naïve, very innocent. I'm not any longer. We need to start again, spend more time getting to know each other. Right now, I've got to concentrate on the Pageant so it's best if we say our goodbyes now."

✳ ✳ ✳ ✳

I busy myself preparing for the Pageant, trying to force the scene with Javier out of my thoughts. César flutters around like a newly hatched butterfly, anxious to get me ready for the contest. He is always dragging me off to beauty salons to try new hairstyles. Then he races around the city, searching out just the right clothes he thinks I should wear, with the hairstyle du jour he'd chosen. Some of the gowns are rather exotic, one is a long, brown, clingy crêpe number that bares one shoulder and is slit up both legs to the top of my thighs. "Isn't it fabulous?" He says.

"Really, César, you expect me to wear this?" I laugh when he asks me to try it on.

"For God's sake, Sweetheart, you'll grab the judges' attention—don't you get it? I want you to stand out from the others."

I am starting to get it. "I'd certainly stand out in this dress. Or maybe fall out. I'm not wearing it. I'm a conservative girl. My mother raised me that way, and that's how the judges will see me. I'll stand out from the others in the simplicity of my dress if all the other girls look like hookers."

He fumes, storms around the studio for the next twenty-four hours, and treats me like I have a contagious disease, but in the end, he concedes. We settle on a medium blue gown with a halter top cut deep enough to show what César judged is an ample amount of cleavage. It has sapphire sequins sewn on the bodice and a more modest slit in the skirt. Conservative? Not exactly. But I'm comfortable enough that I can wear it without fear of tripping or something flopping out. César finds the perfect heels to go with the dress and has them dyed to match.

"This will get you through the local pageant, Sweetheart," he says, hands on hips, in a bit of a huff, inspecting me as I walk around the studio trying to get used to the shoes. "But Carmen will put you in something more daring if you make it to the next level."

The next level? Who is he kidding? I don't even think I should be at this level. Does anyone really think this is a career path? Who thinks a beauty pageant is so important to begin with? Beauty pageants aren't for me. So why am I about to parade half-naked in bikinis (the thought still sends chills up my spine) and tight-fitting, low-cut dresses in front of ogling Mexican men I don't give a hoot about?

Strangers have taken over my life. Carmen is almost constantly on my mind. There are a lot of questions she has to answer the next time I see her. Not just mine, now Rico's, too. The thought of Rico hanging around Vivian in Mama Gorda's porno house is too troubling for words, but what other options are there? He'd made it plain he didn't want to see papa. In fact, he isn't going to leave Vivian at all.

All these uncomfortable thoughts weigh on me, constantly intruding on my waking hours, dulling my enthusiasm, while César bustles around trying to get me ready. And yet, impossible as it is to explain, the thought of winning a beauty contest still gives me a chill whenever I let myself think about it. Isn't it every young girl's fantasy? Isn't it every woman's desire to have men admiring her? Secretly, the thought of parading around the stage thrills me just a little.

Who am I kidding? Certainly, not the other girls entered in the local pageant. "I know you," one of them says when we are all gathered around the organizers to hear instructions the first day. She is the model we photographed at *La Valenciana*. "You were César's gofer who did my hair." Her eyes harden. "I suppose you think your photos will help you?"

"What photos?"

"Come on, don't be cute. Those pictures are all over Guanajuato. In one of those sleazy tabloids, probably on Instagram, too, all over Mexico by now."

"What photos? You must have me confused with someone else."

"No, *chica*. No mistake. They're your tits. Take a look."

She pulls a folded paper from her large shoulder bag. I cry out when she shoves it in my face. I throw the paper down, embarrassed beyond all belief. She's right, it's me. I look again. Staring back at me is me, bare breasted in my apartment wearing

265

only the skimpy bikini thong. I throw the paper down and run back to the studio.

"How could you?" It's all I can say.

César stands with his back to me at his workbench, tinkering with a light panel.

"What are you talking about?" He says over his shoulder. "I want you to run out and get me some lunch."

"No chance! Not till you explain those pictures."

"What pictures? ...Oh, those pictures."

"Those pictures! What right —"

"For God's sake, don't get so upset. They'll help you in the pageant."

"You took them without my permission."

"Permission? You were in my studio. What permission do I need to take pictures in my own studio?"

"In my apartment! Not your studio! You must have a camera hidden there."

He moves away from the bench and stares straight at me. He put his hands on his hips and cocks his head off to one side. For the first time, I see an earnest look come over his face as he scowls at me.

"To begin with, Sweetheart, they're great pictures. You are enchanting, beautiful and sensual. The judges can't help but notice."

"Can't help is right."

He pays no attention. He's missed the point entirely. He's exposed me to who knows how many people and doesn't care. I mumble a plea to the Virgin, but César isn't finished.

"Over and over, I tell you, you don't get it, Teresa Maria Diaz. And you still don't. Maybe you should pack it in and go back to California. We have one goal here: to get you in the Miss

Mexico Pageant in Mexico City two months from now. That's what we're all working toward. The photos are a publicity stunt, so the judges will know your name even before the contest starts. Get it?"

For a moment, I'm frozen where I stand. "What do you mean? Who are all the people working for me?"

"Who do you think?" he says, hands on hips, with a look plastered across his face that treats me like a kid. "Who do you think is paying for all these gowns and other clothes? Hairdos and everything else?"

Opened-mouthed, I stare at him. I'd never thought of it, never even questioned who was paying. There's a huge lump growing in my throat. I'm scared. I want to run to my room and sob like a teenager. I'm not a teenager. I'm growing up fast.

It takes several seconds for me to get my emotions under control and feel I can talk. I put my hands on my hips, facing César, letting my anger show on my face.

"Did you get paid for them?" I ask him. "The pictures?"

"That was just a side benefit. The goal was to get you noticed. And I did."

✳ ✳ ✳ ✳

I search my apartment for the camera César used to spy on me and tear it from its hiding place when I find it, feeling sick. I get on my knees in a far corner of the room and have a long conversation with myself, and with Our Lady. I tell her how lost I've become in a world that doesn't make any sense to me. I tell her my life is falling down a dark hole. I pray for her guidance. Then I stay silent for a long time and pay attention when she speaks to me.

The next day, I go back to the pageant office and join the other young women in a practice dance routine. Other girls shoot me angry looks. The model refuses to speak to me. I return all their looks without any explanations, keeping to myself, studying the others, and trying to decide where the competition will come from. When our first practice is over, I go straight back to the studio.

Calling out to César, I say, "Take the sequined blue gown back. Find something sexier. I have an image the judges will expect of me now."

He reaches for his hat and heads out the door with rooster feathers flapping like a hungry pigeon in the plaza. He returns an hour later with a gown that makes me blush, but I don't let him see that.

Two weeks later, it is incredible how easily I win the *Nuestra Bellesima Guanajuato* title. Standing before a cheering crowd on the stage of the ancient Teatro Juarez, with most of my breasts exposed, the winner's sash is draped over my shoulder. A crown of fake diamonds sits on my expensively coiffed head.

CHAPTER 34

FLYING IN TO Mexico City, the yellow haze obscured the snowcapped mountains The foul air is thick in my throat. City's streets are clogged with unmoving cars. Stalled, their horns blare a loud off-key fugue, and their exhausts penetrate the window of my cab as we rock and jolt our way along Paseo de la Reforma.

I have a note from Carmen when I check in to the Miss Mexico Pageant hotel. She says to meet her at noon the next day by the flagpole in the Zocalo. She doesn't say why, only that any cab driver will get me there from any place in the city.

The Guanajuato Pageant is already more than a month in the past. The excitement of winning has diminished. César is still boasting to anyone who will listen how he secured the title. My pictures have been plastered on the pages of the newspapers for miles around. Even on a couple of local billboards. The local TV Azteca station interviewed me three times. Each time, I wore a different outfit César picked out. In a way, they were job interviews. On our third meeting, I was offered a starting position in the station's news department. Being interviewed at the station was a great learning experience. César calls it all necessary preparation for the big show in Mexico City. But it is much more.

At first, it felt strange to realize and accept that I'm no longer the ugly duckling Veronica Estrada had said I was. More than that, I have a growing feeling of personal strength that comes from deep within. I'm a woman men look at longingly—I saw that from the stage in Guanajuato. It's a powerful feeling. I'm also an intelligent voice the TV station people want on their team. In winning the local pageant, I've shed the cocoon of girlhood. I think I'm free to pursue my future no matter what happens here in Mexico City. I think I'm ready to face Carmen.

* * * *

Hundreds of people mill around the Zocalo in the bright early May sun. Absorbed by the hustle and buzz of the square, I wander for a few minutes basking in the sense of history I've now become a part of.

"This is our center, our core." A hand reaches out to touch my shoulder. Turning, Carmen is smiling at me. "Congratulations," she says, her bright red lips part in a big smile. "You are a lovely Miss Guanajuato."

I try to smile back. It isn't very successful.

"I wanted you to see this spot that's so important to the people of Mexico. If you win, you'll be representing us."

"It's only a beauty contest, Carmen." I feel distanced from her because she's withheld information from me. I want to be angry, but I can't help still being fond of her, and grateful for what she's done.

"You'll see," she says. And it's clear in her voice she's seeking some common ground so we can move forward, too. "The people will look up to you, honor you. Just as the Aztecs honored their emperor right here where we're standing." She tells me as if I'm something new to her.

"This was an island when Cortez arrived with his mistress, *La Malinche*, to translate for him," she continues. "Imagine, Teresa, Cortez, *La Malinche* and his small band of soldiers standing here face to face with Moctezuma in Tenochtitlan, his capital, surrounded by thousands of warriors. Picture Moctezuma adorned with wild bird feathers and brilliant flowers. The city held more gold and silver than the Spaniards had ever seen before."

"I *can* picture it, Carmen. I've been studying Mexican history the past couple of months, so I won't embarrass myself. I can see Aztec priests making human sacrifices of young women. Ripping their hearts out," I say in a snarky voice.

She doesn't respond, but I see her face grow tense, wrinkles deepening across her forehead, her penciled brows flatten. She holds me steady in her stare for a long, silent interval.

"You're angry with me. Vivian said so."

"Anger's part of it," I tell her. "So are confusion and hurt. I thought you were my friend, but friends don't withhold information the way you've kept things from me."

"I don't know if I can satisfy you with an explanation, and I won't apologize. I did what was best," she says.

"Best? Best for whom? How could you possibly think it was best for me? You withheld news about Javier. Over and over, you treated me like a child, like one of your porno girls. How could that be best?"

"We were worried the truth would bring you harm. There are people..." She stops to find words before continuing. "There are people who would hurt you just to get to Javier and Felix." She shudders. "They tried on the border, didn't they? Felix wants to protect you. He thought the less you knew, the safer he could keep you. He told me to keep quiet. So, I did."

"That was six months ago. You've kept quiet ever since, even though you knew Javier was safe. I guess I should thank you and Felix for saving me, for helping my brother and getting me back into California to see him, but I feel used. If I weren't in this pageant, I think I'd walk away from all of you."

"Walking away wouldn't be that easy." Her voice is inflected with warnings, almost threats. "You're part of us now. We need you, and you need us. No one expected Javier to fall in love with you, but he did. That makes protecting you important to all of us."

Hearing her words, I tremble. My hands clench into fists. I struggle to keep them at my side. "How could you?" It's both a shout and a sob.

"You need to hear all this from Javier. He'll make you understand. He wants to tell you the whole story if you'll listen."

The thought of seeing Javier again makes me hesitate. I don't know how I'll react. That scares me.

Carmen tries to reach out for my hand, but I flinch, like a small, frightened dove.

"He'll be at the Museo de Anthropologia in Chapultepec Park. If you want to see him, go now. He'll be in the Olmec heads room. He'll be there until two o'clock and then leave. It's up to you, Teresa."

CHAPTER 35

IT IS UP to me. Wrestling that thought, I walk away from Carmen and start down the Reforma. I need time to collect my feelings before seeing Javier again.

How *do* I feel about him? Conflicted. In the seven months, almost eight, since I've known him, he has never been far from my thoughts. The image of his face comes to me whenever I start to think of him—handsome, strong but gentle, romantic, everything I've ever dreamed of. I know it's a romantic vision, formed before I knew much about him and Felix Ugalde and Carmen. Is he as much a victim of his father and mother as I am?

The sidewalks are crowded, but I barely notice the people as I hurry along, dragging my dilemma with me like a wheelie suitcase. As hard as I fight it, our love scene in Patzcuaro runs like an endless loop in my mind.

"I didn't plan on this, Teresa." He whispered in my ear as we stood in each other's arms on the balcony, gazing over the moonlit lake. I feel the thrill of his body tight against mine. I'm dizzy with the feeling of him lying by my side, the touch of his hands. "You are special, I'm falling in love with you," he said.

What could I do? Say to him?

"Planned or not, you've completely seduced me," I returned his whisper. "We're a pretty unlikely couple. We might never see each other after I find my father."

An unlikely couple. What an understatement! I'm not sure if we were a couple at all. It didn't feel like we were at the airport in Guanajuato. So, absorbed in remembering my anger at his presumptuousness, I stop abruptly on the sidewalk, and a portly man hustling along bumps into me. *"Lo Siento, Señorita,"* he says with a broad smile and a tip of his cap.

What do I know about men? About Javier? The simple fact is, almost nothing.

And I never will unless I confront him now. Of a sudden, I'm panicked to get to the Museo. I walk faster, starting to run, then stop. I'm not going to run breathlessly into Javier's arms. I step into the street, a cab swerves sharply through traffic to the curb alongside me. The driver smiles, asks where I want to go. He laughs when I tell him, then points to the museum a block farther up Reforma. Apologizing, I jump out of his cab, thrusting a couple of pesos through the window at him. Then I hurry to the Museum.

No time to stop and admire the magnificence of the Museo de Anthropologia entrance I'd heard about from César. "For God's sake, a must see, Sweetheart," he'd said. But now I'm swallowed by the enormity of the place. When I ask a guide about Olmec heads, he looked at me like I'm the village idiot. In unmodulated tones and simple words, he gives me directions in English.

Rushing down the hall the way he points, I duck into a restroom. A quick look in the mirror tells me my hair is tousled from the walk, but it's still okay. I put on a bit more lipstick.

La Paloma

Large stone heads look disapprovingly at me when I enter the gallery. Silent, impassive, the stone men are staring at me with brooding countenances. They make me feel tiny, unimportant. Unwanted. Walking away seems like a good idea.

"Stop, Teresa," a voice calls out behind me.

Javier startles me. He steps out from behind one of the gigantic heads. My old feelings come back; waves of emotion sweep through me.

At that moment, I want to fall into his arms. But I don't. I stay rooted to my spot and give him the best smile I can. Not my very best smile, but anything more would be insincere.

"Beautiful but different," he continues. "You're more sophisticated now, more confident. Señorita Guanajuato."

"And less naïve," I tell him, still feeling the urge to embrace him. I will myself not to.

"It becomes you, Teresa. You're poised, confident, just what I'd hoped for."

"Hoped for?" Now the urged to run comes back.

"When we first met. Before I fell in love with you."

The other urge returns.

"Things are different now," I tell him. "I had to grow up quickly after you abandoned me."

"You blame Carmen for not telling you. I know, but she was only following her instructions. Perhaps you'd like to hear what happened from me. About all of it."

"I'll listen." I feel a bit faint. "Can we sit? Get a glass of water or a soft drink?" I need time to deal with the feelings running through me, but happy we're in a public place. I need to sit down to stop my knees from shaking and gather myself, so I don't act like an idiot, mumbling incoherently at him. Javier needs to understand me.

275

He leads the way to an outdoor patio off the museum café, leaving the Olmec heads staring after us. I feel their stone eyes boring into my back, urging me to run before it's too late.

Javier helps me to a seat at a table near the wall. The waiter takes our order and disappears inside the restaurant. Out of the corner of my eye, I see two men in suits sit down at a table near the door. They don't order anything.

Javier puts his hand on mine as if we were still having lunch in Patzcuaro, a whole lifetime ago. "You are now Miss Guanajuato, about to enter the Mexicana Belleza Pageant. Congratulations."

"Thanks..." I withdraw my hand. "That's not what we need to talk about, is it?"

"I guess not... Where should I start?"

"Right after I fell in love with you and you disappeared."

His eyes brighten. "How can I ever forget that day? That night? And how can I make it up to you, Teresa? I am so sorry. What happened was unavoidable."

"You could have warned me."

"I had to run." The look he gives me turns somber. His sincerity feels real, but I have to stay cautious. Guarded.

"I never planned on falling in love with you," he starts. "It wasn't part of the plan."

"Plan? What plan?" The voice screaming in my head starts again.

"It just crept over me." He continues without answering. "I was torn between staying with you and doing what I had to do to stay alive."

"What plan?" I almost shout. "This is crazy." Anger tinged with frustration rises in my voice. I desperately need to calm myself, but my words come out in a gush. "What is all this about, for God's sake! You scare me, Javier. How can I take you seriously when you scare me?"

"Perhaps you can't..."

He sits straighter in his chair. As I stare at him, he tenses, the veins in his neck tighten. He seems to struggle for words. I'm praying they'll be words that make sense to me. I keep my own eyes expressionless, but secretly I drink in his handsome features that have smitten me from when we first met.

When he starts to speak again, he's very controlled. "I told you at the start, things aren't always what they seem in Mexico. I told you to trust no one—not even me—and I told you I am a smuggler, or at least my family is. I needed for you to know all that. I would have gone further, but my feelings for you got in the way."

"Please, Javier, don't beat around the bush. I'm not a child. Don't treat me like one."

He hesitates again then starts. "My father controls a large organization in Mexico, Teresa. His wife died a long time ago, before I was born. I know you know Carmen Madrazo is my mother. She was Sophie's mother, too. Carmen was my father's mistress long before my mother died. She and my father never married—they couldn't—but they depend on each other. My job is preparing to take over my father's business and protecting him from the cartels that want to push him out. In Patzcuaro, they came after me. I had no warning, no time to tell you, I had to hide from them."

Thinking back about the newspaper headlines I'd read in Uruapan I wonder if Javier is trying to tell me something more now without having to say the words? My response is almost shrill. My anger drives me. "I almost died because of you. I was attacked in the desert!"

Javier's face matches my anger. He spits the words through clenched teeth. "Damn, El Pelon." Then immediately, he softens, and his eyes turn sad. "I will never be able to make that up to you, not if I live forever. But you were foolish, you acted impetuously. I wanted to come after you—kill those men with my bare hands—but I couldn't."

"You keep saying you're sorry you couldn't. Am I supposed to forgive you for everything you do?"

The conversation stalls when the waiter brings our soft drinks to the table. Javier gives me a helpless kind of look, waiting for the waiter to walk back to the bar.

"I still want you, Teresa," he says when we're alone again. "I'll do my best to win back your trust."

"That will be hard, Javier. Maybe impossible. You assumed way too much in Guanajuato."

"I know... Even if we can't be lovers again, I still want you in my life. We need you. My family needs you."

"Need me? I don't think so. Your family has treated me as if I were nothing. They've lied to me and twisted information—"

"But they protected you and helped you out of tough situations," he interrupts. "We supported you through the Guanajuato pageant."

I feel my eyes misting as I look at him. The words are stuck in my throat before I can finally let them out. "I gave myself to you. The first man I ever loved. Then you disappeared. For the last seven months, you've never been out of my thoughts. But I never heard. It made me crazy. I didn't know love could hurt so much."

Javier looks at me, sadness creeping over his face. But he doesn't speak. I compose myself, waiting. Nothing.

"I guess I'm grateful for that," I say finally, feeling drained. "I have a job now. I live in Mexico. Is that what you want?"

His hand comes across the table toward mine again. The gentleness of his fingers caressing my hand seduces me with memories. I try to will them away. At the same time, I feel their thrill and want them to stay.

"Our family needs a better image," he says.

"What? I don't understand."

"It was Carmen's idea. We need to change how people think of us."

"Who is we? I interrupt. "Please, finally, be honest with me."

"My father's cartel. He's trying to change. He wants people to stop being afraid of us. You could help us change our image over time."

"How would I do that?"

"We'll introduce you to business leaders, government men. Let people know you speak for us. It could be fun; you'd attend social functions with Felix or me."

"Hire me, you mean? Like an escort service? Is that what's this has been all about? A job? You call that fun? It's disgusting!"

I get up from the table.

"Wait. That's not what it's been about. Please sit back down. Let me explain."

All the voices in my head yell at me to run. Instead, I sit down on the edge of the chair. "You've used me, Javier. You and Carmen and Felix, even Hector. You've all used me. Now you want to use me some more. You're all disgusting." I'm determined not to let him see how much he's hurt me, but I can feel myself falling apart.

"It's not that simple. Just hold on. Let me explain."

"It better be good."

"Initially, we wanted a well-educated young woman to do some PR work for us—All businesses do that. Hector told us about you living in Monte Vista, going to UCLA. He offered to bring you to meet Carmen. She told me you were a good candidate for us, so I came to meet you. But then it all changed. Once I met you, I was smitten. You are bright and pretty...and so much more. I fell in love with you, Teresa."

He stops. The look he gives me is selling sincerity hard. He really wants me to believe him. I'm not sure. One part of me is desperate to believe, wanting to love him. But only one part.

"What happened in Patzcuaro wasn't planned, but after it happened, I had a lot of thinking to do," he continues. "Did I want the woman I loved to be working for our family?"

"Your crime family—why don't you just say it? Cartel!"

"I came to Guanajuato to ask you to make a life with me, but we never found each other that night. I never got the chance at the airport."

"I was desperate to find you that night in the cemetery. I can't believe you couldn't get a message to me." After I said it, I wished I'd held back.

He doesn't try to explain. Instead, he says, "I don't know if we still have a chance together, Teresa, but we could try. I'd prefer to have you as my wife, but if that can't be, I still want you to be a part of my family."

"Stop calling your cartel or whatever it is your family!"

"After the Pageant, important people will want to know you, and they will know you are part of our... organization. Nothing official, you'll have your job at the Azteca station, but as you progress you can soften negative stories about us. It would be a first step for us toward respectability; others will think twice before they attack us. You'll become an important woman in Mexico, Teresa. You'll have all the fine things you want, live where you want. Everything will be paid for. Your life could be very comfortable."

"That's disgusting," I say again, but the idea is a hard one to dismiss. "You want to own me." The thought, after I've said it, stuns me, turns my stomach. But at the same time, I can see the life Javier is describing. It has an appeal I can't put into words, a sense of power. Isn't that what everyone wants—power and money? At what price? Papa used to urge me to be open to new ideas, and I can't help wondering what he would think of this one. Thinking of papa is crazy at a time like this. So is Javier's offer. But I remember getting another offer like it.

* * * *

One day in my junior year in high school, the assistant principal called me into her office. "Teresa, you're going to be a senior next year," *she said, "I hear you're hoping to go on to college. UCLA, is that right?* *I want to suggest that your college application might look stronger if you* *considered running for president of the Hispanic Students Association. I* *think you would do a fine job."*

"I don't want to do that," I told her directly. "I don't associate with *that group of kids. They're troublemakers."*

"They are, Teresa. Many of the Hispanic kids are troublesome for *us. We'd like to see that change. It could with a strong leader like you."*

"I didn't know the school administration got involved in student *elections. Isn't that unfair?"*

"HSA is a tough and disrespectful group. Those kids disrupt our school."

"I don't hang out with them."

"We feel the situation might change if they had a leader like you. *It would look good on your record. We could perhaps help with college* *interviews. Of course, we're only suggesting, but I do know the Dean of* *Admissions at UCLA pretty well."*

When I told papa what Mrs. Rafferty had said, he urged me to take her advice. "That's the way you get ahead, M'hija. She is offering to help you if you help the school. It would be good for everybody."

"I can't do it, Papa. She's asking me to do something I don't believe in to get what I want. It isn't fair."

"It's not fair, Paloma. But it's the way life is. You have to make decisions that offer you the best advantage. Sometimes you must sacrifice what you believe to get ahead."

* * * *

It was the same kind of offer Javier is making. I hated the HSA kids. Led by Veronica Estrada and Pepe, they terrorized much of the student body. They were the Mexican kids I had tried to avoid ever since junior high.

In the end, I decided I had no chance of being elected president of the HSA, so I went ahead and got myself nominated anyway. Veronica threatened to beat me up if I won. The school helped me with my college applications and told me about the University program for undocumented students. I got beaten badly in the election. I knew I would and didn't care.

"I need to take things a step at a time," I tell Javier when I come back from that memory. "I'm not sure I want to get involved."

When I look at him, I see what I think is an unspoken plea written across his face. It melts me just a little. "I don't know if we could ever recapture what we had in Patzcuaro... We could try... I suppose," I say half-heartedly.

He gets up from his chair and comes to me, throwing his arms around me in a big bear hug.

"Hold on," I tell him, pushing him away, "I said we could try. But I need to get through the Pageant first. I have a lot to think about."

* * * *

Two days later, with only a week to go before the pageant, Carmen takes me to the Palacio de Bellas Artes, an imposing Art Nouveau building on Avenida Juárez. Inside, before I can admire the imposing building, she hustles me along to the entrance of a large, empty theater. She stands there silently for several moments before pointing to the stage.

"I know it's hard for you to imagine, Teresa," she says at last, "but I stood on that stage with an orchestra behind me many years ago and sang to a packed house."

"I wish I'd been here that night," I answer. "I'm sure you were great."

She gives a deep sigh. "I was. But that's not why I brought you here. This building houses the best of Mexican culture. You need to know about it. Come, let me show you."

With that, she takes me on a whirlwind tour of the building. Small galleries house the works of Mexican artists I've only heard the names of before. Murals by Tamayo, Orozco, David Siqueiros, Diego Rivera and many Freda Kahlo paintings are just the beginning of the treasures the Palacio holds. She fills my head with stories about the artists and the Ballet Folklórico that performs in the theater. After a nonstop hour, I need to sit on one of the marble benches, trying to absorb it all. At the same time, the turmoil in my personal life, especially my conversation with Javier, won't leave me. It's all too much.

Carmen sits close to me, studying my face with a severe look narrowing her eyes. "I can see you are still angry with me," she says.

"Carmen, I'm trying to understand all that's happened. Angry is not the right word. I'm disappointed you didn't trust me. I understand you were following instructions. You were doing your best to be a matchmaker weren't you? Still...

"Felix and I have known each other a long time, Teresa." She lets my question go unanswered. Instead, she reaches out to touch my cheek with her fingertips in a token of friendship. She turns her large body slightly to smile at me. "He took care of me back in the days when I was struggling to have a singing career. Before I was good enough to sing here. One thing and another. I got pregnant, but he didn't abandon me. He has always taken care of me. I raised his children, our children. There was never a right time to tell you about those days. It's another thing that's different here. Hard to explain."

"Is that the life ahead for me, Carmen? A mistress?"

She doesn't answer.

Leaving the Palacio, we walk back toward my hotel. My mood stays somber, but I can't help being fond of Carmen, and appreciative of all she's done for me that has brought me to these final days before the Pageant. I try to keep our conversation on a light tone, as she points out things of interest as we walk.

We are saying our parting words in front of the hotel, so I can leave her to prepare for another Pageant rehearsal. Carmen is beginning to embrace me when a taxicab races to a stop in front of us. The rear door bursts open, and Vivian jumps out. She reaches back into the cab to assist Rico. Carmen brought them to Mexico City with her to watch me in the Pageant, and they have been sight-seeing alone every chance they've had.

As Rico emerges, I feel faint, a sense of panic consumes me. His face is beaten, covered with blood. One eye is swollen shut, his jaw is twisted and he's missing teeth.

"Mama Gorda, Teresa Maria, thank God you're here! Vivian calls out in desperation. "Help me. Please help me."

We run to Rico's side. "What happened?" Carmen asks breathlessly.

"Rico and Hector fought." Vivian says sobbing, barely audible. "Hector did this." She turns back to Rico.

"Where," Carmen demands.

"He followed us into the park."

"Hector?"

"Rico stabbed him with his knife."

CHAPTER 36

SHIELDING RICO FROM the people in the hotel lobby, we rush him up to my room. Vivian leads him to the bed and cradles him in her arms. She murmurs quietly to him as tears stream down her cheeks, but keeps her eyes averted from the mass of torn flesh his face has become. I take over and with a damp washcloth, I dab at the blood. Rico is barely conscious, yet he flinches when I lightly touch his cheek.

We're all in shock. Each of us looks blankly at the others, not knowing what to do to end this nightmare. My eyes scan from Vivian to Carmen, hoping one of them has a solution. Neither one does.

Carmen is mute. She walks to the window, stands looking down on the traffic creeping along La Reforma and out toward the park where Hector might still be. She seems defeated, her body seems to sag. It's the first time I've ever seen her not in control, and it dawns on me her worry is as much about Hector as it is for Rico's condition. Hector is the boy she rescued from Mexico City street life. She raised him like one of her own. Now he's somewhere in Mexico City bleeding from a knife wound.

Turning abruptly from the window, she says, "I'm calling Felix."

"No!" It's just one word from me, but it ricochets off the walls as if it were a bullet. "Do not call him," I say.

"We've got to do something," Vivian cries from the bedside. "Listen to him wheeze. He's having trouble breathing. He'll die."

"Out. Everyone out, please. Leave me alone with my brother." I feel I will faint if I have to watch these two women staring down at him a moment longer. "He's my brother, I'll care for him."

Rico's left cheek is caved in. The rest of his face is swollen and discolored in spots. A front tooth is missing, and his left eye is black and completely swollen shut. The right one not far behind.

It's hard for me to believe Hector did this much damage. Harder to imagine Rico stabbing him with a knife. Did the love of a young woman cause them to fight like savages? Rico is in no condition to explain. Instead, I take him in my arms, hug him, beg his forgiveness for not protecting him the way an older sister is supposed to.

After a while, he stirs. He isn't unconscious, and yet he isn't really awake either. He drifts in a twilight world where his pain seems dulled to a tolerable level. He tries to smile at me, but it's a macabre sight.

"Not so bad," he tries to say through his broken jaw.

His words arouse me from my daze. "Oh, Rico, how did we get to this? I should have protected you. We were a normal family living in California. At least we were a family. Look at us now. You lying there... Knobhead..." I don't want to think about that.

"I'm going to take you back to Monte Vista, where we can be safe again," I whisper to him, feeling my throat tighten. "Just as soon as we can get you healed."

Rico's lips hardly move. His words come out slowly, almost inaudibly. "Monte Vista's not safe. It was all fake. Papa lied to us."

"Don't say that Rico!" I gasp at his accusation. "Don't insult our father. He tried his best. He tried to make a life for us. We *were* a family."

"He was living a lie." Rico's voice gains strength as he says the words.

I bend closer to his shattered face. Speechless.

"Papa isn't what he pretended to be," Rico is mumbling. "I found out. I didn't want you to know."

"Don't try to talk so much. Didn't want me to know what?"

He persists, trying to sit up. "Where do you think the money was coming from? All the extra little things? Toys for Connie. Your college books. Our clothes. Didn't you wonder it was too much for a Mexican gardener?"

"What are you saying?" I stare at him, not understanding.

"Papa sold drugs. I found out the day I ditched the wrestling match. Some *chavos* on the street corner told me. They all knew. That's when I got drunk. Papa went to Pasadena and the other places where he had gardening jobs and sold drugs."

"I don't believe you!"

Rico looks at me as best he can through blackened eyes. "Hector was selling papa meth and opioids. That's how he knew about you. Papa was working for Ugalde!"

I'm stunned.

"Is that why you fought?" I ask him, after a long moment when I try to get control of my feelings.

"No. He told me what Vivian does in Tijuana."

A soft knocking on the door stops me from asking Rico more questions or trying to explain. When I open it, Felix Ugalde takes me in his arms, hugging me tightly. I shrink back from him.

"I came as soon as Carmen called. I was in town. What can I do?"

I'm startled by the look on his face. My head is a jumble as I try to process what Rico has just told me while I stand in the man's embrace. "What *can* you do?" As much as I want to cry, I keep my face blank. "A doctor," I plead with him. "Rico has broken bones. He probably needs stitches—a doctor for God's sake. Carmen says we shouldn't take him to any hospital."

"She's right."

Felix's expression is one of intense concern. He looks down at Rico. Then back at me, seeming to study us both as if we're strangers. The silence drags on, and we hold on to each other with our eyes, looking for a solution that will make Rico's face whole again. There are no solutions.

Finally, Felix says. "I brought some painkillers for him. I know a doctor who'll take care of him. The police won't be notified."

I can't help grimacing at those three simple sentences.

Reaching into his suitcoat pocket, he pulls out a small syringe with a plastic guard over the needle. He hands it to me. I take it, then look back at him.

"It's okay," he reassures me. "Go ahead. I didn't think he could swallow pills."

"Very thoughtful." My tone is bitter. I can't help it.

Without thinking, I go to the bed and help Rico roll on his side. He protests a little; protests more when I tug down his pants and boxer shorts. I jab the needle in his butt and push on the plunger. When I pull it out, I'm shaking so hard I drop the syringe on the floor.

"I've never done that before."

"You did fine." Again, Felix reaches out to me, taking hold of my shoulder, smiling in a non-smiling kind of way. "We all rise to special occasions. I'll call for some help, and we'll take your brother out a back way."

"I'll come with you."

"It's better if you don't."

"I want to be with my brother."

"I know you do."

I'm startled by the coolness in his voice.

"It's better if you stay here for the Pageant. We'll fly Rico to a doctor in Morelia."

"I'm coming too," I tell him again. "I'm through with the Pageant." I say it with insistence in my voice, trying to accept my responsibility for Rico's condition.

Felix steps back, eyeing me for several moments with no expression on his face. Then, pulling himself more erect, his face grows hard. Hard like stone. Like an Olmec head.

"No deal," he says. "I'll do the best I can to get your brother taken care of, but you've got to continue with *Mexicana Belleza*."

"You're trading Rico's need for medical attention with the beauty contest?"

"You can't quit now."

I can't believe it. I look down at Rico on the bed then back at Felix's impassive face. Speechless, I stand there a long time. I am forever lost. I shrug agreement.

CHAPTER 37

AS WE PICK up speed leaving Mexico City, the roadside is a blurred canvas of rural life, a paint-by-numbers scene. The bus with all the *Mexicana Belleza* participants is speeding toward Teotihuacan and the Valley of Mexico.

"Have you been here before?" The girl sitting next to me asks. She sweeps chestnut hair, parted just off center, from her forehead over one shoulder, framing the curves of her face as she smiles at me.

The bus's other occupants, thirty beautiful young women, all speaking Spanish, chatter and laugh with their seat mates or hang over seatbacks sharing stories with the girls in front of them. I don't feel a part of it. I'm preoccupied with other images—Rico's pale and purple face with a fleshy-pukey smell leaking out.

My seatmate is Miss Jalisco, a buoyant, full-faced girl with boundless energy who has led the rest of us through a couple of the jazz-dance practice routines. I turn in my seat to look directly at her. Her skin glows warmly as she smiles, striking up

Willard Thompson

the conversation. Dark, arching brows and long tapering lashes accentuate the clarity of her eyes.

I tell her no, I hadn't.

Although Miss Mexico contestants have been introduced to each other, I don't know much about this girl except that her name is Pilar.

You didn't grow up in Mexico," she says. It isn't a question.

"No. I grew up near Los Angeles. How could you tell?"

"You don't talk like the rest of us." Pilar shows even white teeth when she smiles. "All the other girls have accents—I can tell which states most of them come from. Your Spanish don't sound like you come from Guanajuato. That's okay," she adds quickly.

"I don't know if it is okay," I tell her. "Maybe some other girl from Guanajuato should be here instead of me. I feel out of place."

"If you won the pageant, and you're Mexican then you should be here." She hesitates a moment, then adds, "You must have had a very powerful group behind you to beat out the local girls. I did too in Jalisco."

"I was born in Mexico—just barely," I tell Pilar. "My parents were trying to get over the border so I would be American. I was raised in California. So, I don't know what I am, Pilar. I worked for a photographer before the local pageant. I guess some local people promoted me." I wondered if she believes that.

"It's okay," she says, shrugging it off. "We're all different." She skips on to other things. "You'll be amazed when you see the pyramids. They're so ancient, they're spooky. But I think they're beautiful. When I saw them the first time, I almost cried thinking about the people who built them—our ancestors—thinking how they are a part of our history. I think you'll be in awe too."

When we arrive, we pile out of the bus and stare down Avenue of the Dead at the gigantic Pyramid of the Sun. The smaller

294

Pyramid of the Moon is in the opposite direction. Pilar is right, I am awestruck. They cast an immediate spell over me.

"Let's stay together, Pilar." Like a child, I take her hand.

All the Miss Mexico contestants have come to Teotihuacan to tape a dance segment to be shown the night of the pageant. The shoot is our first priority. We've been promised lunch, and after that time to explore the historic site before returning to Mexico City. I can't help but feel as if I am just going through the motions.

We change in the back room of a restaurant called Pyramid Charlie's, as out of place amid the ancient ruins as the souvenir stalls we passed on the way in. It feels to me like the girls' locker room back in high school, with thirty shapely female bodies running around in bras and panties, giggling and laughing, but also checking each other out, making silent comparisons.

We have costumes intended to evoke images of Aztec dancers even though everyone knows the Aztecs never lived here. The skimpy outfits are designed to titillate far more than they are to celebrate our cultural heritage. I'm embarrassed but chalk it up to one more indignity to endure.

We dress in cotton micro skirts in vivid blues and oranges, reds and greens. The bustier tops are strapless and cut low. We are all worried about them slipping. The crowning feature of our costume is a feathered headdress that makes us look like tropical birds. Wild arrays of feathers are set in foil helmets that glisten like silver and appear to be inset with jewels. We wear sandals, with feathered anklets.

When we're dressed, our chaperones herd us to the base of the Pyramid of the Sun where photographers and videographers wait. Tourists milling around the pyramid get an unexpected treat when we take our positions for a group shot. The chaperones keep urging us to smile and act sexy for the gawking spectators and cameras.

"Do you like to pose?" Pilar asks as photographers arrange us on the lower steps of the pyramid.

Looking at Pilar, I wonder again why I'm here. How could I even be in the same class with her?

"I'm getting used to it," I answer. "In the beginning, I felt uncomfortable. Now I don't mind. The photographer I worked for made me strip down to a bikini in front of a group of tourists in Guanajuato. It was a funny feeling, but when I saw the men's faces, it gave me a thrill."

"I love having men look at me," Pilar says without a trace of guile. "I know there are men in Jalisco who will benefit if I win, so I work out several hours each day to have the best body I can. I like it when men admire me. I feel powerful. Beauty gives us power, you know."

I think about that for a moment. She's right, but at what cost? "I suppose it does," I reply.

"What will you do if you win?"

For a moment, several images flash before my eyes. Just as quickly I push them away because I can't tell Pilar the truth. "I'm doing this for all the people who have supported me. I'd just as soon not win so I can go back to Guanajuato and start my TV job. But I have an obligation to those people; I guess a lot of them are counting on me."

"Me too. I think we all do," Pilar says. "The men supporting me are very powerful. They can help my career a lot. Miss Mexico gets a lot of publicity all year long, you know. Naturally, I want to do something for our people. I'd work to improve life for women if I could. We need stronger laws protecting women from abuse. If I became Miss Mexico, people would listen to me."

People would listen. I repeat her words to myself, wondering if she's right. "I was a communications major in college," I tell her. "The station in Guanajuato gave me a job after I won, so I'll be happy to be working in television."

"Quiet down, up there," one of the chaperones calls out. "Pay attention to the photographer so we can finish with this. You're not free till after lunch."

We dance a simple little jota, kind of a modern version of a traditional folk dance, in our sexy Mexican feathers. We sing to the diners at Pyramid Charlie's, too, and then change back into our jeans and explode out of the restaurant like college students on spring break, free to investigate the mysteries of Teotihuacan.

Pilar and I explore the ruins together, talking about ourselves as we walk along the Avenue of the Dead. Her warmth and openness touch me, but I keep my own thoughts well buried, asking questions to keep her talking. She isn't a deep-thinking girl, but she has a clear vision of what lies ahead for her. Winning the pageant isn't important to her, either, she says. "Just being in it is enough. The men backing me will be happy and it will give my acting career a boost when I return to Guadalajara. If the opportunity presents itself, I might move to Mexico City where there are more opportunities."

She stops halfway down the long street connecting the two pyramids and faces me with the sun highlighting her auburn hair. In that instant, I am taken by her beauty. And in the next instant, I throw off my insecurities and accept that I belong as much as she does.

Her face turns serious. "You're a beautiful girl, Teresa. I wish I were as tall as you and had your pale skin—so I don't mean to insult you, but what will you gain if you win?"

Looking down the long road of ancient ruins that seems haunted by the ghosts of the ancient past, with the valley of Teotihuacan melting into the horizon, I'm forced to think about Pilar's question. The truth is too hard to share.

"I want to be proud of who I am, Pilar. When I lived in California, I tried to be something I wasn't. I pretended. I don't want to pretend anymore. I want a career and a family—family is very important for me. I hope to be an investigative reporter where I can improve life for the people in my community. But I don't know what will happen after the Pageant. I think there's more ahead in life for me than just being a pretty woman that men gawk at. That's not enough. I know that men want me, but I want there to be more ...if I can be free to find it."

Pilar bows her head and stays silent. I take her hand. "I'm glad I know you, Pilar. I hope you win. And I hope we can get together after the Pageant. If you don't mind, I'd like to spend some time alone now, walking back through the ruins."

She beams. "That's fine. I need to buy some souvenirs to take home to my brother. I promise to stay in touch no matter who wins. Whoever gets back to the bus first can save a seat, okay?"

I go back to the Pyramid of the Moon and stare up at it for a few moments. Then, I start climbing up, step by step, lifting me away from my troubled reality into a faraway world in my imagination. At the top, I feel as if all of Mexico lies below me. The sight makes me dizzy. I think I might fall off, but the feeling of risk exhilarates me.

I need to be alone for a while to clear my thoughts and listen to what these old stones are saying to me. I'm their captive, a prisoner to the spell they cast over me the moment I took my first step. Who were the people who built these monumental temples? Were they good people? Or bad? How could you tell good from bad?

Is Pilar good or bad? Am I? Am I like these Ancient Purepecha people who had the same blood I do? My eyes sweep from stone sculpture to stone sculpture below me, menacing jaguar heads, feathered serpents, carvings of eagles, nameless creatures from the world below, Quetzalcoatl, the Sun God.

I'm haunted by a feeling I've been here before. Time stops. I tremble. I feel an urge to run back to the bus and climb back into the security of those other young women. The frivolous world without serious consequences. The consequences of my real world make me tremble. But the stones have cast their spell.

I'm the same person I was when we arrived this morning, but I feel different. I was born to a mother in the back of a Tijuana bus. A child of poor peasants, parents who'd always been poor; the children and grandchildren of peasants back as far as time goes. As far back as these ruins? Is there a connection? Did we live here?

No one knows who these people were. They came into the Valley of Mexico and built monuments to their gods. Pyramids where they sacrificed young women like me so their male gods would be appeased. So, life would go forward with sun and rain and ample crops. No one thought about the dead young women after they were sacrificed. Am I the next one being sacrificed to the male gods?

I almost lose my balance. The stones of Teotihuacan are speaking to me, crying out, in fact. How could I not hear? It's my choice. It's always been my choice.

It's a long, awkward climb down with the sun falling toward the mountains ringing the valley, and nothing to cling to. They sacrificed young women who never had to climb down. They didn't need anything to cling to. I do. But when I reach the base, I realize I don't need to be a sacrificial offering.

CHAPTER 38

TEN MISS MEXICO contestants smile down at the adoring crowd. Ten glamorous young women, elegant in short black cocktail dresses, press close to each other, holding hands and basking in the thunderous applause. The looks on the men's faces are hungry. The scene reminds me of the ancient ritual atop the Pyramid of the Moon. My entire body tingles with a sensuousness that sends the fine hairs on the back of my neck aflutter. But it doesn't matter to me anymore.

The past year has taken me to the edge. I can't keep my emotions in check any longer. Tears stream down my cheeks when the master of ceremonies announces I am one of the five finalists. So is Pilar. I knew it was coming.

I run from the stage, tears destroying my makeup, and keep on running to my dressing room, almost stumbling on my heels. I flop on the vanity stool and put my head in my hands. The sobs and trembling come in wracking spasms.

"It's wonderful, Teresa Maria." Carmen bursts through the door, "All your dreams are about to come true."

"Not my dreams. Your dreams. I have only nightmares. I'm not going back out there."

"Yes, you are. In a few more minutes, you'll be Miss Mexico, Mexicana Belleza."

I look up at her as she takes the finale ball gown out of its plastic wrapper.

"It doesn't matter if I go out there or not, does it, Carmen? I've won."

She doesn't answer.

"It's all been arranged, hasn't it? Paid for."

Before she can answer, there's a quiet knocking on the door. She opens it a crack and looks out. "We don't have much time," I hear her say.

"It's okay, the familiar voice answers. "Only for a minute."

Papa comes into the room, as finely dressed as I've ever seen him, holding his hat in his hands.

"*Hola, Paloma*," he said.

"I don't want to see you."

"Just for a minute. One minute."

I give Carmen a look that sends her out into the hall, closing the door, leaving me alone with my father.

"I've got to change now for the finale."

"When you were a young girl, I helped you dress. So pretty."

"A long time ago, Papa. I've grown up."

"Now you know the real world." He touches a speck in his eye. "I always tried to shield you. I wish I could shield you now."

"I'm sure Rogelio and Lupe wish they could've shielded Antonio."

"Poor Antonio," Papa says. "That was the start. How do I explain?"

"I don't want more lies."

"We were poor. We had to live. Your mother worked, I worked in the orchards, then the gardens, and still we were poor. We only did the jobs no one else wanted. I had to do something to support *mi niños*."

"Not drugs."

"I saw the ads, the store windows. I wanted to show I loved you."

"I worshiped you, Papa."

"I wanted to give you nice things."

"You were my world. You were more than my father. You were my hero. Whenever I was scared or needed someone to talk to, you were always there for me."

"And you were my world."

"No Papa, that's not true. Your world was secret; a dark place you kept hidden from all of us. We looked to you for strength. Rico looked to you. Look at him now—he knows. He found out. He kept your secret, but he knows you were living a lie."

"I didn't know what else to do, *Paloma*."

"Don't ever call me that again! A father is supposed to lead his family. Not lie to them. Not pretend to be a gardener while he's really doing drug deals for the Ugaldes."

"You know?"

I feel a catch in my throat that stops me momentarily. "Rico figured it out," I tell him. "It was the only thing that makes any sense. That's how Hector knew you'd been deported. How he knew I was a university student. How he knew you were in Tijuana. How Javier knew you were in Michoacán. How you knew where to look for me. The only thing I don't know is if you encouraged them to ensnare me. Did you, Papa?"

He looks down at the floor.

"I see," I say softly. "You sacrificed your own daughter."

"Don't say that," he says, looking up at me with eyes that seemed to burn. "I wanted the best for you. I saw you try so hard to fit in, but they never let you. A wall we could never climb over. A very high wall. In Mexico, you will live well. The Ugaldes can see to that. We can be together. Rico won't go to jail. Don't you see, *mi Paloma*, it wasn't real for us in California, not for any of us. Here you can have the kind of life you never could've had in California."

"Did you think I wanted to be part of a drug cartel, Papa? Was that your hope for your daughter? To marry a drug smuggler? Raise his children?" I try to keep my emotions under control, but they're slipping. "Is that why you sacrificed me? You have to leave now, Papa, so I can change my dress."

Slowly he stands up from the chair without looking at me again. He goes to the door but stops before opening it. "Will you come home with mama and me when this is over?"

I look at his image in the vanity mirror: smaller, shriveled, more pathetic than he's ever looked before. "You are my father. I will always love you, but the time for being a family is gone. It will never come back."

"Would it have been better if you'd been born to poor peasants in Uruapan? If we'd never gone to California? I'm so sorry, Teresa Maria. Sorry beyond any words I have for you. Your life in Mexico would have been terrible. When I saw how we were treated in Monte Vista... When I saw what happened to Antonio... I knew the bad mistake I'd made. What was I to do, *M'hija*? Whatever was I to do for my beautiful dove? I couldn't change anything. It was too late."

I don't look up when the door closes.

* * * *

Standing side by side, holding Pilar's hand, my knees shaking, we are the two finalists for the Mexicana Belleza title. We are alone in the spotlight at the front of the stage now. The other finalists have drifted to the rear. The Mariachi orchestra is reaching a crescendo and the audience is clapping and cheering along with it. Every fiber in my body is twitching with anticipation as the judges fumble with the envelope containing the winner's name. I try to summon as much composure as I can muster so I don't embarrass myself when the name is read out loud to the audience. At this moment, all my negative thoughts about the pageant are washed away in the anticipation of victory.

I flinch and feel as if I've been punched in the stomach, when Pilar's name is announced. Only the single word, "no" escapes my lips. My face contorts through a whole range of emotions, but probably no one in the audience notices as they burst into wild applause, shouting, "Pilar! Pilar!" over and over.

I look quickly at the back row of the theater, under the balcony. Javier is already on his feet heading for an exit. Felix Ugalde slams his right fist into the palm of his left hand. Carmen and Vivian are dabbing tears from the eyes. Papa's emotion is harder to read, but his face is sorrowful. Rico is there too, brought from Morelia in the Ugalde plane. He is next to Vivian, encased behind a protective layer of bandage so I can't read his emotion. I imagine I see a small boy in short pants, his feet dangling off the chair, swinging back and forth, sitting there with them, oblivious to what everyone is cheering for. A little trickle of blood runs down one cheek. Why did the bullet find Antonio and not me? Antonio was an innocent. So was I then.

When the outgoing Miss Mexico places the diamond tiara on Pilar's head and drapes the sash over her shoulder, I step closer to her and throw my arms around her. "I am so happy for you,"

I whisper in her ear. "You deserve this." Then I step back in line with the other runners up, letting Pilar step forward, alone in the spotlight while I fight off old feelings.

And yet, as I stand in the background of this scene as it plays out, a feeling of relief washes over me. I feel freer—hurt but freer than I have felt since my search for papa began. Things are not always what they seem in Mexico, isn't that what Javier had warned me? Guarded by three men standing along the wall behind them, the inhabitants of the dark back row, fade from my view. I straighten up, put on my best smile, and join the celebration with the other runners up.

I know I still have a choice to make. A hard choice for my future. Which path for me? Am I really free to decide?

I hug the First Runner up's bouquet of red roses tighter to my breast and turn away from the people in the back row to bathe in the warmth of the hundreds of cheering Mexican faces looking up at us. I know I have to choose a path, maybe not now, not tonight, but soon. I give a silent thanks to the Virgin. I ask her for the courage I will need. I say a prayer for Antonio.

The End

AUTHOR'S NOTE

LA PALOMA IS a work of entertainment and should be read as nothing more. The names, characters, places and incidents portrayed in the story are the product of the author's imagination or have been used fictitiously.

The original idea for *La Paloma* came to me about a dozen or so years ago, when I first became aware the California University system offered free tuition to qualified undocumented young men and women. These young people have more recently come to be called Dreamers. For several reasons I put the project aside to work on *The Chronicles of California*, my historical fiction trilogy. But as the United States has become increasingly consumed by immigration issues, border security, our urge to send troops and build walls, and the plight of young people living in the U.S. without documentation, the story kept coming back in my mind with greater timeliness. (Note that our domestic vocabulary has morphed recently from border fences to border walls.)

Teresa Maria Diaz's story is the product of my imagining how these issues might play out when the head of an immigrant family is deported back into Mexico. His undocumented, college age daughter, has to go into Mexico to find him and bring him back in order to keep her family together.

But as we all know, things are not always what they seem in Mexico.

It is Mexico's unfortunate fate to share a border with the world's strongest economy and most powerful nation. The 1994 North American Free Trade Agreement (NAFTA) had the unintended consequence of driving many Mexicans out of work or into criminal activities. Corporate farming along the U.S. side of the boarder and the building of *Maquiladora* factories on the Mexican side combined to drive many Mexican workers into low wage jobs. Americans' insatiable demand for recreational drugs helped build a powerful, deadly cartel culture in Mexico that trades U.S. automatic assault rifles for meth, cocaine, heroin and most recently opioids in a deadly border trade. The new U.S., Mexico, Canada trade agreement (USMCA) is not likely to improve cross border conditions.

We all have a tendency to see our world in a good vs. evil, or us vs. them, our country vs. Mexico, kind of way. If we believe ourselves to be on the good side, we tend to feel protected from the bad, but we are often misled. We have all heard horror stories about murderous cartels, dishonest governments and police that often play for the wrong side when the reward for bad behavior is more money than they could acquire in any "good" way. Good, honest, hard-working people are vulnerable to being seduced over to the bad side; good people can become the pawns of bad. Teri Diaz's story is one such seduction.

In the Spanish language, the word *Paloma* has two different meanings. It can refer a timid dove or an aggressive pigeon, because both birds belong to the Columbidae family; both birds are Palomas, two birds with diametrically opposed perceived personalities. As Javier Ugalde tells Teri, "Things in Mexico are not always what they seem."

Special thanks to José Aguilar from Guanajuato and Sergio Martinez from Michoacán, both good friends for over 15 years, for helping me understanding the states of Mexico from which they have come to the U.S. I have traveled to Mexico many times and never cease to marvel at the unsurpassed beauty of these states, and many other Mexican states. People on both sides of the border have help me to understand the complex, possibly unsolvable issues, on both sides of our common border.

And thanks to my early readers Guy Strickland, Mary Sheldon and Melanie Weisse for substantial contributions to my final draft. And to Dinah and Jerry Baumgartner for careful proofreading of all my books.

As always my thanks and appreciation to James Patillo for his advice on all things literary.

And finally, my deepest debt of gratitude to Jo. She is not only my best and bravest editor and creative consultant, she is also my spouse, lover, helpmate, confidant, and mother confessor. She is my guiding spirit that keeps my life in balance and the rock of reality that knows when to rein in my passions. She is my all.

If you have enjoyed reading this novel, please post a positive review on Amazon, Kindle or Goodreads and your other favorite book sites. Thank you for reading.

Other Novels by Willard Thompson
The Chronicles of California
Dream Helper
Delfina's Gold
Their Golden Dreams
Also
The Girl from the Lighthouse
La Paloma